Read the Leaves

Kate Valent

VALIANT INK

Contents

Prologue

*A*lice's candle flickered in the cool breeze wafting up the basement stairs. The darkness felt like a yawning mouth ready to swallow her whole. She'd never gone downstairs. There'd never been any need to. On a normal day the manor would be in the midst of waking up with servants bustling through the sprawling manor. Today however the manor remained as quiet as a cemetery, making her feel utterly alone.

Had another servant disappeared like the missing maids before her? Soon there wouldn't be any servants left, and any night Alice could be next.

If the hunter was right, the truth lay beneath her feet. Could Lord Hallow be slumbering in his coffin, waiting for the sun to set? She wouldn't know unless she went down into his lair. A distant boom of thunder echoed through the manor, sending her heart thudding. If this wanted to face the Lord she needed to do it now before the storm blotted out the sun.

She had to know the truth. She had to know if... if he was a vampire. A monster who fed on his own servants.

She slid her right foot forward, onto the first step. After one last glance back at the sunlight streaming in through the kitchen windows, she pushed on into the darkness. With each step the air grew cooler, sending goose bumps over her arms and shoulders. Every scrape of *her shoe echoed through the stairwell, threatening to give away her presence. The stones muffled the coming storm.*

Then finally she stepped off the last stair and into the cold cellar. A mouse darted past. She pressed a hand to her mouth, muffling her yelp of surprise. Her ragged breathing filled the room. She could hear nothing except the frantic pounding of her heart.

At the edge of her candlelight a closed door beckoned to her. That must be the room the hunter spoke about. The door creaked as she opened it. She froze, straining to listen for any noise. Time seemed to stand still as she waited, wide-eyed. At best, she'd be punished for trespassing, but at worst, she'd be walking straight into the lion's den. Even so, Alice couldn't turn her back on whatever dark secret awaited her. She steadied herself and stepped into the circular room.

An ornate coffin sat conspicuously in the middle of the space, the very same coffin the hunter sought to destroy. Breathless, she crept forward, resting her hand on the lid's heavy brass handle. Curiosity overcame Alice's fear, and though her knees shook, she managed to silently slide open the sturdy oaken lid just enough to see inside. Dread filled her heart as she cast the candle's flickering light through the narrow opening, yet she could not see the sinister lord's face. The hunter had told her he would be resting here in the soil of his homeland, but that very soil was all she could see.

"Alice."

She whirled, finding Lord Hallow watching her from the shadows.

"What are you?" Her voice shook, as did her hand, sending the weak candlelight bouncing around the room.

~~*He stepped into the light. He looked as handsome as ever, his eyes sparkling pools of emerald and his dark hair as soft as down. His soft fingers wrapped around her wrist, his porcelain skin as cold as a corpse. "I must be dreaming," he said, voice breathy, "for you to be here." Their eyes connected, and he leaned toward her.*~~

"No, no," Mary muttered under her breath as she crossed the paragraph out. "That isn't romantic." She turned to the stack of romance novels she'd pilfered from under Margaret's bed. None of them could explain why her readers found the wicked vampire Lord Hallow to be so romantic. But they could certainly describe kissing scenes.

"He kissed her with a fiery passion," she read. She mulled over the lines before opening her mouth, attempting to mimic the book's description. It didn't feel right. How could a cold dead blood-sucking creature of the night be passionate? Perhaps she needed a more subdued kiss. One that was sweet instead of fiery.

"What is that face supposed to be? Are you trying to taste the air?" Margaret asked as she strolled over to open the parlor curtains wider. The afternoon sunlight flooded the room.

"What would kissing a vampire be like? I don't think it would be fiery, but it is their very first kiss..." Mary pondered aloud before turning to her sister. "How would you describe a first kiss?"

Margaret's face scrunched in distaste. "I'm not telling you about any kissing I've done."

"That's not what I meant!" Mary waved her away. "You know what, never mind. Let me get back to writing."

"On a kissing scene? It's about time something exciting happened." Margaret leaned over her shoulder and Mary scrambled to cover the page.

"Don't look at it! It's not ready for anyone else to see it yet."

Margaret groaned. "Then how am I supposed to help?" Her attention landed on the pile of books and her nostrils flared. "Are those my—" She cut off her own question, hastily gathering up the romance novels.

"I needed them for reference. My editor is begging me to make it a romance instead of the horror I planned. He thinks killing Lord Hallow will upset my readers. If I'm to write this drivel I ought to at least know what it's supposed to look like." She paused, turning her full attention to her sister. "Although I never knew you liked reading about pirates kidnapping innocent maidens." Half of the books in the pile were about pirates. The others involved a mix of lords, highwaymen, and maids finding love.

Splotches of pink crept into Margaret's cheeks. "Shut up. I like the adventures. And don't go borrowing books without asking. I'm not a library." She added the last book to her towering stack. "I say just have Alice stake Lord Hallow and run away with another maid. Like that blonde she was sharing a room with."

Mary scoffed at the suggestion. "My editor would probably stake me if I did that. My readers want romance with Hallow, not more murder."

"I'll stake you if you steal my things again." Margaret stalked out of the room, grumbling under her breath about Mary's thievery the whole way.

Mary returned to her pages. She picked up the quill, preparing to write again, but no words came. Without Margaret's book she had no references. And she felt none the wiser as to what could possibly be drawing all her readers to the blood-thirsty vampire. Whatever his appeal was, she needed to figure it out and quick or there'd be no more *Twilight at Hallow Manor.*

She moved on to a blank page.

Before his lips touched hers, the hunter burst into the room.

"There. That ought to buy me more time."

Chapter 1

Not for the first time in her life Mary wished she wasn't the responsible older sister. Then she could sneak right out of Roquefort's party just like she was certain Margaret already had. By now Margaret was probably exploring the grounds instead of gossiping. Or she'd managed to corner Elizabeth somewhere to pick another fight with her. Those two always got into cat fights at parties.

Mary didn't find the party boring per se, but watching her papa pretend everything was normal with Hawke House was far too painful. She couldn't stand to let him out of her sight lest something happen while she was gone. Being the responsible one meant it was up to her to save him when he found himself in a tight spot.

"Erm, our new stories for next year?" her father answered the two men beside him. He couldn't act to save his life and his sweating brow and distracted mind would raise questions sooner rather than later. They wouldn't be able to delay the news of their dire situation from getting out much longer.

"Papa, have you seen Margaret?" Mary asked as she slid up beside him, giving him a look of wide-eyed worry. "I meant to take her a cookie and she has already slipped away." This was the third time she'd stepped in to save him, and her excuses were getting progressively lazier. Soon she'd have to make up some sort of cataclysm to get him to leave altogether. Ever since her uncle ran off with Hawke's money, they were floundering. They'd already cut back on new stories to save costs. Without more investors they wouldn't stay afloat, but if word got out about what deep water Hawke House was in, it would be even harder to find support.

"Oh dear," he said, relief in his eyes from her interruption. "Shall I go look for her?"

"If it isn't too much trouble. I'm worried."

"You go visit with your friends. I'll check on your sister." He wished the men next to him farewell.

"Thank you, Papa." She beamed at him. They split ways. She made her way across the room to the drinks, pausing to look about every few steps. As she'd already expected, there was no sign of Margaret. While their father struggled to hold the business together, Mary struggled to hold the family together. Margaret spent her nights sneaking out and refusing to say where she went. Mary stared at blank pages while Papa locked himself in his office.

She reached the table of drinks, ignoring the giggling women beside her when a man approached them for a dance. She didn't bother to look up, knowing he wasn't there for her. Only writers ever asked Mary for a dance as they tried to worm themselves into Hawke's good graces. Her gaze jumped across the label on the wine bottles without reading them. She grabbed a small pastry and nibbled on it. It wasn't as good as Clarke's bakery pastries, but few were.

What she wouldn't give for a night to forget the specter hanging over her family. Each day it looked less and less likely Hawke Publishing could survive, and once it failed so too would her family. They could lose their house next. If she was lucky another press would pick up *Twilight at Hallow Manor*, but that alone wouldn't be enough to support her father and sister.

Sometimes she considered begging Charlotte to do something, but she knew that wasn't fair. Mr. Martin Steepe investing in Hawke would only be a short-term solution, another way to stall the inevitable. Plus Charlotte still had her hands full with Martin's cousin trying to ruin their engagement.

She needed more ideas for her story, she thought as her gaze searched the crowd for inspiration. More material would help convince a new publisher to take the story on once she no longer had Hawke. She watched the flirtations between young couples. The glares between two of the maids. Off to her left Mr. Steepe's talking teapot wouldn't quit rambling. And its stories? Too dry and overly detailed, and with such dreadful pacing. Its maker may have been skilled with enchantments, but whoever he was, he clearly hadn't been a writer.

She grabbed some wine and took it to an empty table against the wall. There she glowered at the dancers. She'd rather be dancing like Charlotte. But she didn't know any of the gentlemen well enough to feel comfortable marching up to them and asking to dance the way Roquefort sisters liked to do. Maybe in a disguise, but not as herself. She was far too aware of her family's reputation, and with Hawke in trouble, that was a burden now more than ever. Not that it ever stopped any of Margaret's antics. But her parents had long given up on getting Margaret to behave.

"I wish someone would ask me to dance." She sighed, and from her right a meow answered her complaint. She startled. Then looked down, finding a black cat sitting on the chair beside her, tail swishing as it watched her.

"Oh, um, hello there."

The cat meowed again, its gaze tracking her silver bracelet. Her father had given it to her several years ago. After watching her mother's charm bracelet grow over the years and hearing about Queen Victoria's bracelet, Mary had wanted one for herself. The bracelet came with its first charm, a simple silver circle with her name engraved on it. Since then, she'd added a quill, a book, and a hawk. She'd been considering adding something else to signify *Twilight at Hallow Manor*, but hadn't found the right charm yet. As it turned out, the jewelry stores in the city didn't stock vampire charms.

"Are you supposed to be in here?"

"Meow." The cat batted at her bracelet. She jerked her arm away to avoid the claws.

"None of that," she scolded. A cool breeze blew over her from the open doors nearby. A group of well-dressed magicians stood on the patio. One of them blew cigar smoke into the shape of a curvy woman while the others hooted and laughed. She rolled her eyes. What a waste of magic. "Did you wander in from outside?"

"Meow."

"Is that so?" she said, taking the meow as an affirmative. She sipped at her drink, wondering what to do about the furry visitor. The cat looked clean and well fed. Was it Roquefort's pet? "Do you live here?"

The cat didn't answer this time. The cat's body tensed, pupil's widening as it tracked the bracelet. She reached over to rub its head. The cat launched itself at her arm. She yelped in surprise and jerked away from the table, almost dropping her drink from the attack. The cat jumped down to hide beneath the table in a blur of black fur. A stinging in her arm made her wince. A pink scratch marred her arm, but at least it wasn't deep enough to bleed. More importantly, her wrist was bare. Her heart jumped into her throat.

She patted the tabletop, her chair, and then looked under the table. Nothing. No, no, she couldn't lose the bracelet. If the business failed, she already stood to lose far too much. She patted down her dress one more time, her hands growing more frantic by the second.

Movement out of the corner of her eye caught her attention as the cat crept out from under the table. The little devil headed toward the hallway, its prize dangling from its mouth. The charms swayed as the cat walked. "You little ..." The cat's head swiveled to glance back at her. She shot away from the table and the cat ran for it.

The cat darted between a man's legs, and she dodged around the man. "Excuse me, sorry," Mary mumbled as she crept around a large group of women next. They paid her no mind as they continued gossiping.

"Lord Holiday dead, and so suddenly. How tragic for the family."

"Doesn't that mean the son will be looking for a wife now that he is lord?"

"We can only hope he'll be in a hurry to get settled," a woman in a green dress said.

Mary paused, searching for any sign of the cat. Then a black tail swished out from beneath a lavender dress.

The woman in the green dress continued. "I'll send him an invitation to dinner. My Elizabeth would be a good match for him." The cat's tail swished again, harder this time. The woman squealed, jumping. She crashed into the woman to her right, sending her squealing too.

"Something touched my leg!" the woman cried.

The cat bounded away, making for the doorway. Mary followed it, unable to catch up, but she kept the creature in her sights.

"There's nothing there," another woman said from the group. "Is one of the magicians up to something? You can never trust them. I should have listened to my instincts and refused the invitation."

Mary didn't catch the rest of the conversation as she stepped into the hall. The cat meandered toward the back of the manor where the party goers faded away. It entered the last room at the end of the hallway, squeezing into the crack left by the partially opened door. Its hips caught and the cat wiggled. Just as Mary reached for the cat, thinking it stuck, it pulled itself free.

She peered inside. The library. A large fire in the hearth gave the room a warm glow. A few men sat in the armchairs placed in a half circle around the fireplace, discussing the latest horse races and their predictions for the next one. A half-empty bottle of brandy sat on the nearest table. Mary opened the door wider and slipped inside without the men noticing her. Her pulse picked up. She felt like a detective. Or a spy.

A black tail swished around a corner of a bookshelf, and she padded after it deeper into the library. She rounded the corner just as the cat slipped between the wall and a set of shelves with no back. She bent down, finding the cat staring out at her, green eyes shining in the darkness. Her bracelet still dangled from its mouth. The creature looked far too pleased with itself.

"Please give that back." Mary reached for her bracelet. The cat backed up another few steps, staying well out of her reach. She slid in as far between the wall and shelf as she could manage, but the cat was still a hand's width out of reach. A shelf crushed her bosom, making it difficult to breathe in the tight space. The cat laid down as it watched her. "Come on." She pressed against the bookshelf, but it was too heavy for her to budge it.

The cat backed up, escaping through a gap between the books on the bottom shelf. With a mumbled curse she tried to slide out, but found herself stuck. The shelves assailed her hip next, digging into her skin.

"Oh dear," she whispered. There was no way she was going to let herself be found this way. Her embarrassing situation would be gossip fodder for months. "Poor Mary Hawke," they'd say. "Her father lost the business and now she's gone funny."

Another tug and the bookshelf dug deeper. Her skirts rattled several books on the shelf. She twisted this way and that until she finally freed herself, sending her stumbling forward as the shelf spat her out right into a man's waiting arms.

Or rather not as waiting as she'd hoped. The man jerked back in surprise, but caught her by the shoulders, keeping her from falling on her face. As soon as he righted her, he let go. She paused, confusion falling over her as she stared at a man's chest dressed in an impeccable tailcoat. She swallowed as she searched for her voice and gathered herself. "Sorry, sir. I didn't see you there."

The man was tall. His top hat only accentuated his height. Pale and dressed in all black with piercing green eyes, he looked almost exactly like Lord Hallow, the vampire from *Twilight at Hallow Manor.* His appearance sucked the breath right out of her. Although the man's clothes were far more stylish than the outdated wardrobe of Lord Hallow, and his dark hair shorter, looking into his eyes was just like looking at the grisly character as depicted on the cover of her serial. Everything about this man screamed fashionable from his top hat right down to his gleaming boots. His black clothes highlighted the pink of his lips and the green of his eyes. If he'd been shorter, she might have suspected Margaret of playing a prank on her in disguise.

She pinched her arm to make sure she was awake. His image blurred from her watering eyes. He raised his eyebrows at her and she couldn't help but to find the movement elegant. Everything about this man screamed refined. Her bracelet dangled from his right hand, all the charms right where they belonged.

"My bracelet," she blurted out. "The cat stole it." She looked down but saw no sign of the troublemaker. "I've been looking for it, but the cat seems to have gotten away."

"Miss Hawke," he said, holding out her bracelet. A light accent tinged his words, but she couldn't place it.

She gaped at him. "How do you know my name?" This had better not be one of Margret's pranks. She would kill her. Margaret liked to tease her about Lord Hallow's popularity, but enchanting a man to look like him was too much.

"It is on the bracelet." He spoke each word with care.

She blushed in embarrassment. "Right you are, sir." She accepted her bracelet and slid it back on. A quick check ensured nothing was amiss. "Thank you. I thought I'd lost it to the cat for good. I should return to the party before he steals it again."

"I am heading there as well. Please, allow me to escort you." His speech remained slow and careful, and the lilt it gave his words made her want to hear more. Except her tongue was tied with nerves. Lord Hallow imitator or no, he was handsome. And a gentleman. She'd always liked men with dark hair.

She kept an eye out for the cat. Wherever the creature had hidden, it'd hidden well. It took all of her restraint to keep her attention forward. To pretend to be more composed than she felt. Lord Hallow wasn't real. At least he wasn't supposed to be.

In the ballroom, they both stopped a few steps into the room. She glanced at him, their gazes connecting. She looked away, not knowing what to say. "I ...uh ..." It was hard to think with a handsome man beside her. How much of her predicament in the library did he see? "Thank you again." And please don't tell anyone what you saw, she thought.

"May I have this dance?" he asked, that accent of his niggling at the back of her mind.

Relief shot through her. At least that came with an easy answer. "Yes."

They joined the couples on the dance floor. She didn't miss the stares thrown his way from the women. Did they notice his resemblance to Lord Hallow too? The stares grew by the second, and she found her skin itching from all the attention. Their dance began. Her thoughts scattered as she focused on the steps. The other women turned their attention to the dance, leaving her mysterious partner in peace at last.

He danced well despite his stiff movements. Yet she couldn't shake the gloomy feeling clinging to the air about him. It was all the black clothing mixed with his serious expression as he danced. No tell-tale signs of glamour clung to his features. No blurring at the edges of his crisp, perfectly arched eyebrows or the dark hair curling about his ears. Which meant he couldn't be one of Margaret's pranks. Whoever he was, he was a real-life Lord Hallow lookalike.

She didn't mind the silence of their dance as he concentrated on the steps. All the more time to admire him. She was certain she'd never seen him before. But to be at this party he must be someone, either a magician, lord, or businessman. She couldn't begin to fathom who or what he was or get thoughts of the villainous vampire out of her head.

The dance ended, and she waited for him to make a hasty retreat. Instead he asked, "Are you Miss Hawke of Hawke Publishing?"

"I am." Oh no. Only a writer would be asking for her. That would explain his gloomy air as well. The men always came to her with the same story of misunderstood genius. And unlike Charlotte, they could never handle her critiques of their writing. It was always easier to pretend she knew nothing about writing or the business.

He gave her a somber nod. "Does that mean you are acquainted with Lord Hollow?"

Her thoughts veered off course and right into a wall where they sputtered out. "W-what?"

"Lord Hallow. Do you know him? I was told you could acquaint me with him." His face remained serious.

She composed herself. "I suppose so in a manner of speaking." Maybe this was one of Margaret's pranks after all. If so she'd outdone herself. "Why do you ask?"

A woman behind her gasped and her dance partner's gaze focused on something over her shoulder. She turned, spotting her friend Charlotte. Oh no. The poor thing stood frozen as she received a sloppy kiss, not from her fiancé, but from his insidious cousin. Bertram Steepe was a snake through and through to put Charlotte through this public drama in his latest attempt to ruin her engagement to Mr. Martin Steepe. He definitely wanted to replace Martin as heir to the Steepe fortune. She could think of no other reason for his constant antics.

Then Charlotte slapped Bertram. Hard. Bertram's quick reaction spared his cheek, but Charlotte's hand still caught him on the nose. Mary winced at the strike. Bright red blood trickled out of his nose. Mary's dance partner made a noise of disgust and she turned back to him. He pulled his handkerchief out of his pocket and clenched it in his hand. His eyes fluttered shut, the dark lashes long against his pale skin. His Adam's apple bobbed as he swallowed.

"Excuse me, I must be going." He spun and headed off toward the front door of the manor, his steps hurried as he dodged around other dancers.

It took a minute for Mary's senses to catch up with everything. "Wait," she called out, far too late. Charlotte was already at Martin's side, and Mary's dance partner was nowhere to be seen. She gave chase for the second time, reaching the hallway just as the mysterious stranger disappeared through the front door. She followed.

Outside, a young lady waited for a carriage, her arms folded across her chest as she ignored the older woman lecturing her about her poor taste in magicians. Having the same hair, nose, and eyes, Mary guessed them to be mother and daughter. Some noble family she couldn't remember the name of. Based on their open disdain for magicians, she was surprised they'd come to a party here of all places. Then again, the only thing worse to the nobility than rubbing elbows with magicians was missing one of the biggest parties of the season.

"No woman in our family will marry an untitled magician," the mother said. "They aren't proper, and it's uncouth the way they flaunt magic they shouldn't even know."

"I suppose we'll see what father has to say on the matter," the young lady shot back. "I'm certain he doesn't share your opinion." Their carriage pulled up and she stuck her nose in the air as she flounced toward it.

Mary caught sight of the man further down the line of carriages. He chatted with the coachman, one hand on the handle of the open carriage door.

"You get back here!" the older woman shouted, colliding with Mary in her haste to get to her daughter. The woman didn't bother apologizing as she pushed past Mary.

Mary returned to her task, but the man in black was gone. The coachman sat alone. She lifted her skirts and ran, determined to discover his name and interest in Lord Hallow.

"Wait!" she yelled as she reached the coach. She wrenched the door open. "I want to know your na—" Surprise stole her voice away. The inside was empty except for a folded blanket lying on one chair. She swallowed, refusing to believe her eyes. He'd been right here seconds ago. She shut the door. A white handkerchief fluttered to the ground with gold embroidery in one corner. She reached for it, admiring the quality of the embroidery.

When she looked up, she found the coachman watching her, his stare unnerving. "Excuse me, but where is your master?"

He said nothing, but very slowly raised a hand. He pointed to the manor. She followed the direction of his hand to the front door.

There, in the window beside the door sat the black cat, watching her. She turned back to the coachman, but he offered no explanation. She backed away, tripping over her own feet before catching herself against a tree and slipping the handkerchief into her pocket.

The coachman snapped the reins and the carriage jolted toward the road. When she turned back to the house, the black cat still watched her. She wondered if this was how the prince felt when Cinderella got away.

While the prince used the glass slipper to find Cinderella in the end, she hoped she wouldn't have to go around asking eligible gentlemen to blow their noses for her.

Chapter 2

The page in front of Mary remained blank except for the words "Lord Hallow." It'd taken her all of half an hour to get those down. Whenever she closed her eyes she saw a dance floor covered in fog with Lord Hallow standing alone, coattails fluttering like a bat's wings.

"Lord Hallow ... Lord Hallow stared out at the rain." She crossed the line out. "No, no. Lord Hallow ... Lord Hallow ..." With a sigh, she put the quill down for the fourth time. Her mind couldn't focus on anything but the mysterious man from the party. His handkerchief laid in the corner of her desk. A monogrammed "LH" adorned one corner. Their encounter wouldn't stop replaying in her head. At this rate she wouldn't get any writing done today.

She knew many authors in the social literary circles rather well, from wealthy authors who thought themselves a better writer than Dickens, to the more humble authors who wrote penny bloods and were happy to be able to feed their families with the money made from their scribblings. She sifted through her memories of all the recent parties she'd been to but couldn't place the man at any of them except Roquefort's. Surely no one could miss a man that tall dressed in all black. And to have asked about Lord Hallow, what had he been playing at? It wasn't a sign that he knew her pen name, was it?

Her heart raced. She didn't want to be revealed as M.H. Crane. The anonymity made for a comforting blanket beneath which she need not worry what others thought about her writing or her as the writer. No one could judge her work based on who she was. It took no great stretch of the imagination to think of the insults she'd hear from those claiming she was only published because she was a Hawke. The Hawke name alone would make it too hard to prove herself a worthy writer in the eyes of critics. Worse still would be the cries that it was shameful for a woman to be writing penny bloods and not "real literature."

Seeing the popularity of her stories was indescribable. A long-awaited dream she couldn't believe she'd finally reached. She didn't want any of it tainted by arguments over who M.H. Crane was. She didn't need the accolades attached to her real name either. She simply wanted to enjoy the story's popularity.

And yet nothing in her day-to-day life had changed. She'd always thought success as a writer would somehow change her or her life, but no. She was the same Mary Hawke living in the same house with the same family while drinking the same Steepe brand English Breakfast tea every morning when she woke up.

The only difference was the writing deadlines she worried about meeting. If she couldn't get past today's writer's block, she would have to start worrying about the next deadline. Even if the man revealed her as the author, she'd only be the latest piece of gossip until everyone got bored and moved on to the next scandal. Still, the thought made her skin clammy. She'd never liked being the center of attention or the distractions that came with it. Unlike Margaret, she preferred to observe from the sidelines instead of throwing herself right into the middle of drama if she could help it. More attention would only get in the way of her writing.

She hoped Charlotte was doing better than her after the party. There'd been no talk of any changes to her relationship with Martin. Mary hoped that meant the engagement was secure despite Bertram's attempts at ruining it. And with The Great Exhibition right around the corner, Charlotte's fiancé was busy preparing. Hopefully, not hearing any news meant nothing awful was afoot.

Maybe all the drama would give Charlotte a new story idea—one Hawke could publish. If they were careful, the company could come roaring back. After all, they'd been doing well before her uncle muddled everything up. Mary refused to write Hawke off just yet. She'd rather hold onto her hope than give up.

Maybe she should write to Charlotte to check on her. As long as her next chapter still eluded her, she might as well write something. Besides, Charlotte's friendship had come at a time when Mary desperately needed a friend. She should return the favor. Let Charlotte know someone was thinking of her after Bertram's latest stunt.

The parlor door swung open, and she jumped in surprise. Unlike her father, she didn't have a study of her own, forcing her to write in the parlor or her bedroom. She preferred the parlor with its large windows looking out into the geraniums and morning glories lining the front of the house. The desk drawers made it easy to slip her writing inside and out of sight from any prying eyes visiting.

"Mary, dear, good morning," her father greeted as he squinted against the bright sunlight. His bloodshot eyes spoke of too much alcohol at the party. A bad habit on the rare occasions where his nerves got to him. Hawke's troubles hadn't been easy on him. His slumped shoulders gave Mary a sinking feeling. Surely if he'd made any progress toward saving the business, he wouldn't look so gloomy.

Hawke's troubles were harder on him than anyone else. He'd helped build the company and spent more than two decades on making it a success. More than that, he blamed himself for putting too much trust in his brother. For not having a stricter hand with him.

"Good afternoon," Mary returned. It was one in the afternoon after all.

He spotted the papers on her desk and brightened. "How's your writing coming along?"

She gathered up the papers. "Not as well as I'd like. I can't stop thinking about the party or my friend's engagement."

He shuffled over to her, his expression softening. "Are you sad that you aren't engaged? I can ask around for you. We could host some dinners for eligible gentlemen. I'm sure your aunt would love to help."

"No! It's not that. There was ... an unfortunate incident at the party is all. I hope Charlotte is doing well." Her skin crawled at the thought of letting her aunt play matchmaker. Margaret had never gotten along with her, and Mary had given up trying to sweeten her own relationship with her aunt after listening to her insult those women daring to do 'men's work.' If that old hag had her way, Mary would put down her pen to marry and never pick it back up again.

"Ah. Have any visitors showed up today?"

"Not yet. Are you expecting someone?"

"No one in particular. I thought you might be. Or even Margaret." He ran a finger over the right side of his mustache, tamping down the hairs sticking up at the ends. He needed a trim.

Oh. He'd hoped a gentleman would come calling on her after dancing with her at the party. She'd never been good at playing the flirt.

"Have you been working on your embroidery?" He reached for the mysterious gentleman's handkerchief.

She resisted the urge to snatch it away from him. That would be far too suspicious. Being pitied by other young ladies for not having any gentleman visitors was one thing, but her father's pity was quite another. She'd only ever wanted to make him proud. "It isn't mine. I found it. A man dropped the handkerchief at the party, and I plan to return it."

"A man? Who?" He inspected the cloth.

"I don't know. A gentleman with dark hair and green eyes."

He gave her a sly smile. "And you plan to return this to him? Did you find him pleasing perhaps?"

Mary tried her hardest not to wince. The topic of marriage never failed to be uncomfortable despite her father never being harsh. "I'm not returning it because he is handsome but because it is the right thing to do. The problem is I don't know who he is."

"LH?" He rubbed the stubble on his chin. Then his eyes lit up. "I wonder if this is Luke's..."

"... Luke?"

"Luke Holiday. An old friend of mine." He chuckled to himself. "Well I suppose I should say 'Lord Holiday.' He's never been one to brag about his title."

"The name rings a bell, but I don't remember meeting him." Then again, there used to be so many writers, editors, and old school friends stopping by or inviting him out that it was hard to keep track of all the names and faces.

"I don't think you ever have. Last I heard he was away visiting with his wife's family. I didn't know he was back. Someone at the party mentioned a recent death in the family. I should give my condolences."

"Can you describe him?" She wasn't as knowledgeable of the nobility as she was writers and magicians. Barring the magician parties like Roquefort's, which mixed the classes, the Hawke's didn't often rub elbows with lords and ladies. Not unless they were writers.

"It would be easier to show you. Come to my study."

Mary hid her papers away in the desk before following. His study always calmed her and reminded her of happy times. The room smelled faintly of sweet cigar smoke. The smell was stronger than usual as if he'd already smoked one today. That meant he was stressed. He always smoked when he was stressed. They needed to find a way to resolve the Hawke issue soon before his bad habits caught up to him.

Despite the smoky smell of cigars, more than once she'd considered sneaking into the study to write at his desk. But she could never bring herself to do it. The study was too much his domain. She had no qualms entering, but actually writing at his desk would make her feel like an invader.

As a little girl she'd spent plenty of time playing at his feet or sleeping on the divan while he wrote letters and read manuscripts. Sometimes he read them aloud to her. At night nothing got her to agree to go to bed faster than him promising to read her a chapter from a book. Her earliest memories of her favorite stories were mixed with the soothing sounds of her father's voice. Margaret enjoyed the stories too, but not enough to want to write her own. They inspired her to find her own adventures.

He slid on his reading glasses, the frames too circular to flatter him, before searching through his bookshelves. Those glasses always meant he was working or reading. He had time for little else. "Here." At last, he pulled a book down. "He and I went to university together."

He smiled, a real smile this time, and not one put on to soothe her. "He loved literature and debates. We used to discuss books together. He always loved books full of terror and difficult choices." He flipped through the book. Once he found the right page he set it down. "That's him there." He tapped a sketched portrait of a young man. The enchanted image stirred to life and looked out at them, its head tilting to one side before leaning back again. "Don't be fooled by the stern expression. He was quite the charmer in our university days."

Her heart jumped at the sight. The portrait looked exactly like the man she'd run into, and the resemblance to the vampire depicted on the cover of *Twilight at Hallow Manor* was uncanny. If the enchanted sketch were to bare its fangs and hiss she'd have a difficult time telling them apart. "That was him. He's hardly changed." The portrait had the same somber air as the man she'd danced with.

"Once I get the payments to our current printer taken care of, I'll have to pay Luke a visit. He owns a printing press himself, and he's done impressive work using enchantments on the machinery. Our current printer isn't going to keep working with us with how delayed our payments have become." He took his glasses off to rub his eyes. "We'll need to secure a new press. Assuming any will work with us. Word will get around fast."

She gave his shoulder an affectionate pat. "I can call on him and ask about his rates if you'd like. Besides, you are too well known in the business for anyone to think our troubles are your fault."

He shook his head. "No, my concerns with the business are not yours. It is my fault that I didn't see this coming. Focus on your writing and finding a beau." He shifted in his seat and cleaned his glasses with a handkerchief. "I've been meaning to discuss marriage with you for far too long. It's time we start looking for a good match for you. However, I'm afraid Lord Holiday is far too old for you. And already married. Please don't go getting any ideas about him."

"Too old? He looked exactly like this picture. No more than a few years older than I."

"That isn't possible. Not to mention that back in our university days he was quite the womanizer. He isn't a suitable match for you." His eyes drifted to the portrait of her mother hanging on the wall. It was the only picture that remained. All the other paintings had been sold to repay Hawke Publishing debts. "I would like to see you settled and happy. Your mother—" His breath came out shaky as he pushed his glasses back on.

Mary grimaced. "We don't need to talk about her. In fact, I'd rather not."

He gave her a tight-lipped nod. "Margaret is going to need you more than ever. She's always listened to you. Please steer her in the right direction. She's good at getting herself into trouble, but it's about time you both start thinking about marriage." He crammed his handkerchief back into his breast pocket. "I admit I feel out of my depth here. I want what is best for both of you, and with Hawke's future uncertain, I'd like for yours to be taken care of."

Marriage. She always knew it was a matter of time, but she'd avoided the topic as long as possible. Romance never came easy to her. "I don't suggest bringing up that particular topic to her. She won't take it well." The last time an aunt suggested it, Margaret left the parlor and locked herself in her room for the rest of the afternoon. And now with their business and family imploding, there was no love lost on marriage from Margaret.

He lowered himself into the chair. "She is going to need to learn. If I can't save the business, you'll both need good husbands."

The moving portrait in the book blinked up at her, the man's mouth twitching. It made him look strict, like a teacher. "I will do what I can. I would be of more use if you let me help with the business. If we can save Hawke, there'll be no rush."

"You already do enough by helping read and edit manuscripts. I refuse to drop anything else on your shoulders." He picked up his nib pen. "I have some letters to send. Please go back to your writing or any visits you have planned for the day."

"If you change your mind ..." Mary said, pausing at the door.

"I'll handle the business. I don't want you and Margaret worrying over it. And speaking of which, I haven't seen her yet today." His pen hovered over the ink pot. "Is she out?"

Mary searched for a believable lie. In truth she had no idea where Margaret had gone off too, but her father didn't need that worry on his plate. She would handle her sister. "She went out to a luncheon I think."

He rubbed his thumb along the pen. "She has never shown interest in any particular bachelor. I should start introducing her to more eligible gentlemen."

"That isn't necessary," Mary said in a rush, "I think she already has her eye on someone." Margaret would have to be dragged to the altar kicking and screaming, and that wasn't a conversation she felt prepared to have with their father. The best she could do was save her sister from an unhappy marriage. If Margaret preferred a life of business and taking care of herself, then so be it.

Relief filled his eyes. "That is good. I hope it works out." He dipped his pen into the ink and started scribbling away. She took one last glance back at her mother's portrait, making a mental note to take it down once he left. None of them needed the reminder of the pain she'd caused. Mary didn't think she would ever understand her mother's decisions. Her uncle had always had issues with gambling and money. The only thing he had in common with Papa were the good looks that ran in their family and a love for books. Papa had always been the more responsible brother.

Her mother however ... it wasn't worth dwelling on. Nothing could explain away the pain and hurt of the past few months or them choosing each other over the rest of the family. Nothing would excuse their actions.

A thump drew her down the hall to the last bedroom. The door hung open a crack. Mary opened it further at the sound of a curse from inside. "Are you all right? What is going on?"

Margaret froze, one leg still dangling out the window.

Mary sighed. "You've been sneaking around again, haven't you?"

Margaret pulled her leg inside. "I wanted some fresh air is all. I was gone less than an hour."

"In glamour no less." Mary gestured to Margaret's loose trousers and coat. "It's not safe to go out alone, even if people mistake you for a man." Plenty of working women in the area wore trousers, but Margaret never wanted to risk being recognized. Mary suspected her sister liked pretending to be someone else entirely to escape her troubles.

Margaret scoffed. "Your lectures are getting stale. I'm always careful and rarely alone."

"Nothing you can say will keep me from worrying." She tugged on a strand of Margaret's hair. "Make sure you do your hair. You're coming out with me."

Margaret's head snapped up. "What? Where?"

"Father was worrying. I told him you had plans today, which means you are staying with me so he doesn't keep worrying. I have business with a printing press to attend to." Father was wrong. She could help by helping Hawke and she had every intention of doing so.

Margaret wrinkled her nose. "That sounds boring. I don't want to go to a printing press. I bet it's dusty and loud. I'd rather sleep." She cast a longing look toward the bed.

"If you don't come, I'll tell father you've been sneaking out. He'll send you to live with Aunt Beth." Aunt Beth was their father's oldest sister. She was also rather old fashioned with no fondness for magic or women writing or doing anything that didn't include looking after their house and family. She didn't know about Mary's writing. Or the glamour she and Margaret used.

Aunt Beth's heart would give out if she saw the way Margaret dressed as a man to sneak about. Ever since they went to the docks with Charlotte, Margaret's sneaking out had only increased. She hadn't always been this way. Not until their family imploded. But running away wouldn't fix Margaret's worries.

Margaret groaned long and loud. "Aunt Beth is appalled we aren't both already married off like brood mares. She'd make me spend hours embroidering."

"Father already considered sending us to stay with her once Mother ..." She cleared her throat. "I talked him out of it, but don't force him to change his mind. If you want to stay here, you need to at least act like you are on your best behavior to keep him from worrying. And this way I can make sure you don't cause any problems today."

Margaret grumbled but quit arguing. "I'll be your coachman," she declared as she slid a fresh shirt on. "That's far better than getting stuck talking about printing presses."

"Coachman?"

"Yes. I'll drive our hansom cab since we can't afford a driver any-more." She deepened her voice to mimic their father, "We must be careful with our expenses, dears."

Mary stifled a laugh. The spot-on impression left her impressed, but she refused to admit it out loud. No need to encourage Margaret. "Fine," she said. As much as she hated to give into Margaret's antics, having a coachman would be convenient. It would save her a long day of walking.

Surprise crossed Margaret's features. "Really?"

It was the best way she could think to meet her sister halfway. As long as Margaret stayed within her sights, she wouldn't need to worry. "It'd be a long walk otherwise. Keep your hat down and don't let anyone we know get a good look at you."

Margaret grinned. "I'll make sure no one knows it is me." She plopped the hat back onto her head. "So, where are we going?"

"To Holiday Printing Press. For Hawke business. Unless you want the whole family badgering you about marriage again while Aunt Beth lines up suitors, we need to save Hawke."

Margaret saluted her. "Of course, M'Lady!"

Chapter 3

H oliday Printing Press wasn't hard to find. It sat just down the road from Clarke's bakery and several streets over from the current printer Hawke Publishing used. The ride on the other hand was a different matter. Mary clung to the hansom cab's sides as Margaret sent them careening past a slow carriage. They'd only ever gotten their own cab at their mother's insistence. Back then it had been a luxury they could afford with careful spending, but no longer. Seeing how Margaret drove made her wish their mother had never gotten the idea in the first place.

"Are you certain you can drive this?"

"I've done it plenty of times."

Mary added that fact to her list of things to interrogate Margaret about later. Their coachman had always been a careful man, preferring a smooth ride over a quick one. Margaret was the opposite, pushing the hansom cab to its limits as she took them around a corner with a whoop. Mary held in a scream, certain the cab would tip. It didn't, and Margaret was finally forced to slow thanks to the line of traffic ahead of them. When they finally reached Holiday Press, Mary's shaking legs were eager to be on firm ground once more.

Once they fixed the business, she'd start paying fare instead of letting Margaret play coachman. It was far too terrifying. She couldn't believe the shy little girl Margaret used to be had grown up with such a dangerous thirst for adventure. One would have thought that she would grow up to be the quiet writer in the family rather than its boisterous thrill seeker.

The front of the building didn't look half as gloomy as its owner. The late afternoon sun lit up the front room, giving it an inviting air. A weather-worn sign depicting a printing press hung above the door.

Mary's uncle had handled the payments to their current printer among other responsibilities. It'd taken three months before her father found out about the missing payments and all the money his brother made off with. It was only when the press refused to print anything else that he realized something was amiss. He used to check in on the finances monthly, but he'd grown too comfortable over the past year. It was all the leniency Uncle had needed to take advantage.

Her father confronted his brother and the next day he was gone. Mary's mother too. And all the unpaid debt had been left for her family to clean up with what little remained from the plundered business. They'd been struggling to pay the debt back ever since. Securing Holiday for their printing meant one less problem for her father to worry about. One more step to put the business back on the right path while increasing her say in Hawke.

"Shall I escort you, Miss Hawke?" Margaret said, amusement dancing in her eyes as she climbed down.

Mary took a deep breath to steady her nerves from the ride. "You've done enough already. I'll feel much safer with both my feet on the ground."

"So dramatic."

Mary shook off the lingering stress. "Let's go in and see if we can get any information on their printing. Hawke needs to find a new printer, and Holiday is the fastest one around. If they have fair prices, they could be a good option. Plus, Papa knows the Holidays. Maybe we can get a better deal than our current contract."

"What happened to the current printer?"

"Father is paying everything we owe them, but they are refusing future business past their original agreement. Which means if we get no one lined up in the next few months, we won't be able to get any stories printed when the agreement ends. We need another contract in place to avoid having to cancel any stories or miss any release dates."

"Whatever keeps Aunt Beth away. She'll marry you off to the first man who looks at you."

"I don't want to talk about marriage or Aunt Beth." She clenched her hands. There was also her writing. If she could convince her father to let her take a more active position within the business, even better. This bump in the road could be the beginning of her stepping up her role in Hawke."I'm going in," she announced to stop the whirlwind of worries. "I'll see what I can find out."

She marched inside. The smell of ink and paper washed over her in the small room. Two men stood at a desk, haggling over the printing times of a book. The customer waved his hands about as he argued to get a run of his book a day sooner. He tapped a stack of papers on the desk in front of him. His manuscript, Mary guessed.

Her uncle had always dealt with the printing of Hawke serials and books, and had consistently thwarted her attempts to become more involved in the process. He would complain to her father about what a tiresome burden the business of printing negotiations was, insisting it was no place for a "meek young lady." No doubt this was to keep Mary's prying eyes from his own thieving hands, but now the damage had been done twice over. If only she could get Papa to understand the business wasn't a burden to her. She wanted to see the serials fresh off the presses. To help create the perfect lineup of stories..

The closed door to the back couldn't silence the clanging of the presses. There was supposed to be a new printing press unveiled at The Great Exhibition, Applegath's vertical printing machine. It was steam driven and allowed for faster printing compared to earlier models. And yet their steam presses still couldn't keep up with Holiday's. She'd heard talk of the closely guarded enchantments that made it impossible for other presses to compete. No one had any idea of how Holiday did it, and no one outside of publishing cared or knew enough to guess.

"Wednesday is too soon," the reedy worker in glasses said. "An unreasonable demand."

"I thought you had the fastest printing presses in England," the customer, a squat man dressed in a finely tailored suit, taunted. He dumped a stack of papers onto the desk.

The worker didn't take the bait. "We do, but we have too many projects in front of yours. You are giving us short notice while they scheduled theirs ahead of time. You are lucky we have time for this project at all." The man checked a schedule book. "We can do next Thursday but no sooner. That is the best I can offer you."

The customer thought about his options, but the man in glasses didn't budge. He stood with the bored patience of a man accustomed to the demands of poor planners. If his perfectly cut curly coarse hair and clothes were any indication, the man was meticulous in everything. No wonder Holiday's printing was considered the best.

"Get it done by Thursday night and we have a deal," the customer said. The men shook on it, and after the impatient customer left, the bespectacled clerk turned his attention to Mary. Ink stained the apron he wore as well as the tips of his fingers. Apparently his meticulousness couldn't combat his years of printing work leaving its mark.

"Can I help you?"

"I'd like to speak with Lord Holiday."

Surprise flitted over the man's face, but it quickly disappeared behind his stoic expression. "I'm afraid he's unavailable. We're not expecting him here today. Is there anything I can do for you?"

"Can you give me his address? I'd like to call on him."

The man pursed his lips, looking her up and down. "I don't feel comfortable giving that information out."

"Then when can I find him here?"

"Some days he visits after dark, but I don't know when he plans to visit next." He picked up the manuscript and shoved it under one arm. "If there isn't anything else, Miss ..." his gaze strayed to the door. She couldn't fault his work ethic, but her growing frustration threatened to spill over. She squeezed her hands together to force it back down.

"Can I see your printing presses? My father's company is interested in doing business with Holiday."

The man pushed his glasses up the bridge of his nose. "No visitors are allowed to see the presses. Only our workers are allowed in the back."

Then what good are you? Mary wanted to ask as her frustration continued to boil.

"Please, miss, if there's nothing else, I have work to do." And with that he dismissed her as he slipped through the back door. She craned her neck to see, but she spotted nothing except a white wall decorated with covers of books Holiday had printed. Of course they wouldn't make it easy to see the presses. As much as her curiosity gnawed at her, she knew she couldn't risk sneaking into the back. With Hawke Publishing on the line, she wasn't about to start off by getting the family business blacklisted from yet another printer.

She blew out a breath of defeat and stepped out. She'd have to go home and try to weasel Holiday's address out of Papa. Or snoop through his study.

Raised voices from two men bickering somewhere in the alley beside the shop put an end to her sulking. "...Well I don't care! These papers need his signature, so if the boy doesn't show up, you take them to him yourself!"

"I haven't got a horse. You want me to spend a whole bloody week walking to his manor?"

"If that's what it takes, then yes! It'll be your head if Holliday doesn't get this by the end of the day!" With that, a door slammed, presumably on the hapless middleman without a horse.

"Damn delivery boy. Where the hell is he?"

"Right here," a familiar voice answered.

Mary wheeled toward the alley to find Margaret holding out a hand for the stack of envelopes from another worker in an ink-stained apron. She held in her groan. As always, Margaret had found a way to get herself embroiled deeper. It was as if she took an interest only when she knew it would annoy Mary.

"You're late," the man said, looking Margaret up and down, "And who are you? Where's Johnny?"

"Oh, he died recently." She barely missed a beat.

"He did?" A look of horror crossed the man's face. "I didn't hear about that. Are you sure?"

Margaret gave the man a somber nod. "A tragic delivery accident just the other day."

The man frowned and tugged at his apron. "What happened?"

"Overturned wagon. He was crushed by a pile of books." Margaret leaned forward, holding a hand over her mouth to one side as if to hide the secret she was about to tell him. "They say books will ruin the minds of the youth. Let me tell you, they have no idea."

The man nodded, looking stunned. "The poor lad..."

"If his twin, John, comes by for deliveries, don't remind him about the accident. It upsets him."

"Of course." The man shuffled. "Carry on then. Oh, and this small crate too." The man gave the box to Margaret before backing away as if he couldn't wait to escape the awkward situation.

"Right away, sir."

As soon as the man stepped inside, Mary rushed Margaret. "What do you think you are doing?"

Margaret wobbled beneath the weight of the crate. "Help," Margaret wheezed out, her cheeks reddening. "Heavy."

Mary grabbed the far end of the box and between the two of them they carried it to the hansom cab. "Why?" Mary finally asked once they'd hefted it up.

"I heard the man refuse to give you Holiday's address, and this seemed like a good way to get it. I saw no reason to miss the perfect opportunity."

"Sure, except I could have asked Papa instead. He knows Holiday."

Margaret pouted. "Perhaps you could have, but that wouldn't be as fun, would it? And what happened to not worrying Papa?"

Mary folded her arms over her chest as she settled onto the seat, hating to admit her sister was right. "We are here now. Might as well get on with it."

Margaret grinned as she climbed up in triumph.

"Take the turns slower this time, please."

"I don't know where this address is exactly." Margaret shoved one of the letters at Mary.

"That's near Roquefort's. It will be the manor past his."

"Never been that far. There's nothing out there except forest, farms, and villages."

"Which means it is going to be a beautiful ride." Mary smiled at the stack of envelopes. She loved the moors. They not only made a great setting for her story, but she found them beautiful. After growing up on a busy road in the city, she loved how much more peaceful and quiet they were. There was nothing she would enjoy more than sitting at a desk looking out over the countryside and writing. What wonderful ambiance!

Once the city finally gave way to the countryside, Mary sat up straighter to get a better look. Hyde Park couldn't compare in her opinion. Birds twittered and sang from the trees lining the road. She leaned back, letting the scenery wash over her. It was easy to imagine her protagonist running from a vampire hunter across the moors. Or a vampire stalking the shadows at night.

"I could never live out here," Margaret said as they passed a farm.

"Why not?"

"It's too boring. I want the excitement of the city. Out here everything is too quiet."

"That's what makes it peaceful."

"The quiet is too lonely." She lowered her voice, forcing Mary to strain to hear her. "Just like home these days."

Mary twisted around to look at her sister who stood at the back of the hansom cab. "I know what you mean about home," she said, keeping her voice gentle. Charlotte's visits were the highlights of her week. With mother gone, her friends no longer paid them any visits. There were no more dinner parties with Father's business associates or writers. Distant family no longer came either, as if they were too afraid to step into the rift between brothers. Altogether, it left the house quiet. Stiflingly so. She wondered if that was why Margaret kept sneaking out, to escape the house.

"That's Roquefort's manor. We must be getting close. We'll be late for dinner though after taking this long of a trip."

"It doesn't matter. Papa is dining elsewhere today. Some business dinner he is attending." Another road opened up between a cluster of trees so dense they almost missed it. "I think Lord Holiday is down that way."

A few minutes later the trees gave way to gentle rolling hills with a large manor sitting in the middle of them. The manor was similar to Roquefort's. Curtains hung over most of the windows. Horses grazed in a pasture off to their right and to their left sat a small pond. The rose bushes lining the drive were wild and needed a good pruning, as did the rose bushes butting up against the road. Mary twisted this way and that once she was on the ground, taking in every detail she could. Replace the manor with an old castle, and it would have been the perfect setting for Lord Hallow despite the rose bushes that lined the property. Somehow the gorgeous blossoms only added to the sinister air of the whole estate.

"Are you sure this is the right place? It looks ... empty." Margaret shuffled behind the horse, putting it between her and the manor.

"He might be out. If he is, I'll keep coming back until I get a chance to speak with him." Mary started toward the door. When Margaret didn't follow she stopped and turned.

Margaret waved her on. "You can go inside, but I'm staying out here." She stared at the manor. hugging herself with a frown.

"I thought you liked adventure?"

"Yes, but that is different from creepy old houses. It looks like it could be haunted. I don't want to run into any ghosts. I never liked ghost stories."

Mary loved listening to her father tell ghost stories during Christmas, but Margaret had always gone and hid during them. That explained why her sister tended to shy away from the scarier stories Hawke published. Margaret liked adventure and excitement, not terror. "At least help me get the crate to the door. That thing is far too heavy for me to carry alone."

Margaret relented, but as soon as they dropped the crate on the doorstep Margaret rushed back to the horse, leaving Mary to face the imposing front door on her own. The place did look haunted, Mary thought. Right down to the curtain on the second floor above the door that shifted as she approached. A shadowy figure peered down at her. Or perhaps it was just a shadow. Mary certainly hoped so.

She reached for the heavy door knocker, but the door swung open before she could grab it. She gaped at the butler who answered. His impeccable uniform didn't match the haunted outside, but the dusty floors did.

"Can I help you?" His dry, raspy voice gave her goosebumps. Now he matched the manor.

"Delivery," she squeaked out. She handed the letters over. "There is a crate too."

"Where is Johnny?"

"Johnny?" Oh, right. The delivery boy. "I don't know. He didn't show up. I offered to bring the crate with me since I was on my way here anyway." The butler's mouth pursed, and she rushed on. "Is Lord Holiday available? I was hoping to speak to him about his printing business." She held out her calling card.

"I can check to see if the lord is awake." The butler gave it a quick glance before pocketing the card.

Awake? She couldn't imagine why anyone would be asleep mid-afternoon. "The parlor is to your right, Miss Hawke. You may wait there." He hefted up the crate and headed toward the back of the manor. Mary crept into the parlor. All the other doors were shut, making it impossible to snoop.

Unlike the dusty hallway, everything was immaculately clean in the parlor, making her feel as though she'd stepped into a different home. Except the old furniture gave the room an air of forgotten disuse. Some updates would keep the room from feeling like a relic of the past. As it stood now however, it only made Mary feel an eerie sense of discomfort.

The hairs on the back of her arms rose. She glanced about, feeling as if someone were watching her. But no, the parlor was empty, a crack in the curtain being the sole source of sunlight in the dim room.

The tapping of footsteps returned to the parlor, stopping at the door with a creak. She waited, but the butler didn't reappear. "Hello?" She stuck her head out into the hallway, but no one was there. She hugged herself, wishing Margaret had come in with her. What if the manor was haunted? She sucked in a deep breath. This wasn't a penny blood. And despite all the ghost stories she'd ever heard and read, she'd never seen a ghost herself.

A terrible wailing started somewhere upstairs. The noise echoed through the hallway like a tempest. Mary ducked back inside the parlor, flinching from the noise. Her legs tensed, her instincts telling her to run, but fear held her in place. The air felt too heavy. A draft around her ankles made her imagine the house breathing.

"Miss, you must go now," the butler announced as he shuffled into the room.

"What?" Mary asked, unable to hear over the wailing. Was the lord all right?

"You need to leave! The lord isn't home." The butler headed right for the door and opened it, waving Mary out impatiently. Mary headed out the door. "Is there a better time for me to visit to see Lord Holiday?"

She received no answer. The door shut behind her, cutting the wailing off.

"What was all that noise?" Margaret asked, rubbing her right ear. "It sounded like someone was being murdered." She made a face at the manor. "I knew I made the right decision staying out here.

"I ... I don't know." Mary swallowed. The manor felt more foreboding than ever.

"Based on how long you were in there I'm assuming you didn't speak with Holiday."

Mary's shoulders sagged. "No, I didn't. The butler didn't tell me when to come back either. Based on what he said, the lord might be sleeping."

"In the middle of the day? Is he sick?"

Margaret was one to talk with her late nights and mornings. Mary looked back up at the window, but the shadowy figure was gone. In its place sat a black cat watching them. Her hands trembled. Something was wrong with the manor. That heavy air and the wailing ...

She grabbed Margaret's arm and pulled her behind the hansom cab. "Listen, Holiday looks exactly like Lord Hallow. What if he is? What if it's all become real, and he was feeding? All that wailing could have been his latest victim."

Margaret stared at her, mouth flopping open. Then she threw her head back and laughed. "Are you listening to yourself? Vampires aren't real!"

"Oh and I suppose hauntings and ghosts are?"

Margaret's expression soured. "I don't know which ghost stories are real, but I know for a fact you made up Lord Hallow."

Mary blushed, embarrassment rushing up."If you'd seen him and the inside of this place you'd understand."

"The outside is creepy, but that doesn't make him a vampire. Although he does need a new gardener. And some of the chickens got out." She pointed at two chickens pecking at the dirt near a clump of geraniums surrounded by weeds. "Roquefort would be embarrassed if his manor looked like this. Believe me, I went poking through that man's garden and stables. He keeps everything well taken care of. He's desperate to look like nobility. Funny how the magicians build reputations on eschewing the old-fashioned norms of the nobility while being desperate to join them."

Her lingering embarrassment sent Mary clambering into the hansom cab. Margaret was right. She was being over dramatic. One of those writers so obsessed with their own work that they couldn't see life past it. "We should head home. They got the delivery, and Lord Holiday has my calling card. I'll talk to him another day." She continued babbling, not caring what she rambled on about. Talking kept her nerves at bay and her mind off the wailing.

Hawke needed a new printer. If they could get a good contract, the wailing and other oddities about the manor wouldn't matter. There had to be a logical explanation for all of it, and it wouldn't matter anyway since she'd never need to come back. So what if she'd just heard a vampire murdering and feeding on an innocent victim?

Secure the contract, and she could forget all about it and focus on the family business. And her story. Alice still needed to choose between Lord Hallow and the vampire hunter, and those pages weren't going to write themselves.

Chapter 4

"I want to go to the Steepe cafe," Margaret whined as she flounced down the stairs, now clothed in one of her dresses. She did a spin at the bottom, her skirts bouncing. "I'm pretty again, so let's go out to eat. Cooking dinner ourselves will take far too long. Holiday's was a long trip without any refreshments. I'm dying."

"You'd better not be picking the café to glare at Elizabeth the whole time. Our last visit was embarrassing. I thought you two were going to start growling like dogs at each other."

Margaret puffed out her cheeks. "I happen to want their soup."

Mary noted Margaret had done her hair up, including a butterfly pin on the side. She preferred Margaret in these clothes not because she didn't like the men's clothes, but because Margaret didn't hide her face when she dressed this way. Mary would rather be able to look her sister in the eye without either of them worrying about being judged. Sometimes dressing as a man felt freeing. Other times it could feel even more restricting due to the fear of being found out by someone who would recognize them.

It made her envy the daughters of magicians who were expected to flaunt expectations. As the daughters of a respectable businessman, she and Margaret would be judged more harshly if they didn't follow the social mores expected of them.

Her stomach growled, and Margaret cast her a look of triumph.

"See? We're both starving. Let's go eat." Margaret wrapped a shawl around her shoulders.

"Fine." If she didn't get the books she'd been hoping to buy this month, she could put the money toward dinner out instead. It would be a good opportunity to talk with her sister too without their father overhearing. They couldn't keep sweeping everything under the rug and acting like life was normal. Not with Margaret sneaking about and Papa hiding his grief instead of being honest with them. And Mary, well, she felt hollow inside whenever she thought about her mother and uncle. Hollow, because she was afraid to face the betrayal and preferred to push her emotions away.

"I want some of their amazing soup and tea," Margaret said as she pranced toward the door.

"We'll share a pot." The walk sent Mary's stomach growling with renewed vigor. Despite the setting sun, the cafe remained busy. They picked their way through the busy space, swooping in on a free table as soon as the previous occupants vacated it. The inside of the cafe was clean and tidy unlike far too many areas of the city that weren't. Plant boxes lined the windows, and the displays of tea could be seen from the table. She caught hints of bergamot mixed with something smoky clinging to the air.

Unlike Holiday Manor, this was an inviting place that made her want to linger. The cozy space made for a great place to plot out her stories or edit manuscripts. Here she could unwind instead of feeling lonely. There was no worry her mother would suddenly walk back through the front door. There was no floor creaking overhead as Papa paced in his study. And Margaret sat across from her instead of disappearing into the night.

Arjun was there in a flash. "Good evening. May I get you ladies some tea?" There were some ladies who worked part-time at the shop now, but she always preferred Arjun. No one knew the tea as well as he, and he was good at making sales without being too pushy. He could, however, be rather insistent on offering samples of Steepe's various tea blends. It wasn't uncommon to see someone leave with at least one tin of tea after their meal, sometimes many more. Arjun had convinced her more than once to branch out from her usual favorites, and he never led her astray.

"What do you think?" Margaret asked, pulling Mary from her thoughts. "The vanilla tea or Earl Grey?"

"Hmm." Both sounded good. Both were her usuals, and tonight she wanted one of her comfort teas. "One pot of the vanilla black, please."

"Right away, ladies." Arjun hurried off to get their order.

"What if we got a pot of Earl Grey next?" Margaret pored over the list of teas. "Or the breakfast blend."

"No. I told you one pot, and I'm holding us to it. Every little bit we save helps. Besides, we have both of those at home. You can drink it when we get back."

Margaret crossed her arms with a huff. "Wherever Uncle has run off to, I hope the tea is horrid. The coffee too. In fact, I hope he is suffering immensely."

"Let's not ruin dinner by thinking about him. He's caused enough problems." She doubted he cared. Certainly not for the family. Not for his quality of hot beverages either.

The waitress came by with their tea. They each ordered their favorite, a soup for Margaret and a sandwich for Mary.

"Say you managed to negotiate a deal with Holiday Press," Margaret said as she folded her arms on the table, "would that be enough to save Hawke?"

"It would be a start. If Papa can secure even one new investor it will help pay the rest of our debts. We'll have to continue to be careful with our spending, but we'll rebound if we are careful enough. We have plenty of popular writers and serials. We do have a chance, however small it may be." Perhaps too small to allow for any mistakes.

"Except he hasn't had much success getting a new investor. Plus, you didn't get to talk to Holiday today either. We spent a day on the road for nothing." She poured their tea.

Mary looked away, hating how fast her sister poured. At least she no longer splashed tea all over the place. "Not yet, but I'm not ready to give up. We can't afford to."

Margaret scowled, bending the tea menu. "And I won't let Mother or Uncle back into my life. They don't deserve forgiveness for what they've done to us. I thought all those comments about how she married the wrong brother were said from anger. And all her nitpicking over you and me not being proper ladies enough for her tastes. She preferred to foist us off onto our nanny. Now I know better. She doesn't want us, and I don't want her either."

Mary reached across the table for her sister's hand as much for her own comfort as Margaret's. "She never wanted marriage, and wasn't given a choice. But no matter what Mother and Uncle do or have done, I'll always be here for you. Papa too." She swallowed the lump in her throat. Too many times she'd worried she'd wake up and find Papa gone too. Some days she worried Margaret wouldn't come home either.

"Don't you see?" Margaret said, bending the menu further with her free hand. "That's why I'm furious. She and I have always argued, and I gave up on being enough for her long ago, but it wasn't only me she hurt. Have you noticed how little Papa leaves his study? Or how you spend hours every day staring at blank pages in lieu of writing?"

Mary swallowed. Having that pointed out made tears sting the corners of her eyes. She loved to give Charlotte writing advice because it made it easy to ignore her own struggles. It made her feel like even if she wasn't getting any words out, she was still doing something. If she didn't get another chapter finished soon she'd miss the deadline. Losing one of their most popular stories would mean losing money that Hawke desperately needed.

"Papa's worried about us. About our future." She paused. "And with you sneaking about, I'm worried about you too. What if you get hurt? What if you wind up in an opium den or something worse?"

Margaret pulled her hand away with a huff. "I refuse to discuss this. I can take care of myself. I'm going to go look at the teas."

Mary sighed as she watched her sister go. Margaret bumped into a table where a man sat reading the newspaper. Mary didn't know how she was supposed to help Margaret. With her mother gone, she couldn't shake the fear of the family splintering further. It was why she refused to go stay with Aunt Beth. She didn't want to lose Father too, and she feared how he might crumble if he wound up all alone. She rubbed her thumb along the rim of her saucer.

Margaret stood in front of a display of tea, but her head was turned, letting her stare daggers at Elizabeth who sat near the window. If Elizabeth had noticed her, she didn't show it. She kept her attention on her tea while she nodded along to the chatty young lady across from her. Elizabeth was only the daughter of a baron, but her attitude of acting like she might as well be royalty had always set Margaret off.

She didn't know how to soothe Margaret's hurt when she wasn't even sure how to feel about it all. The sense of betrayal she felt was at least easy to understand, but she couldn't fight a guilty sense of relief of knowing she wouldn't have to hear any of her mother's disappointed lectures again. That was why she couldn't marry too soon or she would risk winding up in an unhappy marriage like her mother. She couldn't stomach the thought of carrying the pain forward to push it onto others, the suffering multiplying with each new person it touched.

"Miss Hawke, may I join you?" a soft voice asked.

The voice startled her. She'd been too lost in her thoughts to notice his silent approach. The man staring at her looked as gloomy as the first time she saw him in his black outfit. Even the umbrella in his hand was black as was his cravat. All the black highlighted the pallor of his face.

Past him the last rays of sunlight disappeared behind the buildings. In the darkness of night, he'd be easy to mistake for a shadow stalking the streets. Hadn't the printing press worker said he sometimes visited after dark? Odd. Almost as odd as a lord wanting to sit with her. Or the way all the young ladies at the tables around them stared at him. His attention on the other hand was solely on Mary. Those piercing eyes of his made her heart speed up.

"Lord Holiday, good evening."

"May I join you?" he asked again.

"Yes, of course," she clarified.

Only then did he sit down.

"I'm glad to see you," Mary said as he got situated. "I just came from your manor."

Surprise sent his eyebrows shooting up. "Whatever for?"

"You are Lord Holiday of Holiday Press, are you not?"

He hesitated before answering, as though he didn't want to admit it. "I am. I must have just missed you. My butler didn't let you inside, did he?"

"He did."

Holiday blanched. "I apologize for the state of my manor. I haven't been home for very long." Embarrassment tinged his quiet voice.

She decided to pretend she hadn't heard the wailing for Hawke's sake. If he truly hadn't been at home, then the wailing may not have been his fault. She'd already jumped to one ridiculous conclusion. No need to do it again. "I stopped by because I was interested in discussing your printing press. I hear it is the fastest press in London, if not all of Great Britain."

"It most certainly is." There was a brief uncomfortable pause. "I too was hoping to speak with you, Miss Hawke."

Margaret appeared behind her empty chair, gawking at Lord Holiday. Mary couldn't help but to feel smug after the way her sister had laughed at her. He glanced between them as if he wasn't sure how to respond to Margaret's appearance.

"Lord Holiday, allow me to introduce my younger sister, Margaret."

"A pleasure to meet you." He bent his head as if bowing, a perfect match for his slow, formal tone.

Margaret slid into her chair just as Arjun appeared with their food and tea.

"Might I get you some tea, sir?"

Lord Holiday frowned. "I'm fine, thank you."

"Come now, sir! We have the best chai in the city. Our vanilla chai is very popular this time of day."

Holiday hesitated, his gaze bouncing around the other tables. "Well I—"

"A cup on the house, sir! I insist. One taste and I know you'll be enthralled!"

Holiday raised a hand to protest, but Arjun was already walking away. Margaret pounced. "Why are you talking to my sister?"

Mary nudged her foot under the table, but Margaret ignored her.

Holiday turned his panicked expression from Arjun to Margaret. He swallowed. "I'm looking for someone. At Roquefort's party your sister said she was acquainted with the gentleman."

"A gentleman? Which one?"

"Lord Hallow. I'd hoped she could introduce me. I don't know where to find him."

Margaret gave him a wolfish grin that made Mary squirm. "My sister knows Lord Hallow better than anyone."

He lowered his attention to their teapot, the movement highlighting his long lashes. "Then, Miss Hawke, you are just the person to help me."

Mary couldn't decide how to react to the sincerity in his voice. Did the poor man really not know about Lord Hallow? Then again, that light accent in his voice made her wonder if he was even from around here. Margaret elbowed her in the side and Mary considered telling her sister to go look at the tea a little longer.

Finally, she cleared her throat. "Why do you want an introduction to Lord Hallow?"

He took a moment to mull over the question before giving an answer as careful as the slow way he spoke. "Ever since I returned home I have been mistaken for Lord Hallow more times than I can count. I've never met him and was hoping to clear up the confusion. I thought meeting him would be a good start."

Margaret turned, her shoulders shaking as she held in her laughter.

Arjun returned with a cup of chai, setting it before Holiday with a loud clack that made the man startle. Once more he raised a hand as if to protest the cup, but Arjun was already rushing back off to the shop counter. Defeated, Holiday sniffed at the tea but didn't take a sip. The smooth vanilla scent made Mary regret not getting a cup for herself.

"Is something wrong with your tea?"

"No. It simply isn't what I'm accustomed to drinking." He gave the tea a dubious look. "I got a letter the other day addressed to this Lord Hallow. Unfortunately, I don't have his address to forward it to him."

"Someone sent you mail for Lord Hallow?" Margaret asked, mouth agape. "Seriously?"

Holiday shifted in his seat, keeping one hand wrapped around the warm cup. "Yes, and it would feel impolite to make sure the letter doesn't reach him. Miss Hawke, can you tell me where to find Lord Hallow?"

His earnest expression made her take a deep breath to steady her thoughts. He really was being serious.

"Lord Hallow has no address."

His forehead wrinkled. "I'm afraid I don't understand. Has he moved?"

Margaret looked away again, clapping one hand over her mouth.

"No, Lord Hallow ... well he isn't real."

His expression turned to bewilderment. "How is that possible?"

"He's a character in a popular penny blood, *Twilight at Hallow Manor*. Hawke publishes it."

His cheeks turned a light shade of pink that she almost missed. His fingers twitched. "I admit I'm not familiar with the story."

"We could have guessed that much," Margaret said. "Or else you wouldn't be asking about him."

The pink on his cheeks deepened. "I can't imagine why anyone would mistake me for a fictional character."

"You do bear a great resemblance to him," Margaret said. "You might want to read the story to understand."

"I haven't had much time for reading since my return. What is it about?"

"The story is about a maid who takes a position working for Lord Hallow," Mary answered.

"Don't forget the best part," Margaret added. "Lord Hallow is a vampire."

The color drained from Holiday's face. He looked away, and his hand tightened on his cup. "I see."

Mary followed his gaze to the priest sitting at a nearby table. The priest stared at Lord Holiday, one hand on his open Bible. In his other hand he clutched a rosary. His lips moved in a silent prayer. "Who is the letter from? The one addressed to Lord Hallow."

The cafe's clock chimed. "A young lady I don't know handed it to me in Hyde Park and didn't give me time to explain once I saw the name." He pulled out his pocket watch and checked the time. "I apologize, but I need to be on my way or I'll miss my train." He stood, his gaze darting back to the priest. He hastily dropped a few coins on the table, presumably as payment for his complimentary chai. He then tipped his hat farewell and then left, the heads of all the young ladies craning to watch him go.

"Wasn't he dressed like Lord Hallow?" someone behind Mary whispered.

"He's getting your fan mail," Margaret said with a sniff. "That's a little unfair, don't you think?"

"We don't know for certain he received fan mail. I have some supportive readers yes, but none quite so ardent. I don't expect any of them would think Lord Hallow was real." Then again, she'd never expected her story to become so popular let alone one of Hawke's biggest stories. "He wasn't supposed to be the one everyone falls for."

"That's because you don't sit at the tea parties and hear how the ladies talk about Lord Hallow. They would marry him if they could despite him being a bloodthirsty vampire. I told you the brooding mysterious man will always be the favorite instead of your godly, virtuous vampire hunter. He's too preachy. It's like you don't read romance." She clicked her tongue.

"I don't! And the story is meant to be a horror, not a romance."

"Which makes the romance all the more enthralling. And besides, how could it be anything other than fan mail when it was addressed to Lord Hallow?" Margaret grabbed Holiday's chai.

"Margaret!"

"What? He didn't drink any. No sense in letting it go to waste."

It was a good point. One she had no comeback for.

A man walked past them. Something about him she couldn't place felt familiar. Mary squinted at him, her suspicion growing.

"Roger! Is that you?"

The man pulled his hat down lower as he tucked his newspaper under his arm.

"I knew it. You'd better not be watching us."

Roger didn't turn. He quickened his pace, heading off in the same direction outside that Lord Holiday had gone.

"Who is Roger?" Margaret craned her neck to watch as Roger stepped out of sight of the cafe.

"He was that man who was following Charlotte. Remember the one you saw out your window the night after we visited the docks to find out what Bertram Steepe was up to? I bet it was him then too. He hired Roger to investigate Charlotte to find a way to destroy her engagement to his cousin."

Margaret wrinkled his nose. "Sounds like an awful man."

"Indeed." She chewed on her bottom lip and glanced at the door. "Stay here. I'll be right back."

"Where are you going?"

"I've let Lord Holiday slip away too many times. I won't allow it this time."

Chapter 5

She couldn't see Roger. He blended in too well with all the other men wearing similar hats and coats. Lord Holiday's tall frame on the other hand was easy to spot as he headed down the sidewalk.

Mary rushed after him. "Lord Holiday!" She narrowly missed a puddle, too focused on him to see it. She dodged around a street vendor next, closing the gap between her and Holiday.

Lord Holiday jumped as she stepped up beside him. "Miss Hawke." Her name sounded more like a question than a statement. His brow creased in confusion as he halted.

"Lord Holiday, please wait. I wanted to speak to you about your printing press. I'm interested in doing business with you. I mean for Hawke," she clarified. His pretty eyes made it hard to think with their attention pinned on her. Her mind kept wanting to wander to his lips next.

He checked his pocket watch. "My train will be here soon. I don't have enough time to discuss all the details at the moment." They both shifted closer to the wall of a store to avoid a group of gentlemen wandering past on the busy sidewalk. Between all the shops, pubs, and street vendors, there would be no chance of having a private conversation here. Too many people.

"I see a handsome man in your future," a woman a few steps away predicted to a young lady. "And a courtship." The lady's friends giggled in anticipation.

"What will he look like? Will he be rich?" the lady asked. Mary ignored the scene. She was no stranger to the mediums on this street. They were as pushy as the street vendors. Anything they could say to lure in customers was fair game to them. Ladies were prime targets for them, Mary included.

"Come into my shop for a reading and I can tell you," the medium told the giggling women. "I can give you a discount."

A month ago, one of the mediums predicted a mysterious stranger for Mary, as if she would believe a vague prediction like that. She saw strangers passing by on the street every day. And she had more important issues to worry about, like Hawke and her story. She didn't care how mysterious a stranger could be.

She shifted her attention back to Holiday. "Then can we meet sometime for tea or dinner? Hawke needs a new press, and I'd like to explore our options as soon as possible." She handed him one of her calling cards, hoping he didn't notice the nervous tremble in her hands. Botching this would mean destroying Hawke's chances of securing a new printer. "Whenever you are available, please let me know."

He glanced down the road before looking at her calling card. "I will send you an official invitation once I double check my schedule at home."

"That sounds wonderful." She smiled at him. She didn't know how Papa chose what was best for each of his business meetings, but as long as she managed to get a chance to discuss the press with Holiday she would be satisfied no matter who did the hosting. She knew the prices of the current press. If she could manage a similar deal with Holiday it would prove she could handle helping more with Hawke.

He pocketed her calling card. "I might have time in a few days for a meeting. Are you available this Wed—"

"Ah, what a lovely young couple," a voice drawled. A woman stepped up to her, crystal earrings and necklace catching the light of the nearby shop.

Mary cringed. Not the medium. Two of them worked across from each other, making the road dangerous to tread unless Mary wanted to hear promises of either spinsterhood or marriage. Neither medium seemed able to make up their minds on which one awaited Mary. She was convinced they never recognized her or remembered all their previous predictions given to her.

"Uh," Holiday said, glancing back and forth between Mary and the medium. He shifted on his feet, the discomfort on his face obvious.

"It isn't like that," Mary said. "It's more of a business relationship."

The mediums eyebrows rose. "Oh?" She looked Mary over, nose wrinkling. "I didn't realize Madame Beaumont's ladies had become so ... brazen these days. They usually stay away from this street."

Holiday perked up, the discomfort falling away as he smiled at Mary. "Madame Beaumont. Is that your mother's name?"

"No!" She waved her hands in front of her in a panic, cheeks blazing. "I have nothing to do with Madame Beaumont or her kind." Mary only knew the name thanks to overhearing a conversation between her uncle and father in which Papa chastised him for spending money on Beaumont's ladies instead of settling down. "I didn't mean that kind of business."

"Well then, would you like a reading? I'm the best seer around, unlike others." The medium glared at her rival across the street who was in the midst of waving goodbye to the group of giggling women leaving her shop. "I can read your palm. Or offer a séance. Everyone has someone they miss." Thanks to the rise in spiritualism, so had the claims of those who said they could speak to the dead. Mary had never seen it for herself. Then again, there were no dead she wanted to disturb.

"No thank you. I already had a reading last month," Mary said, deciding it was a polite enough rejection. If she could get the woman to go away, she could get back to securing a meeting with Holiday. Thanks to the train schedule, her time with him was ticking away.

"I would like a reading," Holiday said, offering his hand. "I would also like to come back for a séance some other time. You do them at midnight I presume."

Both women looked at him in surprise.

"I have questions about my father," he added.

The medium collected herself. "Not unusual to have questions about the secrets of those dear to us. Let me see what your palm has to tell." She peered down at the lines of his hand.

It may have been Mary's imagination, but for a moment she thought the crystal at the woman's throat glowed. Just the reflection from the lantern of a passing carriage, she assured herself. That was a more comforting thought than the woman using magic on them. Charlotte's poor cursed cousin was proof of what could go wrong when magic was used by untrained hands. Poor clumsy Claude was a warning to not take curses lightly, but if this woman ruined her chance to do business with Holiday, Mary would be sorely tempted to pay the other medium to curse her.

The medium traced one of the lines of Holiday's hand. "You come from an old, prestigious line."

Mary wanted to roll her eyes. Anyone could tell by looking at his clothes that he was well off. The compliment would please anyone full of themselves.

The woman let out a dramatic sigh. "I see ... grief. So much grief," she said, voice cracking on the last word. "And ..." She dropped his hand. The color drained from her face. Her eyes started to roll into the back of her head. She stumbled back a step before regaining control.

"Did you see something?" He asked, hope lighting up his eyes.

The woman shook her head. "I saw nothing." She took another step back, holding both hands out to keep him away. "Stay away. Don't come back." The medium fled into her shop, slamming the door behind her. She peered out the window at them before flipping the open sign to closed. Then all the curtains slid over the windows.

Mary couldn't decide whether to feel pleased the woman was finally out of the way or disturbed by her behavior. Mary's grief had never gotten that reaction.

Holiday sighed. "None of them have been able to give me answers."

She hadn't taken him for the type to be interested in mediums. He seemed far too serious a man to be interested in such frivolities. "There is another medium across the street. Her readings tend to sound more believable." Mary pointed across the road. She mentally slapped herself. Time was ticking down to the train arriving and she'd gone and lost herself more time to get their meeting settled. She blamed his good looks for making her eager to please. The pallor wasn't becoming, but his bright eyes, pink lips, and refined features were.

The medium across the road met their gazes. Her eyes widened. Instead of fleeing into her shop, she ran.

"That's ... new." Mary said. She'd never seen them react in such a way to anyone before. She peered at Holiday out of the corner of her eyes, wondering could have given the mediums such dramatics. "Do they all react that way to you?"

"No. The last one told me she could do nothing to help me as soon as I stepped into her shop. I tried to explain I was there for a reading, but she wouldn't listen to me. Told me to get out." Holiday checked his pocket watch again. "Are you available Wednesday for tea? I will make sure my schedule is clear."

"Oh, uh, yes. Wednesday would be fine."

He tipped his hat to her. "Wednesday it is, Miss Hawke."

"I'll look forward to it." She watched him go, wondering if she'd just made a grave error agreeing to meet with him alone. The curtain in the first medium's shop moved, but when she looked it fell back into place.

She headed back to the cafe. She'd been badgered by the mediums enough to not put any stock into what they had to say. Come Wednesday she'd get a contract with Holiday for Hawke, and Hawke would be that much closer to getting out of hot water.

Mary set down the stack of submissions on her desk. Her father always brought them home with him to read, and over time reading them became Mary's job. Mostly because she would steal the manuscripts out of his study to read. She passed any promising stories on to Papa, and despite his initial misgivings, he eventually learned to trust her judgement. If Wednesday went well, they'd need to start thinking about their next stories.

"Anything good?" Margaret leaned over the desk to peer down at the manuscripts.

"Another whining letter from the man who wants to complain about the historical inaccuracies he finds. Hasn't he ever heard of suspending your disbelief?" She scanned the letter before tossing it into the garbage. "Yes, we get it. Abraham from Oxford Street knows more history than all of us."

"It's not him I'm looking for. His complaints are insufferable. There's word going around that the author of *The Great Garden Gnome Detective* has been hard at work on a new story. Is it in there?"

"We are not publishing a serial about garden gnomes no matter how many times you insist." Margaret always went for the odd submissions whenever she interfered with Mary's reading. The ones with rough writing or bizarre plots that wouldn't go over well with readers.

In truth most submissions weren't of publishable quality to begin with. Many new writers were satisfied to send in their haphazard first drafts and were clearly unfamiliar with the concept of proofreading their own work. Some would, however, stick with writing and improve enough each story that eventually they would submit something Hawke could use. Those ones were the story artisans who didn't let the rejections scare them away from their craft.

Mary also wrote a lot of awful stories in her early days of writing. It was all part of becoming a good writer, or at least that's what she told herself. That notion dulled some of her embarrassment whenever she remembered her older works.

"Of course not, but he sends something every six months like clockwork. I don't want to miss anything. Besides," she grumbled, "it would be nice for something to continue on as normal around here."

Mary adjusted her shawl. A spring chill had set in, made worse by the cold misty rain. "I haven't looked through the whole stack yet. I don't know what is in here." She was hoping to find Charlotte's story. But lately the stack of unread manuscripts had become unwieldy. She could tell Papa hadn't read any of them. He always made notes when he read a story, and he kept a stack of the stories he liked best on his desk. A stack that had remained empty since Uncle had run off.

Margaret flipped through the manuscripts, face scrunched in concentration. "Ah-ha!" she held up a fistful of pages. "The next installment in the series. I'm going to enjoy this over a pot of tea." Margaret was proof enough that even the oddest stories could find an audience, albeit a small one, to enjoy them.

The tell-tale creak of the front door echoed through the room. "Girls?" their father called out.

"In here!" Mary answered.

Their father stepped into the room, his cheeks red from the cold air. A fervent excitement shone in his eyes. One Mary hadn't seen since

Hawke's troubles began. In fact, she hadn't seen that look since her story first soared in popularity.

"What is it?" Margaret sat up, exchanging a worried look with Mary. "Has something happened?"

"I had dinner with a certain Mr. Steepe tonight." He tossed his hat onto the empty chair.

"And?" Mary and Margaret said in unison.

"And we're saved!" He threw out his arms, unable to contain his excitement. "Mr. Steepe has saved us. Everything is going to be all right."

"Mr. Steepe invested?" Mary asked. Martin hadn't shown any interest since the initial letters Hawke sent. Had Charlotte finally convinced him?

"Even better."

"What could be better?" Mary wrung her hands. Somehow, this news didn't feel good.

"He bought Hawke! We won't need to worry about the business anymore, and I'll have more time at home to spend with you girls." His smile fell. "Your mother always complained I wasn't around enough."

"That doesn't mean you needed to sell Hawke!" She clutched her pen, her grip tightening until it snapped in half, the sound like a gunshot in the quiet room.

His face fell. "It was the only choice I had. More importantly, we have no debt to worry about. There was far too much of it to make the company as successful as it once was."

"But—"

Margaret shot her a warning look. "That's wonderful, Papa. Perhaps instead of imposing on Aunt Beth for dinner tomorrow, we can celebrate instead?"

That was just like Margaret to weasel out of seeing their aunt. Mary would rather keep Hawke even if it meant putting up with one hundred nagging aunts.

"Great idea. We'll go out somewhere." He frowned at the stack of manuscripts in front of Mary. "No need to trouble yourself over these any longer. You can focus on your own writing now." He grabbed the stack of papers and carried them up to his office, leaving Mary gaping after him. The broken pieces of pen dug into her fingers. The hollow feeling in her gut grew, gnawing away at her insides.

Chapter 6

The drizzling rain gave way to cloudy skies by dawn, making it a good morning for a walk as the sun peeked through the clouds. Mary walked as fast as she could manage after getting a late start. She'd awoken hoping Hawke being sold was just a nightmare, but it wasn't so. Worse, Papa truly seemed happy, and it made her feel selfish for wanting to cry over the news.

Charlotte waited in front of a dress shop in Piccadilly Square, her attention glued to a royal purple dress full of lace and bows. On the other side of the door an exhausted man sat on a bench. A girl no older than ten tapped on the window from inside as she squeezed between two mannequins. He waved back to her before letting out a long yawn.

The shop was a short walk from Charlotte's bakery and a longer, but pleasant walk for Mary, making it one of her favorite spots to meet with friends. She would usually meet up at the tea room across the street, which of course had taken to serving Steepe brand tea. However, judging by Charlotte's interest in the dress shop, she'd been too distracted to make it that far.

"I'm sorry," Mary apologized as soon as she reached Charlotte. "I haven't found your story yet. We have so many unread submissions that I'm going to need to sort through everything to find it. I promise to let you know my thoughts as soon as I find it."

"That's all right." Charlotte shifted on her feet, her fingers worrying a button on her dress. "Have you heard the news from your father yet?"

"That Mr. Steepe has bought Hawke? Yes. Although I was hoping for an investment, not a sale." Her life had always been intertwined with Hawke Publishing. She couldn't fathom a life without the business. And if they didn't own the business anymore, would she have less control over her stories?

"I'm afraid it gets worse. It wasn't Martin who bought Hawke, but Bertram."

"Bertram?" Mary gasped. "Not that devil! Papa didn't say which one it was. I'd assumed Martin."

"Yes, I'm sorry," Charlotte rushed on. "I didn't know what he was doing or that he was aware of Hawke. Rest assured I've already spoken to Martin on the matter. He has promised to see to everything. We'll do what we can to get it out of Bertram's hands at least."

Mary hugged herself. "It was my father's decision. It is his business to do with as he pleases, but it does hurt to know that it's gone now. I always wanted to take over for him one day, but now ..." All she would have left was her writing.

"I will talk to Martin and see what can be done with the business."

"I appreciate it, but at this point I don't know if Hawke can be saved." Her stomach ached as much from the realization as from her skipping breakfast. She'd always viewed the business as something intertwined with her family and her future. Now it was just another part of her life which had suddenly been torn away from her.

They headed down the road, stopping to look at the storefront displays until Mary's gaze glossed over. She'd never expected to find a new friend at Mr. Steepe's tea party, but with her publishing friends no longer visiting, it was a comfort to know she still had one friend willing to see her. Even if she was merely Mary instead of Mary of Hawke Publishing. "Why did he buy Hawke? Do you know?"

"He thought I was chasing after Martin's wealth purely to trick him into buying Hawke."

Mary smirked. "To be fair, you did consider it."

"Perhaps at first, but things do...change." She grimaced from guilt. "I just wish Bertram would change. No matter how many times he fails to ruin my engagement to Martin, he still refuses to give up. Buying Hawke is just another of his schemes."

"What a snake." She'd never realized what cruelty lay beneath his handsome face. Now he'd pulled her family into his cruel game of ruining Charlotte's engagement. It was too late for her to stop him. All she could do was find a way to move forward.

She stopped outside of a jewelry store. "Can we go inside this shop? I want to look at their bracelet charms."

"I've considered getting a charm bracelet too. I like yours, but I don't bother with jewelry since I can't wear any while I work at the bakery. Although I suppose if the wedding isn't called off, I won't be baking quite as much anymore." Charlotte stopped beside a display of charm bracelets. "That is hard to imagine." She reached for one of the bracelets, admiring the craftsmanship.

"Your wedding will not be called off. I refuse to live in a world where that horrible man ruins it for you. His cousin has to see the truth eventually. Even Martin can't be that obtuse."

Charlotte gave her a nervous giggle.

Mary wound her way around a man shopping for an engagement ring and several young ladies looking at necklaces. Her parents had never been happy together as far back as Mary could remember. Their marriage had come about from pressure from both families thinking it would be an advantageous match, except they never went well together. That left their mother moping about the house when she wasn't out socializing and Papa spending long hours at Hawke. She pitied her mother for getting trapped in a marriage she didn't want, though it was hardly an excuse for the way she'd always treated them.

She wanted to believe at least one couple could be happily married. That love was real and not a mere fairy tale. She desperately hoped Charlotte could prove as much to her despite the odd start to her engagement. She'd never heard of anyone else getting engaged over having the same favorite tea, but it suited Martin Steepe.

"I'm going to talk to Martin about it again at The Great Exhibition opening. I promise you we'll sort all of this out."

"I can't believe the Exhibition is opening already." Her hand brushed over a rose charm. "This spring has flown by in a flash." Burning paddle boats, escaping tavern fights, and having a lord walking around looking like Lord Hallow made time rush by. If not for Hawke's troubles, it would have been one of the most wonderful springs of her life. At least it was never boring. "How is Martin?" She watched Charlotte closely.

Charlotte smiled, a dreamy look overtaking her expression. "He is well. Excited and nervous about The Great Exhibition, but well." Her lips quirked up and her hold on her parasol went slack. The handle started to slip from her grip, and Charlotte snapped back to the present. Mary made a note of the dreamy expression. It would be perfect for Alice when she spoke to Lord Hallow.

"Charlotte, I ..." She swallowed and then tried again. "Can I tell you a secret?"

"Of course." Charlotte gave her an inviting smile. The sweet air about her made talking with her easy. Knowing she had been through her own unexpected twists and turns ever since first fainting after her surprise engagement announcement in front of strangers made Mary feel like Charlotte could understand.

"What I said about my uncle ruining the business wasn't entirely the truth." She inspected several charms while she gathered her thoughts. "He did his best at ruining Hawke, but he didn't run off alone. My mother went with him. She hasn't sent word since then, and at this point I hope she never does. I don't think I have it in me to forgive her. I wanted to step up and help my father run Hawke, but—" her voice cracked and she swallowed

Charlotte rubbed her shoulder. "I can't imagine. I'm sorry. I won't pretend to know how you feel, but you are always welcome to visit the bakery if you need to get away. I can save you a pastry. And next time I visit I will bring you fresh tea. I've been getting acquainted with all the Steepe tea flavors better."

Mary smiled through the weight of her grief. "Thank you."

"If you ever need help, let me know. But don't tell my mother, or she will ply you with more bread than you can ever possibly eat until you can't stand to see another loaf."

Mary laughed. "I'll keep that in mind. She sounds sweet." She picked out a miniature mirror charm. "What do you think of this one?"

Charlotte blinked at it. "It's, uh, bright? I suppose it would be hard to lose."

Mary nodded. "Yes. I like the gold frame of the little mirror. It's pretty."

"Ah," the shopkeeper said as he sidled up on the other side of the counter. "This is one of our most popular charms. Even in the dark, it still shines brightly!"

He held his hand over the charm to shield it from the morning light. Runes within the gold frame began to glow gently, and the mirror remained as bright as it had in sunlight. Perhaps even brighter.

"Lovely isn't it? And practical too! Young ladies have told me it makes an excellent mirror for applying makeup at dimly lit parties."

Mary frowned. She hadn't put much time into her makeup this morning. Neither she nor Margaret had shared their mother's belief that a woman's highest calling was to be beautiful. As little girls they did take quite naturally to her lessons on glamour magic, though they much preferred using it to turn themselves into characters from books, like Oliver Twist and the Hunchback of Notre-Dame.

The shopkeeper seemed to notice the change in Mary's mood, and without missing a beat changed tactics. "For others, it's also a reminder to remember who you are, no matter how bad things may be."

"No matter how bad things may be..." Mary considered the charm one last time. "That is indeed something worthy of remembering. I'll take it."

"Excellent choice, miss."

It hadn't been much, but it was the first time she'd bought herself anything since her mother left. Now that the business was gone, she didn't feel guilty spending money on something so frivolous. No box was needed. The shopkeeper added the charm to her bracelet for her before she left the shop.

Outside, a never-ending line of carriages drove past them beneath the darkening sky. While she loved the thought of writing on the moors, sometimes she wanted to be surrounded by the bustle of the city and other people. Piccadilly was always busy and bursting at the seams with street vendors and visitors.

The delicious scent of eel jelly and fried fish wafted through the air. The mouth-watering aromas reminded her of her childhood when father would buy both every week from his favorite street vendor and get some for Mary too. Once Margaret got old enough to join them, she was only brave enough to eat the fish.

"I've been wondering, did you ever find the man you were looking for at Roquefort's party?"

"Yes. Apparently he is a lord. Lord Holiday." They walked past a vendor hawking fresh flowers. It was the very same vendor her father used to buy flowers for her mother. More than once, Mary saw her throw them away as soon as Father walked away. Each time Mary fished them out and hid them away in her bedroom to dream of a day someone might bring her flowers.

She couldn't see Charlotte throwing away flowers. Not with the way her eyes sparkled when she talked about Martin Steepe. "He may look a great deal like Lord Hallow, but it turns out he's just a humble businessman. He owns Holiday Printing Press. I had asked to meet with him in hopes of securing a new deal with Hawke but now ..."

"Do you have a meeting set up?"

"He said he'd send an invitation for tea. He lives out on the moors, and it's a long way to go without any business to discuss."

"You should still go."

"You really think so?"

"Yes." Charlotte stopped to smell the lilies the vendor was selling before continuing. "You'd get to dine with a lord. I've never done anything like that before. Besides, Hawke may be Bertram's for now, but you are still a writer. Why not keep making connections with those in publishing?"

"I suppose it would make for good book research too." The next few chapters of *Twilight at Hallow Manor* hadn't gotten any easier to write.

"Exactly!" Charlotte linked their arms. "I didn't want to go to Martin's first tea party, but I did because of my mother and a friend insisting I go. You never know what may happen." She lowered her voice. "Is he handsome?"

Mary groaned. "Yes, but according to my father he is unavailable."

Charlotte sighed. "What a shame. A man who looks like Lord Hallow must be fascinating. Introduce me to him someday, okay?"

"If I get a chance. He's rather elusive. A bit out of touch with the world as well, it seems."

"What do you mean?"

"The poor man didn't know Lord Hallow wasn't real. It seems some of my readers have been handing him letters addressed to Hallow, and I don't think all of them were merely joking. He was hoping I'd get him in touch with the real Lord Hallow to clear up this little bout of mistaken identity."

Charlotte pressed her hand over her mouth as she laughed. "He must be a very popular man indeed. I can't believe I missed him at the party."

"I had written him to be a villain, you know. But between all the young ladies begging to work as his maid and now a lord hoping to meet him, I wonder if I'm doing something wro— "

Charlotte cut Mary off by grabbing a hold of her arm. She squinted up ahead. "Is that Roger?" She pointed to a man sitting on a bench with a newspaper in hand. He checked his watch before folding up the paper and standing.

"Seems so. I ran into him at the cafe the other day. I think he is still keeping tabs on us."

Charlotte chewed on her bottom lip. "Bertram got what he wanted. There is no need for Roger to keep spying on me let alone you too. There is nothing else for him to learn."

An idea struck Mary and she grinned. "I know one way to find out what he's after. Let's follow him."

"Why is it that I always end up in a chase when I'm with you?" Charlotte asked as Mary hid behind a vendor stall, leaning out to watch Roger as he got up and ambled down the sidewalk.

"You are the one that got us followed in the first place." She tugged Charlotte behind her, hiding both of them from sight. "If Bertram is trying to dig up blackmail on you, you should do the same to him."

"An interesting idea." Her brow knitted in thought. "Maybe I should try a detective story next."

"Still have writer's block?"

"Yes." Charlotte adjusted her parasol. "No idea I've considered has felt right yet. And my head keeps getting sidetracked with thoughts of Martin." Her cheeks turned a light pink. "I'm not going to give up. I just need to find the right story."

Mary hoped it was the same for Lord Hallow. There was the matter of what to do about him being a vampire to figure out yet. Would he turn Alice? Or keep her mortal? Or sacrifice himself in a tragic ending? Or would he be an irredeemable villain that drove Alice into the arms of the vampire hunter? She didn't want to continue the story indefinitely until readers grew too tired to keep reading it. She wanted to give Alice and Hallow a proper ending.

Roger continued down the sidewalk with that ever-present newspaper of his tucked under one arm. Had he ever actually read it, or was it merely part of his disguise? He stopped at a drink vendor. Mary halted in front of a cobbler's store, angling her parasol to hide her identity if Roger happened to look their way. "Where do you think he is going?"

"I don't know. Can you spot who he's following?"

Mary peeked out from behind her parasol. "He is drinking … ginger beer I think." He sipped on the drink, turning to peruse a theater advertisement. He checked his pocket watch and then browsed the selection of hats for sale by a nearby street vendor. "I can't tell who he is following. He doesn't seem to be watching anyone in particular." If she'd had the money earlier to hire a detective to find her uncle and mother, she would have. But now she wasn't so sure she wanted to know where they were. Coals of anger burned in her chest. She'd rather have her uncle stripped of everything he stole and then some.

"Roger is simply too good for us to figure out his target." Charlotte watched Roger in awe. "I wonder what it's like to work as a private detective."

Roger tried on a hat. He adjusted it, wiggling the hat from side to side. Then, deciding against it, gave the hat back to the vendor and moved on to buying a sandwich to go with his beer.

"Are you all right?" Charlotte gestured toward Mary's hands. "Your parasol handle is creaking."

Mary loosened her grip. "I'm fine."

"Oh!" Charlotte grabbed Mary's arm. "He is on the move again. And he's carrying something in his hand, but I can't see what it is." Roger crossed the street and they followed. Charlotte giggled. "Following the detective. It feels as though we are getting our revenge on him."

The darkening sky opened, and fat raindrops fell. Around them dozens of umbrellas opened. Charlotte switched from her parasol to her umbrella.

"Can I share? I only brought my parasol." Mary huddled under the umbrella with Charlotte. Roger took refuge under a store awning, which was already sagging from last night's rain. The crowd around them scrambled to shelter indoors or under awnings as the rain grew heavier. The foot traffic pushed them closer to Roger.

"We are getting too close," Mary said, but a man pushed them forward as he nudged his way through the crowd. An omnibus pulled up to the street corner and passengers spilled out, thickening the crowd and pushing them closer yet to Roger.

"He is going to see us," Charlotte said in a hissing whisper.

Mary took another step forward to avoid a man's swinging briefcase as he dashed down the street, a newspaper over his head in a poor attempt to stay dry. Shopping bags whacked the back of Charlotte's legs as the woman pushed through the crowd to get to the omnibus. Mary and Charlotte shuffled closer to the buildings, but the stream of passersby continued to bump into them.

"We need to get out of here," Mary said.

"We can go to the bakery to get out of the rain."

They stepped away from the building but got caught by the crowd again as it carried them toward Roger. He shuffled forward to let a group of ladies take shelter under the awning, putting him at the front edge of the shelter. Mary tried to scramble out of the flow of traffic and away from Roger who stared down at his pocket watch.

Suddenly, he looked up and about, and his gaze connected with Mary's as she jerked toward the shop door, pretending she merely meant to go inside. In her haste she bumped into the one of the side supports of the awning, sending it shaking overhead. The shaking dislodged the puddle of water sitting on top. The water came pouring out of the front in a waterfall right onto Roger. Everyone nearby scattered to escape the onslaught. The women behind Roger squealed as they ran away.

The sidewalk around the awning emptied except for Charlotte and Mary. The waterfall splashed their skirts. By the time it was over, Roger stood alone, soaking wet with water dripping onto the top of his head as the rain poured down the awning. He clutched a soggy sandwich in one hand. His right cheek stuck out from the clump of sandwich in his mouth. A steady drip, drip of water fell from his hat and coat.

Mary clapped a hand over her mouth. "Roger, I'm so sorry. I didn't mean for that to happen."

He finished chewing the bite of sandwich in his mouth.

Mary offered him her handkerchief. He looked at it as if to say "what am I supposed to do with that?" A water droplet clung to the end of his nose.

Mary retracted her hand. "Is there anything I can do for you?"

"A new sandwich perhaps?" Charlotte offered.

A priest appeared from behind them like a guardian angel. The shade from his broad black umbrella made it difficult to see his face.

"Let me help you, sir. My church is nearby. You can dry off by the fire there."

Relief crossed Roger's face.

"Are you sure there is nothing we can do for you, Roger?" Charlotte asked. "There has to be something we can do to help."

The priest's kind smile peeked out from under his umbrella. His features were much more youthful than Mary had expected. "I'll take care of him, miss. You ladies get inside and stay dry."

"Yes, Father," Charlotte said, snapping to attention. "Thank you."

His attention switched to Mary and his smile fell. "Here, take this." He slipped a rosary into her hand. "The world can be a dangerous place for young ladies." The priest walked off with Roger beside him.

"What?" Mary murmured.

"Good day, Father," Charlotte called out in farewell. The men crossed to the next street as Roger slipped a damp envelope out of his coat and handed it to the priest.

An incredulous Mary turned to Charlotte. "'Father?' The man can't have been as old as all that."

"Well of course not, but that's just what you call a Catholic priest."

"I didn't know you were Catholic."

"I'm not, but my mother's parents were from Ireland."

"Then do you know what I'm supposed to do with this?" Mary asked, holding the wooden rosary. The beads were smooth and glossy and the crucifix looked hand-carved. Something this well crafted could not have been cheap to produce.

"Well I don't know how to pray with a rosary, but it certainly looks pretty." She chuckled. "Maybe it will keep you safe for your teatime with Holiday."

"Don't remind me. Thinking about it is making my stomach hurt. I don't feel prepared to have tea with a lord."

Charlotte laughed. "Well come on, let's get to the bakery before we get drenched like Roger. You can have some tea with us common folk to prepare for the big day."

Chapter 7

This time Mary took the train to Lord Holiday's manor. She should have thought about it the first time. Then again she and Margaret would have struggled to haul the crate on board. She just hoped Johnny didn't find out his employers thought him dead. That would be uncomfortable to explain on her next visit to the press.

At first the morning ride proved to be peaceful and gave her time to sit in silence with a book she'd been meaning to read for far too long, *The Scarlet Letter*. So far the story had done nothing to improve her already dim view of marriage and romance. She found it harder and harder to envision a happy ending for Lord Hallow. Yet still she had to try to do just that. Too tragic an ending would infuriate her readers, and her career couldn't afford to be making new enemies.

She thought of Charlotte and how happy she seemed. Time would tell if her marriage worked out, but the dreamy expression she got whenever she talked about Martin caused that hollow feeling in her center to start gnawing again. Part of her desperately wanted to fall in love too, while the rest of her found it terrifying. Maybe Margaret was right. Other women were taking to magic and business to escape marriage. Perhaps that would become her fate as well.

By the second stop the train station proved to be too distracting for her to keep reading. Being on a train reminded her of the day she got the idea for Alice's story when she went on a family trip to visit distant relatives. *Twilight at Hallow Manor* started with the maid Alice on a train heading toward her new employer, nervous about what to expect and wondering whether the rumors about him were true.

At first she had meant for the story to be a horror where the vampire hunter won. In fact, she'd never written a romance before. But as Lord Hallow's popularity grew, the story morphed into a budding romance, and as the story changed, the popularity exploded. Her uncle then used the unexpected windfall to go gambling and lost. He stole from Hawke to repay his debt and then ran away. Until then, he'd never touched Hawke's money. Part of her couldn't help but to wonder if it was partly her fault.

The cramped towns gave way to the moors. Her stop was next, and it wouldn't be long now. Much faster than taking a carriage all the way out to Holiday's manor to be sure. Not enduring Margaret's terrifying driving was worth the train ticket too. She returned to her book until the train began to slow again. Only three other people got off at the same stop, making it easy to spot Holiday's silent coachman waiting for her. The same one she encountered at Roquefort's party.

"Are you here for me?"

He gave her a single nod before turning and heading for the carriage. Well at least she wouldn't have to make awkward small talk. Instead, she sat and squirmed from nerves as she watched the view through the window. Had she dressed up enough for a social event with a lord? Should she have brought Margaret along to act as chaperone? Was Holiday an old fashioned nobleman who scoffed at the magicians pushing social boundaries and expectations? If so she was bound to offend by coming unchaperoned. Then again, Margaret would probably find a way to cause more scandal than she'd prevent. Her absence was for the best, Mary thought. Or at least she hoped.

It was a short ride to the manor. This time a gardener was hard at work battling the bushes out front. His hedge trimmers looked too small to win as the man struggled to cut a branch off one of the thickest bushes. After a minute of pitched battle one of the longer branches wrapped around the clippers and yanked them out of the man's hands. The gardener threw his hat down in exasperation.

Mary took the moving bushes as a sign of magical wards. Sometimes strong magic could seep into the land over time, causing any number of surprises. It was unfortunate for the gardener, but it surely meant that the Holidays knew more magic than printing press enchantments.

The gardener stalked off as the coachman pulled the carriage to a stop and offered her a hand, all without saying a word. The closed curtains gave the manor the same foreboding feel as last visit. She began to feel less certain about her decision to leave Margaret behind.

The butler greeted her at the door. "Miss Hawke, welcome." He spoke even more slowly than his lord in his rasping voice. "Please allow me to see you to the parlor." He walked with a strange gait as though he were swaying on the deck of a ship.

She peeked into the dining room that sat across from the parlor. All the chairs had been piled onto the table and covered, but the rooms looked less dusty than her last visit. As soon as she stepped into the parlor the painting above the mantle drew her attention. It hadn't been there before. Or at least she couldn't remember it being there. The pale peach curtains were different too, and the threadbare rug had been replaced. New pillows sat on the furniture as well.

Everything looked clean and tidy. The overall effect gave the room an inviting air. Instead of feeling forgotten and haunted, the room felt ready to host at a moment's notice. A small table had been set up near the fireplace where a low fire burned, completing the room's transformation.

"Please wait here. His lordship will join you shortly." The butler ambled away.

Mary crossed the room to stare up at the new painting. The Holidays, she guessed. They all wore somber expressions, even the two young boys. The younger-looking boy sitting on the woman's lap seemed more bored than despondent the longer Mary looked. Instead of looking straight at the viewer, he gazed off to the side with a pout, as if distracted by whatever had been there.

Beside them sat a man with the older of the two boys standing beside him. The boy rested one hand on the man's knee. Dark hair framed their pale faces. And the man, he looked exactly like ... like Lord Holiday. It had to be a portrait of him. Yet the Holiday she knew from the party and the tea shop was always dressed in the finest and latest fashions. The colorful clothes the man in the portrait was wearing would only have been considered fashionable ten or twenty years ago.

Her blood froze. It couldn't be possible. But her father had said he went to school with Holiday. The man she knew couldn't be much older than herself. Which meant ... No. There had to be an explanation. Perhaps they'd fallen on hard times like so many others and couldn't afford new clothes for the portrait. Yes, that must be it. Her shoulders relaxed, and she chided herself for jumping to conclusions. Still, precautions wouldn't hurt. She slipped the rosary out of her pocket and slid it on above her charm bracelet.

"Meow." Something rubbed against the back of her legs. She peered down. A black cat stared up at her with the same eyes as the furry demon who'd stolen her bracelet. She reached down to rub its head. The cat spotted her bracelet and batted at it. The very same thief indeed.

"No!" She yanked her hand away. She waited for the cat to put its paw back down before petting it with her left hand. The cat sat, closing its eyes and purring while she scratched its head. "You got away from me last time, and you almost got away with my bracelet too. What were you planning to do with it?" She tapped the cat's nose, and in response it cocked its head, letting out a loud meow.

Then the cat rubbed against her legs and disappeared behind her. "Where—" she started as she turned in search of the cat and almost stepped right into Lord Holiday. She squealed and jumped back. He was as handsome as she remembered.

"I apologize, Miss Hawke. I had no intention of scaring you."

"I hadn't heard you come in. I was looking for the cat." She peered around him, but it was already gone.

"I hope he didn't bother you or steal anything this time. I've been more careful about making sure he doesn't hitch a ride in my carriage when I leave."

"Not at all. Is stealing a habit of his?"

"Stockings mostly. Was your journey here all right?" His soft way of speaking made him feel less intimidating.

"Yes. The train was quite comfortable. I was just admiring this painting." She turned back around to look up at it. "Is that you in the painting?" she hedged. She watched him out of the corner of her eyes, but he didn't react, making him difficult to read.

"It is. I had the portrait moved from the library yesterday. This one has always been my favorite." He gave the portrait a fond smile, the expression making his pale features seem less severe.

Mary's family only had one portrait with all of them in it. The rest her mother always had an excuse to skip, leading to several paintings of Mary and Margaret with only their father. In fact, most of her childhood memories included her governess or nanny in place of her mother.

No wonder she and Margaret had grown up favoring their father. From what she understood, her mother had married young after much protesting. Her family hid the protesting from Papa, making him think she was happy to marry until it was too late. She'd only been twenty when the families arranged the marriage. If she'd been given more time and more say in who she married, maybe things would have turned out differently with less heartache for all involved.

"It's a lovely family portrait."

He gestured toward the table. "Please, sit. I will have my butler bring us tea." He pulled out a chair for her. He wore black again, but less of it this time. A cream cravat had been tied neatly at his throat, breaking up all the dark fabric along with the gray waistcoat. The colors added a brooding air of mystery to him that she found captivating.

She accepted the seat, running a nervous hand over her charm bracelet and rosary. There were no other seats. Only the two of them then. The quiet of the manor made it feel as though they were the only ones in existence.

Right on cue, the butler appeared with the tea cart. He set a tray of sandwiches, cheeses, and fruits in the center of the table and then poured them each a cup of tea from two different pots. They each had their own little cup of honey and cream.

"Excuse me, could you open the curtains a little more?" Mary asked. "It's a bit dark in here."

"Right away, Miss Hawke."

"Thank you. And, my lord, thank you for the invitation."

"My pleasure."

She reached for her teacup as the butler threw one of the curtains open, sunlight washing over her half of the table. Holiday jerked back with a hiss, raising a hand to cover his eyes.

Her rosary! The crucifix lay against her charm bracelet, front and center. Wait, no. Right beside it lay her newest charm, the mirror. A bright beam of light reflected off it and right into Holiday's eyes. "So sorry!" She hid her hand under the table.

"What was that?" he asked as he slowly lowered his hand.

"A charm on my bracelet. It's a miniature mirror. I hadn't realized it was so bright." She slid the bracelet onto her other hand and then reached for her teacup again, keeping the rosary in place. He didn't react this time.

She sipped on her tea, using the moment to ground herself. "Like I was saying," she said as she lowered her teacup, "Thank you for having me. I was interested in learning more about Holiday Press." She struggled to figure out how to explain her situation. The eerie quiet of the manor didn't help.

"We are the fastest printing press in London. Is there anything specific you want to know?"

A splotch of red marred his cream cravat. Mary tried to avoid looking at it, but her gaze kept getting drawn back to it. Some jam perhaps. Or a bit of red wine? Yes, that had to be it. A logical explanation.

"Originally, I'd been interested in seeing if you'd had any interest in working with Hawke. I believe you are acquainted with my father, the owner of Hawke House."

"Your father? Um, yes. Of course," he said, sounding unsure. "Did he wish to meet with me?" He stirred honey into his tea.

"No." She tensed as she struggled to keep her gaze on him instead of the painting to his right. He couldn't be old enough to have gone to university with her father. Impossible. "The truth is someone recently bought Hawke since we last spoke, and so I am no longer in need of Holiday's services for Hawke."

"I see." His brow knit in confusion.

"I'd still like to know more about your press though." She suddenly felt keenly aware of the fact that she sat across from a lord. A lord! He'd invited her for business, and not talking business would make her feel like she was taking advantage of his hospitality. Or worse. He would mistake her for a desperate bachelorette looking to marry up. "Depending on how the sale pans out, I may need to take my writing elsewhere."

"Are you considering having it printed and sold yourself?"

"I'm not sure. I haven't had time to think that far." It could be an option. Instead of moving to a competitor who might tell her no when they discovered her identity, she could handle the business side herself. All her years with Hawke meant she knew exactly what that entailed. She could do it ... "Does your press ever work directly with authors?"

"Sometimes, yes. Publishing houses are our biggest customers, but we take on other printing work as well. Since our press is fast, smaller projects fill in the gaps between the bigger print run orders."

That was good to know. Their current press didn't like bothering with small projects, believing the time it took to set up the press wasn't worth the small payout. "I publish under a pen name. Would that be a problem?"

"Not at all. Holiday Press does its best to keep our prices fair and quality high. We have some of the best book binders around. If you get a page count and know how many copies you need printed, I could give you a quote to give you an idea of what we would charge."

"That is very good to know, thank you." She bit into the egg salad sandwich. Holiday kept his hands on his teacup. Silence passed between them. She kept her hands busy to prevent them from trembling. She didn't know how to impress a lord, or if her desire to impress him extended beyond Hawke. She could feel his heavy gaze watching her, as if he was analyzing every movement.

Once she started on her second small sandwich, he broke the silence. "I'm sorry to hear about Hawke. I believe my father was a fan of your serials. I used to read a few of them myself."

She smiled at him. A lord admitting to reading penny bloods, how marvelous. "I am sad to see Hawke go. I enjoyed helping my father run the company." Her face heated. "Oh, but I don't want to sit here and sulk the whole time and ruin tea."

"You have nothing to worry about. We all have our troubles."

Silence hung between them as she wondered what troubles he had. She nibbled on a slice of baguette slathered in a cucumber spread. The crunchy crust came as a surprising delight compared to the usual, more traditional crustless tea sandwiches on offer. Like the egg salad. He sat and sipped on his tea, the deep red liquid reminding her of blood in his white cup. "Erm, that painting above the mantle, how old were you?"

It was time to know the truth. The portrait wasn't enchanted, but she couldn't escape the weight of it. Escape the impossibility of it.

"Four. That is probably why it is my favorite. I don't remember having to stand still while it was painted. I was never good at that." The memory brought a warm smile to his lips. "My father wasn't keen on sitting still for them either." He pointed to his parents. "I'm named after my father, Luke. My mother chose Lucas for me."

Relief washed over her, as well as a touch of embarrassment. He was the little boy then in the portrait, not the man. Obviously. "You look just like him."

He gave her a melancholy smile. "Yes, people often used to mistake me for him."

"Used to?"

His attention turned to the portrait. "He passed away a few months ago. That is why I've returned home, to look after the estate and company." He waved a hand in a circle, the lazy movement graceful. "My father was running Holiday Press. It was his wish for me to continue his work."

"I didn't know. I'm sorry." That explained his black clothes. He was simply in mourning. Another obvious clue she should have been able to put together if not for all the wild conclusions she preferred to jump to. "I ..." Should she tell him? Word would get out eventually. "I recently lost my mother." It was close enough to the truth. He didn't need to know that she was alive and gallivanting off wherever she'd gone with Mary's uncle. Thinking her dead felt less painful.

"Ah. My condolences to you as well."

"If there is anything I can do to help, please let me know. I'm embarrassed that I didn't know. My father mentioned he went to university with yours. Apparently they were good friends." A thud from above startled her. She dropped her half-eaten sandwich onto her plate in surprise. Holiday continued sipping at his tea as if he didn't hear the thud at all.

"Do you want more tea?" he asked, gesturing to her empty cup.

"Did you hear that?"

"Hear what?"

Another thud. Then another, this one louder than the previous ones. "What is that? It sounds like someone is dancing up there." She studied the ceiling, but it told her nothing.

"Oh. That noise would be George. He can make a surprising ruckus for his size."

"George?"

"My cat. Technically he was my father's cat. I inherited him with the manor."

A meow answered him from the doorway. The black cat meandered in, stopping to rub against Holiday's legs before making his way to the window. Another thump came from above.

Holiday frowned as he watched George.

"It isn't the cat," Mary pointed out, her suspicion deepening by the second. What was he hiding?

He glanced from the cat to the ceiling. "Please excuse me. I'll be right back."

He hurried out of the room as another thump hit the ceiling. Her gaze fell to his teacup, still half full of red liquid. She leaned over the table to get a better look. The color of the liquid was striking. Surely it was only tea...

To make sure she picked up the cup and sniffed it. The cup smelled sweet. Did blood smell sweet? Lord Hallow described it as such at one point, didn't he? Or had she edited that out? On second thought, it might not be the best descriptor of blood.

The floor creaked as the butler stopped a step into the room, staring at her. She put the teacup back down, ashamed at being caught. "Erm, might I get some more tea?"

"Right away." The butler left her cup behind, but took both pots and Holiday's cup with him.

Before her suspicions could spin out of control at the evidence being carried off, Holiday returned, looking flustered.

"Is everything all right?" she asked

He returned to his seat. "Just the library as I thought."

"You have a library?" She perked up, all oddities forgotten as her mind focused on that one word. Library. She'd always wanted one of her own, but their townhouse was too small. Her father's study full of Hawke serials was the closest they'd ever come to one.

"Yes. My father attempted to add to the library wards but something went awry."

"Is the library big?" She leaned forward, eager to find out more.

"I suppose that depends on what you consider big."

"Well how many books do you have? Do you have any rare ones?"

He pondered the questions before answering. "I'm not sure how many exactly are up there or if any are rare. I haven't had time to go through the catalog."

She couldn't hide her disappointment. Her shoulders sagged. "That is a shame, but you are lucky to have a library."

"Would you ..." He trailed off, looking lost in thought. After a pause, he returned his attention to Mary, his internal debate settled. "Would you like to see it?"

"I would love to visit the library." She beamed at him. "With your family running a printing press, I'll bet it is very impressive." It would be a good chance to check out the suspicious thumps for herself.

"Very well."

Before he could stand the butler returned with a fresh pot and teacup for Holiday. Mary on the other hand got the same pot as before.

"We'll be back shortly," Holiday told him. "Miss Hawke wishes to see the library."

The man balked. His messy mustache quivered as his mouth hung open before he found his voice. "Now, my lord?"

"Yes. Miss Hawke wishes to see it."

The butler looked ready to argue but he kept whatever thoughts plagued him to himself. "As you wish."

Chapter 8

Mary squinted into the darkness of the upstairs hallway. The library stood at the very top of the stairs, and good thing too because she couldn't see well enough to navigate the hallway. The ominous atmosphere of her first visit was back with a vengeance. All the closed doors and covered windows made the gloom oppressing. It was the same atmosphere of despair she'd expect from a church during a funeral. Even the air itself felt heavy.

Lord Holiday didn't speak as he led the way. Any time she caught sight of his face, he appeared deep in thought. Quiet returned to the manor, but her curiosity didn't die with the thumps. Whatever was making all that noise, she wanted to know, or it would nag at her for months. She'd have to live with the regret of not investigating.

"Are those runes in the door?" The etchings covered the edges of the door, creating a frame of runes. She didn't know enough magic to understand them. Anything beyond a few glamour tricks was where her familiarity ended. She'd never had a need to learn more. Stories were enough magic for her, and magical tutors were much too expensive.

"Yes. They protect the books. Keeps them from moldering, getting eaten by bugs, or stolen. My great-great grandfather put up the protective enchantments, and my grandfather added to them. My father ... well I don't know what he did exactly, but the whole library has become infused with magic."

"Your bushes too."

He raised an eyebrow at her. "Bushes?"

"Yes. On my way in I saw one grab the shears away from your gardener."

"That is going to be a problem." He cast a worried glance toward the windows behind them.

Mary rose on her tiptoes in anticipation as they reached the door. But the closed windows made it impossible to make out anything other than the shapes of covered furniture as the door creaked open. Then the butler flung open the curtains on the far window, letting in enough light to bring the rest of the room into focus.

Sheets covered the furniture save a single chair by the fireplace. The chair struck her as lonely. The stale air told her the room hadn't been aired out in a long while. Dust motes swirled in the sunlight. But the books! Shelves lined the walls, all of them brimming with books from thin tomes to ones thick enough to knock a man out if they fell on him. The previous painting from the parlor hung over the library fireplace. Despite all the thumping, everything looked to be in order.

Just as she wondered if the thumping had actually come from the library, a book toppled off a set of shelves to her right. Holiday bent over to pick it up. "My apologies. The room needs some work done to it yet, but I haven't had time to tend to it since my father's passing." As he slotted the book back into its place, the book below it toppled out. He glared at the second book and straightened without picking it up.

"This is my father's collection here that he started on these top two shelves. We have separate shelves for books our press printed. As far as rare books go, we do have the first book Holiday printed. Although I don't know where it is shelved at the present."

"What is the book about?" Was it something about magic? Or a gothic romance?

"Sheep farming."

"Oh." She blinked, shifting on her feet. "Well, no need to go digging for it on my account." Mary stepped up to the shelf, taking care to not step on the fallen book. She recognized most of the books. Many she'd read herself. Some of the early Hawke serials had given her nightmares as a child. Her mother banned her from reading them, but Mary sneaked them out of her father's study in her own form of rebellion. The nightmares didn't stop her.

She reached for a copy of *The Vampyre* by John Polidori, a tragic tale in which too many young ladies died to feed one man's hunger and the only man who knew the truth was powerless to stop the monster. When her fingertips brushed the pages, the short story flew off the shelves. She jumped back with a squeal as the book flapped around her head, its spine facing the ceiling as it circled her head. Then all at once chaos erupted around them. Other books leapt from the shelves to fly in circles or meander from shelf to shelf.

Holiday shook his head in exasperation. "Sorry. The books are unruly and don't understand that flapping about isn't good for their bindings. I'll have to have them repaired soon." He snatched *The Vampyre* out of the air and tucked it under one arm. Despite the chaos around him, he appeared less stiff than during tea. "I was mistaken in believing they could behave for a guest," he said in a tone she'd expect from a disappointed father.

Another book passed within grabbing distance, and he snatched it up, holding it under his arm with the other one, squeezing it as it tried to wiggle free. He gave her a forced smile, his discomfort making it look more like a grimace.

"I always found books magical, but your library makes that quite literal." She reached for a nearby book floating past, but it dodged her fingers.

"If the books weren't such pests when enchanted, I would appreciate the magic more." He shoved the books under his arm onto a shelf. In response the bookshelves began to rearrange themselves. It was as though an invisible librarian worked on setting the shelves right.

"How do you find anything in here?"

"I don't."

The butler headed for the door, plucking books out of the air as he went and shoving them onto the shelves without looking. He did it with the motions of a man accustomed to tidying up flying books. But his tidying made no difference. The books stayed on the shelves for only moments, sliding back out of their places once he'd moved on to the next books.

A thick leather-bound volume flapped in a way that made her think of a wheezing old man. It began to turn as it headed for the wall near the fireplace, but the book wasn't fast enough. It bumped into the wall and tumbled down several feet before catching itself. The top corner caught against a sheet covering a small mirror, dragging the sheet down with the book as the two tangled together. Then the book bumbled back toward its shelf, dragging the sheet with it. The sheet trailed along the ground, giving the impression of a misshapen ghost floating about the library.

Holiday sighed, mumbling "honestly" as he yanked the sheet off the book. He stepped up to the mirror to cover it back up. Mary's eyes narrowed. He cast no reflection upon the cloudy glass. She shifted, searching for a better angle with no luck. She couldn't see anything at all in the glass. He covered the mirror and turned toward the fireplace. He kicked aside the rug in front of the fireplace, exposing a chalked rune circle underneath. He kneeled, fixing the smudged runes and edges before mumbling in Latin.

All at once the books paused. Then they returned to the shelves, some bumping into each other as they made for the same spot. A few of the slowest books flapped around a minute longer as they searched for open spaces to shelve themselves.

"I assume magic keeps them on the shelves?"

"Yes, but the books don't like it. They always sulk for a few hours." He tossed the rug back over the runes. "But at least they are quiet when they sulk."

"How does a book sulk?" She reached for *The Vampyre* again, but the book fought against her, wiggling and refusing to leave its spot as it pressed itself against the back of the shelf. "I see." The idea of a magical library had always made her picture something that was...well a lot less frustrating. She'd always imagined books that came on command and reshelved themselves more gracefully than the flapping, bumbling books of this library. What good was a magical library where you couldn't find the book you wanted and when you finally did, the book wouldn't let you read it?

"I plan to contact an old friend who might have some idea of what has gone wrong with the magic in the manor. Martin always did love a good magical riddle to solve, and I've never met a magician who knows runes as well as he does. I hope with his help I will actually be able to read in here again like when I was a boy."

"You don't mean Martin Steepe by chance, do you?"

Surprised, he glanced up from fixing the rolled edge of the rug. "Yes. Do you know him?"

"I'm friends with his fiancée, Charlotte. How do you know him?"

"We studied magic together one summer. I did hear about his engagement the other day, but I almost didn't believe it. I hope Charlotte has plenty of patience."

"She does. She finds him charming, his eccentricities included."

Holiday chuckled. The happy sound took Mary by surprise. It didn't suit his somber air. "That couldn't be said of most women. I'm glad he found someone. I hope they are happy together."

"I do as well." She crossed the room to the windows. A sprawling overgrown garden sat on the other side. At the end of a row of trees stood an old stone tower connected to ruins. The sight took her breath away. Lord Hallow had a tower just like that one. She planned for it to be the place where he tried to drain Alice's blood, only for the hunter to save her. That ending no longer felt right, not with all the adoring Lord Hallow fans the story accumulated each month. "What is that place behind the garden?

"The old castle?" Holiday asked without approaching the window. He stayed in the shadows.

"I don't see a castle. Only a tower."

"The castle crumbled a long time ago. The tower was the only part of it left standing when my father fixed it up."

"Those clouds behind the tower look ominous." Dark gray clouds painted the sky, adding to the tower's desolate air.

"Please allow me to escort you back to the train station. The spring rains along with the melting snow sometimes wash out the roads."

She perked up at that statement. Whenever a storm washed out the road and the heroine had to return to the spooky house, there were always vengeful ghosts or murderers waiting. That was when all the secrets the owner had been hiding came to light.

The tower left her feeling unbalanced. As if her story had meshed with reality and she found it unnerving. Writing was supposed to be safe. She could make anything happen without anyone in real life getting hurt. And she could dream of anything without anyone else knowing unless she published it. "The rain will be upon us any minute."

"Then we should get you back to the train station."

With two hours left before her train arrived, her suspicions came slithering back. Why was he eager to be rid of her? Was the library some sort of elaborate ruse to distract her?

The gloom grew darker with the approaching storm. She squinted as she made her way down the dark stairs, using the railing as a guide. Her foot caught the edge of a stair and she threw her weight against the railing, holding on. Then a large snap rent the air. The railing gave way beneath her and she tumbled forward with a scream.

Holiday grabbed her, hooking one arm beneath her. She blinked down at the stairs, her body hanging in midair. The broken section of railing tumbled down the stairs, clattering against each stair. Two jagged posts stood where the railing had been. Mary wound her arms around his, holding tight as he yanked her back onto her feet, her legs trembling.

"Are you all right?"

She could scarcely hear him over the pounding of her heart. "I-I-I—" She swallowed. "I think so?" She met his eyes, finding her terror mirrored in his. They stayed there, frozen in the aftermath. The pounding of her heart subsided as she focused on the warmth of his arm and the way it was now wrapped around her back, the front of her pressed against him. Their closeness was deliciously scandalous. "Th-thank you, my lord." Her voice trembled as much as her legs.

"There is no need to call me 'my lord,' Miss Hawke. Please call me Lucas."

"Mary."

"I'm sorry, Mary. The manor is in disrepair, and there is much for me to fix. I didn't know about the railing."

Hearing his gentle voice say her name made her feel warm all over. "It is all right. I'm fine." He was shaking worse than she was. "Are you okay?"

"I ..." He cleared his throat. "A fall killed my father." His gaze drifted up the stairs toward the library, his eyes going distant. "I will have a carpenter attend to the railing as soon as I can to ensure this never happens again."

"I didn't mean to cause you trouble."

Her apology brought him back to the present. "It isn't your fault, but mine. Allow me to lead the way down."

They pulled apart, leaving her feeling cold from the loss of his warmth. He went down the stairs first this time, and she stuck close to him. At the bottom he called for the butler. "Send for a carpenter as soon as the storm clears. "Miss Hawke needs to return to the train station."

A flash of distant lightning lit up the window.

"The storm is already here. Perhaps I should wait it out. I would hate to get caught out there if the road washes out." She schooled her features into the best look of innocence she could muster.

They all looked to the window by the door. The rain outside was a light drizzle nowhere near heavy enough to wash any roads out. "I'm sure you have someone waiting for you. Don't you?" He raised his eyebrows as he settled his attention back onto her.

"My sister and father will understand if I'm late due to this weather." There. Now he knew not to try anything because they would come looking for her. "I'd feel more comfortable waiting here than alone at the train station," she hedged.

His attention traveled back to the rain, but he relented. "I wouldn't want you getting stuck in the storm. Shall we return to our tea?"

"That would be lovely."

They settled back into their seats. The rain grew steadily heavier and within minutes the thunder arrived. Perfect. She could bide her time until she needed to catch the train. Or worm her way into a room for the night to explore right under his nose. Lucas sent for more tea. When the butler returned he carried a stack of envelopes. "Your mail, my lord. Shall I put it in the study?"

"More maid applications?" he asked.

"They appear to be, yes."

"Leave those with me. The rest can go to the study. And bring down the stack on my desk, please."

"Right away." The butler set the stack down on his tea tray.

Once he stepped away Mary spoke up. "Are you looking for a maid?" If he was in need of one, she could give him recommendations. It was the least she could do after he'd saved her on the stairs.

"No. Are you?"

"No."

"Then I suppose neither of us have any use for the inquiries. However, all these applications are addressed to Lord Hallow, not me. Seeing as how Lord Hallow is published by Hawke, I thought I should pass his mail to you. I read the first few not realizing they'd been misaddressed."

"Thank you for the thought." She flipped through the letters. All of them were addressed to Lord Hallow, the writers speaking as though he were real. The butler appeared with a second stack, another ten maid applications. All those letters... the speed of gossip was impressive. Even she couldn't have guessed at how popular Lord Hallow would become with the ladies. She could no longer deny the direction the story was heading. *Twilight at Hallow Manor* needed to officially become a romance. A real love story that left Alice reeling and unsure of whether to choose Lord Hallow or the vampire hunter.

"I didn't realize anyone would send you mail for Lord Hallow. If you get any others, send them to me and I will take care of them."

"I will do so. Your maid must not be a good one." He poured himself a fresh cup, the same red liquid as before.

"Excuse me?"

"The applications." He gestured toward them. "The ones I read all claimed they could do a better job. I've never seen anyone write with such passion about cleaning before."

"I don't think they are interested in...cleaning." She skimmed the first letter, fighting down a blush at the woman's insistence that she was the best at "cleaning all manner of knobs."

"These are maids who don't intend to clean?" he asked, confusion creeping across his face.

"I believe they're trying to..." Mary struggled to find the right words. She stifled a chuckle, finally settling on "...seduce you."

He coughed, reaching for his napkin to keep from spitting tea everywhere. "Seduce me?" he said, voice hoarse once his coughing subsided.

"Yes. *Twilight at Hallow Manor* is becoming a romance. Lord Hallow is quite popular."

"I thought it was a vampire story."

"It is. He's a vampire who enthralls his maid." She watched him closely. His appearance, the tower out back, it all felt too much like Hallow to believe he knew nothing of the story.

His eyes widened and he spilled his tea in his haste to set his cup down. "Is that what is popular nowadays? I had no idea. I am more out of touch with publishing than I thought." He checked his pocket watch. "I'm afraid you'll need to leave soon to catch your train or you'll miss it. I should attend to some business." His brow creased in thought. "Maids, really?" he murmured under his breath.

"You are going to send me away in this weather on a road that washes out?" she said, aghast. That was a popular cliché in Margaret's romance novels. A storm would blow in, forcing the lead to stay with the love interest. As for the horror versions, well she'd rather not think about those. Of course the rain was still too light to be of any real danger to her should she leave, so Mary put on the most worried expressions she could muster. She wasn't about to let this opportunity slip away from her.

He flushed. "I'm sorry I could ... perhaps I could ..." He trailed off, eyes wide like a rabbit caught in the sights of a predator. Mary worried she'd taken her plan too far.

"Shall I have a room prepared for Miss Hawke?" the butler offered.

"Yes!" Lucas said, turning to nod with great vigor at his butler. "Excellent idea. Would that be okay?" He turned to Mary. "The butler can escort you to the first train in the morning."

"That would be perfectly fine."

He shot onto his feet. "Please enjoy the tea for as long as you wish. I'm afraid I have some... some business to attend to." He stumbled over his words in his haste, his accent thickening. "I'll have a room made ready immediately."

She smiled at him while he made his escape, mumbling apologies as he went, never turning his back to her. "Thank you for your hospitality," she answered in a cheerful tone. Once he was out of the room he fled, leaving her to wonder what had spooked him about her staying. Whatever it was, she wanted to know.

Chapter 9

The storm returned in the middle of the night, a loud crack of thunder jerking her awake. She yanked the covers over her head, but the flashes of light broke through the fabric. She buried her head under the pillow, muffling the booms until they finally moved into the distance.

By the time she peeked out, her fire was nothing but glowing embers. Jagged lightning lit up the crumbling tower beyond. She blinked the flash of lightning away, but the light in the tower remained. She crept over to the window, the floor cold against the bottoms of her feet. There appeared to be a glowing lantern in the highest window.

What on earth could Lucas be doing out there at this time of night? Unless ... unless it was his vampire lair. He could be out there this very minute drinking the blood of his maids. No, that was her writer's mind being ridiculous yet again.

She'd already attempted to explore the library, only to be chased out by a hoard of flapping books. As for Lucas, he didn't appear until she'd finished eating dinner alone in the dining room. He gave her a quick tour of the dusty downstairs rooms after some prodding, avoiding eye contact the whole tour, before disappearing off again.

His stories of Holiday family history had been interesting, but by the time she'd gone to bed, she'd found nothing new. Maybe he really was an innocent man who simply happened to look like Lord Hallow.

A man grieving his father with no dark secrets to hide. Boring, but human and understandable. That angle made her pity him, being all alone while he grieved with the family business to look after on top of it all.

Yooooooow!

She jumped. The strange noise came again, and she pressed her back against the wall, pulling the curtain in front of her. This time the lashing of the rain almost drowned the noise out. She lurched for her candle. It took her several tries to light it. Then she tossed another log onto the fire. The extra light bled courage into her.

The noise seemed to be coming from somewhere in the manor. Below perhaps? She couldn't tell. After she first read *A Christmas Carol* by Charles Dickens, she feared ghosts would come force her to watch all her past sins, like when she ate the last of the strawberry jam. Or that time at ten years old when she shoved a boy into a mud puddle because he'd been teasing Margaret. But it was spring, not Christmastime. Surely ghosts would pick a more thematic time of year if they were to begin haunting her.

Yooooooow!

Or maybe not. Unlike Scrooge, she wouldn't wait around until the ghost came to her. She'd find it first. And then maybe interview it for a future story. Once Lord Hallow and Alice's story ended, she could pivot into a ghost story next. Spice it up with some possession and an exorcism. She'd need to ask Charlotte if she knew how Catholic exorcisms worked.

She stood in her doorway, unable to get her feet to move. Reading about spooky noises in the night was easier than facing them. Discovering Lucas's dark secrets didn't feel fun anymore. What would she even do if she discovered a shrine dedicated to Lord Hallow somewhere? Or maids he lured in to feed from? Hawke was out of her hands, and it felt like her story was growing out of her control too.

Yoooooooow!

But if he was pretending to be Lord Hallow, she wanted to know. And if he was doing it for nefarious purposes, she'd stop him. Lord Hallow was her creation and therefore her responsibility.

She turned around and grabbed the fire poker before stepping back into the doorway. The long hallway was as dark as the grounds outside, the heavy air growing damp from the storm. The floorboards creaked beneath her, and she winced at the noise. In the quiet of the manor, the creaking echoed down the hallway.

She took a moment to gather her courage again and steady her quickening heart. Other than her room, none of the other doors hung open. She stuck to the wall, holding her candle out as far as she could to light her way, wincing at every creak and groan of the floor. In the darkness the hallway felt longer than it had during the day.

At the top of the stairs she paused, listening. The odd noise came again, louder this time. She jumped, sucking in a breath as her candle sputtered. The flame didn't go out, but that didn't stop her racing heart. "You can do this," she whispered to herself. "You should at least find out if he's a murderer before you do business with him."

She started down the stairs, sticking to the side opposite of the destroyed railing. In every room she passed all the curtains hung closed. There was no light except for her candle. All the shadows made the house feel too empty. Too quiet, like monsters waited in the darkness to gobble her up. Or a bloodthirsty vampire masquerading as Lord Hallow.

The quiet wailing led her into the kitchen. Here the curtains on the middle window were open, letting moonlight spill into the room. The woodsy scent of rosemary and thyme filled the room. Embers glowed in the hearth. The extra light made the room feel safe after the dark journey through the manor.

Skrtch. Skrrrrtch. "*Heeelp.*"

Goosebumps shot up her arms. She turned in circles, but in the dim light she couldn't spot anything. "Who's there?" She kept the poker held out in front of her as she crossed the room. At the other end she stopped in front of a plain door. The scratching came again, faster now as if whatever was on the other side had heard her.

Was it a ghost? A murderer lying in wait for her? Or a vampire's victim trying to escape? She pictured bloody fingernails scratching at the door. Her stomach tightened, bile rising up her throat.

"I have a fire poker," she told the darkness.

Yooow!

"Attack me and I'll stab you." She straightened her back, but her hands trembled. Something brushed against her legs and she froze, a scream caught in her throat.

"Meow."

Her breath left her in a rush, and she slumped against the wall. Just the cat, George. His green eyes peered up at her. *"Heeelp."*

No, that wasn't a help, just the cat's odd, impatient meow. She scratched his head and he leaned into her hand, purring. Once he'd had enough he sauntered over to the door on the far wall and ran his paws over the wood as if he were trying to dig his way through. *Skrrrrtch*. He paused long enough to cast her an expectant look.

Just the cat. All of it. The realization made a laugh bubble out of her. She'd gone traipsing through a lord's manor in the middle of the night after a black cat. "Do you want in there?" She'd come all this way, she thought. Might as well finish and find out what the cat wanted.

"Mrooow."

She leaned the fire poker against the wall and set the candle down on the counter behind her. The cat twined about her legs, and she had to watch each step to keep from stepping on him. She yanked on the door, but it barely budged. The thing was far too heavy than any door had the right to be. She tugged harder, digging her heels in. The door scraped against the floor, the wood swollen from the dampness.

George squeezed through the gap and disappeared into the darkness beyond. She had to force the door open more to follow him, putting her shoulder into it. The worn stone stairs descended into a large cold cellar. A cold draft sent her little candle flame flickering. She held her hand over the flame to protect it.

As she stood there at the top of the stairs, she couldn't help but recall her latest unfinished chapter of *Twilight at Hallow Manor*, where Alice finally gathered the courage to venture into the basement to find the vampire's coffin. She chuckled, complimenting herself on how accurately she had portrayed the scene now that she found herself in a similar situation. Unlike Alice, however, she had no reason to descend into the cellar. The cat had been the source of all her terror. Surely the most frightful thing she'd find down there would be a bug or a mouse. Maybe an errant book flapping its way back to the shelves.

"Then again," she thought aloud, "It can't hurt to look." The library had been an interesting surprise. What other secrets might this manor be hiding? If nothing else, venturing further would be good research for her writing. Satisfied with her rationalization, Mary stepped boldly down the stairs, her curiosity matched only by her wild imagination.

Yet at the bottom of the stairs, no imposing door or grand chamber stood before her. Only shelves lined the walls, most of them empty. The set closest to the door was filled with fresh ingredients from potatoes, flour, eggs, sugar, honey, and other vegetables. They all looked fresh, like the pantry had been stocked within the last few days.

A dim glow behind an empty set of shelves caught her eye. *Bang!* She jumped and the cat yowled. Then she heard something. A muffled groaning.

"G-George?" She headed for the glow, tightening her hold on the fire poker. Another long groan answered her. At the edges of the circle of light against the far wall a lantern sat on the floor with a long wooden box. A coffin.

The lid on the box squealed as a hand reached up from inside the coffin, pushing it open. The musky, decaying scent of dirt tickled her nose. She tensed as she saw a dark figure rise, sitting up straight and turning to face the light. George's eyes glowed from where he hid beneath a shelf. For Mary, it was too late to hide. Lucas had seen her.

"Lor— Lucas?!"

He stood up and brushed himself off, stepping out of the box with a lordly presence. It would have been terrifying if not for the surprise in his voice. "Miss Hawke? What brings you to my pantry?" His eyes narrowed in suspicion."Are you looking for something?"

Mary did her best to steady her nerves. After being called Mary, Miss Hawke sounded cold. "George did. He was at the door yowling. I could hear him all the way from my room."

"George can be demanding when the mood strikes him." His gaze stopped on her fire poker. "Are you cold? I can carry more wood to your room."

"I'm fine. The cat's yowling sounded like wailing, and I thought someone might be ... well, never mind. George gave me a bit of a fright is all." She shivered. Goosebumps covered her head to toe. "Might I ask what it is you're doing?"

"I couldn't sleep with all the noise from the storm and couldn't stand to stay in bed."

"And you ended up ... down here?" The pantry was the last place she expected to find the lord of the manor, let alone in the middle of the night. This should be the domain of his cook.

He rolled his shoulders. "I wanted to do something productive. I've been making a list of everything I want to check on and everything that needs repairs. There is a lot to do and after your near tumble I can't put some of it off any longer." He squinted down at the cat as George batted at his foot. "Was jumping under my feet necessary, George?" In response George sprawled across them.

A perfectly mundane answer. One which didn't answer the most important question. Channeling Alice, Mary felt confident enough to ask, "What's in the box?"

He turned back to the box and closed the lid. "Dirt from back home." Didn't vampires like to sleep in the dirt of their homeland? "And mushrooms."

"Mushrooms?" Did he actually expect her to believe that? Who grew mushrooms in their cold cellar? Though now that she looked at it more closely, the box was rather plain and didn't seem wide enough to be a proper coffin. She'd heard of odder hobbies, like her mother's friend who liked to paint little statues of ducks for her garden, but paired with all the other oddities ... she didn't dare think the word.

"Yes. My mother insisted on sending it. She loves to pick wild mushrooms and wanted me to have one of her favorite pieces of home with me. I'm lucky my fall didn't crush them all."

"Your mother isn't staying here at Holiday Manor?"

"No. After my father's passing she decided to stay with her sister. I think the company is good for her. She missed her. Holiday Manor would be far too lonely for her. It would remind her too much of my father." The melancholy notes to his tone made her think he was speaking as much about himself as his mother.

"It is sweet of her to think of you."

"Yes. I wish I could give her one of our rose bushes. They were always her favorite."

Mary shivered. George jumped up on the box, and then prepared to jump on Lucas next. Lucas grabbed him before he could. "We should all get back to sleep. Dawn isn't far off."

"Good idea. I didn't realize how late it'd gotten." She stepped back toward the stocked set of shelves as George batted at her loose hair. Lucas shifted as he reached for his lantern and George, hanging onto the cat with his free arm. Once Lucas passed, Mary acted quickly to get whatever protections she could.

She passed a shelf with hanging dried herbs and recalled that rosemary was supposed to fend off wicked spirits. It was too dark to see clearly which herb was which, so she plucked a few stalks of whatever she could and hoped for the best. Spotting the large bag of salt, she looked for a smaller one. Seeing none, she settled for shoving fistfuls into the pocket of her dressing gown. Most important of all was the garlic. She grabbed a couple of hanging bulbs but couldn't stash them away before Lucas looked back, raising an eyebrow.

Mary froze, embarrassment welling in her cheeks, "Erm, a late night snack. Do you mind terribly?"

"Not at all. I don't much care for...garlic." He spoke the vegetable's name with contempt.

She finished tucking the garlic into her pockets and followed. He stopped by the stairs, ushering her out of the pantry first. In the kitchen, the distant booms of thunder were no longer jarring. Lucas pushed the cold cellar door shut. The way he watched her out of the corner of his eye made her own suspicions rear up.

"Were you in the tower earlier?" she asked. "Awful night to be outside, isn't it?"

He met the question with a look of confusion. "The tower? What makes you think I went to the tower?" He set George back down. "I wouldn't want to go anywhere in this weather."

"When George's howling woke me, I saw a light in the tower." She crossed the room to the windows. Blackness stood on the other side. Wherever the tower was, she couldn't tell in the darkness. "It was at the very top." A distant streak of lightning lit up the edges of the tower, but the light didn't return.

"I wasn't out there. I never go to the tower."

"Then was one of your servants out there? I know I saw a light."

Another distant crack of lightning streaked across the sky, outlining the tower. He took a step back.

"You must have been mistaken. No one is in the tower." Grief washed over his face, giving him a haunted look. "Now, I must insist you return to your room. As you've already experienced earlier, this manor isn't safe for exploration. I can escort you back myself."

"That is all right. I can find my way back on my own."

"Go straight back. I don't want you falling through the floor somewhere."

George batted a wooden bowl across the floor to Lucas's feet. The cat chased after it, batting the bowl right into his foot. Lucas sighed. "Yes, George, I'll feed you, you little monster."

George meowed as she shuffled out of the kitchen, her steps quick as she thought of the warm fire and bed waiting for her.

"You could try hunting for a change. Isn't that why you're here?" Lucas's voice drifted from the kitchen.

A shiver wracked her frame, and she quickened her pace more. The pile of salt weighed down her pocket. The garlic tickled her nose. Was salt supposed to work against vampires? She couldn't remember. If he sneaked into her room, at the very least the salt would sting his eyes when she threw it at him.

As she beelined for the sanctuary of her room, light from her fire spilled into the hallway and danced across the window. She stopped at the threshold, turning around to glance out the window. Had she been mistaken about the light in the tower? Perhaps it was just a play of the light reflected in the glass. As she looked out, all she caught was her own reflection, dimly lit by the fireplace. The image of her face seemed to grow brighter as her eyes strained against the darkness. Not just brighter, but the pale yellows and oranges framing her face seemed to turn a bluish green. But she looked closer and finally realized what she was seeing: the face in the reflection wasn't hers.

It stared back at her with empty eyes, mouth agape. The waxen pallor of the spectre's face made it look ill. Its lips moved slowly, as if speaking, but the only sound was that of the whipping wind outside the window. A hand reached forward in the glass, and seemed as though it would come through the window. For the second time that visit Mary screamed, all the nervous energy of her late-night adventure releasing at once.

She fell backwards, swinging her poker at the window. Her swing went wide, but it seemed to drive the vision away. She dared not chance another look, scooting into her room and slamming her door shut, wishing she'd grabbed the whole bag of salt instead of fistfuls.

She arranged the salt in a line in front of the door. If penny bloods had taught her anything, it was that salt kept away the ghosts and demons and other bad creatures. If it didn't work on vampires, well that was what the garlic was for. For good measure, she used the candle to light her bundle of herbs ablaze, filling the room with wisps of aromatic smoke. Rosemary, sage, tarragon. One of those had to be good for repelling whatever it was she just saw.

Once there was an unbroken line of salt across the room's threshold, she stepped back to inspect her work. The thin line looked flimsy, but it would have to do. And if it didn't, she was willing to bet a fire poker would stop an attacker in their tracks. She gave the air a few jabs, as if she were fencing.

"That's right," she mumbled, "no one haunts Mary Hawke." She knew for certain the face she had seen. Lucas's. It had to be. The features, though dim and ghastly, were unmistakable. Although in the light of her room, she felt less sure she'd seen a ghost at all. He may have just been some poor Holiday relative woken up by the storm too. And the dim light reflecting off the window could have played tricks on her eyes. The stress of wandering the manor must have gotten too deep under her skin. In any case, she wasn't going back out there. No, she would stay in the light of her fireplace and behind her line of salt.

She slid back under the covers, hiding the garlic under her pillow and leaning the fire poker against the wall within easy reach. Then she opened the drawer of the nightstand and pulled out her notebook and the loose papers she'd tucked inside.

Ghost outside her door or no, this was all too good to miss writing down.

Chapter 10

In the morning she startled awake to her papers scattered across the bed. The fire had burned back down to embers and she felt as though she'd gotten less than an hour of sleep since returning to her room. Light poured in between the crack in the curtains, blindingly bright after a day and night spent in the gloomy manor.

What time was it? If she missed the morning train she'd be stuck here until the evening. After last night, she didn't care what secrets Lucas was hiding. He could keep them to himself. No way was she going exploring through his house at night again.

She stumbled out of bed, a crick in her neck sending a dull throb through her stiff shoulders. A quick stretch relieved her of the tension. Then she gathered up the pages and notebook that had fallen to the floor. One by one she sorted through her late-night notes. Each page became harder to decipher until her scribblings became incoherent by the last page.

"A bowl of warm milk in a circle of salt? What does that mean?" Below it she'd doodled a black cat drinking from a bowl. The proportions were all off, the tail twice as long as it should be and the paws too thick. Then again she'd never carried any talent for art. That'd always been her mother's talent. Both Mary and her sister took more after their father, she with her love of books and writing, and Margaret with her mind for numbers and finance. She shoved all the scribblings into her bag and got to work preparing for the day.

Her hair smelled strongly of garlic. She began to understand why vampires were so averse to it. Pulling her hair into a bun kept the worst of the smell away from her nose. A floorboard creaked outside her door, and she froze. A meow at the door was followed by a black cat paw curling through the gap between the door and floor.

"George, stop. You'll ruin my salt line." She opened the door to shoo the cat off, but instead he laid down, tail swishing as he ignored her waving hands. With each swish he scattered more of the salt. She bent down to shove him away. He let her push him aside before rolling onto his back.

"I'm not falling for that," she grumbled. "As soon as I touch your belly I bet you'll attack my hand, won't you?"

The way his pupils dilated as his eyes tracked her charm bracelet told her the hunch was right. When she didn't take the bait he climbed back onto his feet to dart between her legs. He grabbed the stocking lying on the floor and ran for it. She shut the door before he could escape. They wrestled over the stocking. Once she pried it from him she hurried to put both stockings on before he could make off with the other one.

Once she'd finished dressing, she opened the door again and tried to shoo George out. He chose to sit on her bed and watch her, refusing to budge at all.

"George, what are you doing? I'm not letting you have my stockings."

"Master George, please do not bother our guest," the butler said as he appeared, pushing a food cart with a breakfast tray and tea. He looked like he'd gotten even less sleep than she had. Dark circles looked permanently etched around his eyes. The air of exhaustion surrounding him and his jerky movements made it hard to tell his age. "Pardon him, miss. He loves attention, and this house has been too quiet lately."

"Don't any other Holiday relatives live here?"

"Only his lordship." Then who was the man she'd seen? Mary's mind raced to find a logical explanation. Perhaps there really was a relative, but he was someone they wanted to keep away from prying eyes. But for what reason? Well a strange man looking so much like the lord of the manor who liked to prowl around outside and peer in windows at night would be worth keeping hidden. It was a stretch, but it was much better than considering the alternative."Your meal, Miss Hawke." The butler bowed as he stopped the food cart a step away from her door.

"Thank you. I'll have it in the room if that's all right."

"Very good, miss," he said, lifting the lid from the plate. The steam from the plate carried with it a powerful aroma of garlic. Had her hair not already inundated her with it, the scent might have knocked her off her feet. The butler however was clearly much less prepared. His nose wrinkled and his eyes watered. It was the most lifelike she had seen him."Quiche with cheese, mushrooms, and...garlic."

"My, my," said Mary, trying to smile as politely as she could. "It certainly is fragrant."

"My lord insisted it would be very much suited to your particular tastes."

Of course. He'd seen her take a whole bulb of garlic as a late night snack. "Indeed. My compliments to the chef." She'd have to choke this quiche down to avoid suspicion. Then again, the aroma wasn't entirely unpleasant. "Is Luc— Lord Holiday awake?"

"I'm afraid my lord has some pressing matters to attend to. He won't be available until evening."

"Oh." After the events of last night, it was perhaps best to leave as quickly as possible. Still, she couldn't help feeling a bit disappointed in not seeing Lucas once more before departing. "Then do give my thanks for his hospitality. I think I'd like to head to the train station once I've finished."

"I will have the carriage readied for you." With that he bowed and shambled down the hallway.

Once out of sight, Mary eyed the quiche with suspicion. Holiday was determined to make her believe the box truly was for mushrooms. Adding them to breakfast was a clever play. She wouldn't be so easily deceived. But her stomach was rumbling. Just one bite to calm her morning hunger. As she took a forkful, to her surprise the overpowering garlic scent translated to a pleasant flavor when combined with the rest of the dish. Each bite made it a little easier to believe he'd been telling her the truth last night.

The sunny day sent all thoughts of vampires and ghosts to the back of her mind. In the sunlight none of them could get her. The normalcy of the train station made Holiday manor feel like a distant dream. The crowded train station however took her by surprise. Ah, that was right. Everyone was heading to The Great Exhibition. Beside her, two young children fought over a doll. To her left a group of men talked about the business and magic they expected to see.

"...and I hear they will be showcasing a model train to show the magical enchantments coming to make rail travel faster," one of the men said.

Another man chimed in, "Still a bit too risky an investment I think, but the stability of the market..."

The man's concerns were drowned out by the crowd as Mary moved closer to the edge of the platform. The train would be full at this rate, and she wanted a good seat. Margaret had promised to pick her up yesterday. Hopefully she came back for the morning train.

Right on time the train approached the platform. Only a handful of people got off, then the new wave of travelers descended on it. She headed straight for the back away from all the noisy families pouring into the seats near the front. She slid into an empty compartment and sat beside the window.

Her head swam from the lack of sleep and her hand cramped from last night's writing session. She pulled her pages out, but couldn't concentrate long enough to make sense of them. Her hurried writing made her tired rambles all the harder to decipher. She yawned. At least the train ride would be short. At home she could nap before getting back to work writing.

As unhelpful as her spending the night had been in figuring Lucas out, she couldn't forget the eeriness of making her way through the dark manor alone. If she could channel that experience into her story, she would have the makings of a new chapter to work on. Alice had yet to see Hallow's true nature, to see him feeding. After last night, today felt like the perfect time to tackle the reveal.

The compartment door slid open. "May I sit with you, miss?" asked a man clothed in a priest's cassock. The ends of his dark hair curled around his face. His serene smile enhanced his good looks. "The other compartments are full."

"Yes, of course." She gestured to the empty seat across from her. A priest would be a safe traveling companion, she thought. At the very least his presence would keep any leering men away.

"Thank you. I was beginning to worry I wouldn't get a seat."

She turned back to the window, watching the train station fall away as the train continued on, putting Holiday manor far enough away that it was no longer a threat. With each passing minute she found it harder to believe she'd seen a ghost. The Lucas she met had been a perfectly fine host. With distance and a more calm mind, all the similarities between Holiday and Hallow seemed like mere coincidence. The portrait of his father, the suspicious thumping and wailing in the manor, even the "coffin" full of mushrooms. All of it had a perfectly logical explanation.

"Has he enthralled you?"

"Excuse me?" She turned from the window, unsure if she'd heard him correctly.

The priest's smile fell away to a stern expression. "Has Lord Holiday enthralled you?"

"I wouldn't say that." He might have strange hobbies, but he had saved her. And he'd felt so warm doing it. And his library! She grinned at the memory. She wished she could spend days writing in that library. "Well ... wait a second. How do you know I was visiting him? I don't know you."

The priest jumped over to her seat, sliding in beside her, and next thing she knew he held a crucifix between his hands. He leaned toward her, aiming the crucifix her way, almost rubbing it against her left cheek. "Pater Noster, qui es in caelis, sanctificetur nomen tuum."

It took a minute for Mary's tired mind to catch up with reality. She'd had no idea the Catholic Church had gotten this aggressive with their tactics. "I'll give you a half penny! It's all I have on me!" She searched through her bag. "I can't offer you any more than that."

The priest paused, his brow furrowing. "What?"

"You want a donation, right?"

"No!" He slid away from her, as if finally coming back to his senses. "I don't want money. All I want is to save your soul."

"I'm Anglican, and I'm not interested in converting." Mary had been a young girl when the Catholic Emancipation Act was passed. Having only encountered a few in her lifetime, she never quite understood what they were, or why her older relatives, most notably Aunt Beth, so often accused them of being wicked and sneaky. Seeing the priest's behavior now, she finally began to understand why.

His lips pressed into a thin line as he considered her. "He hasn't gotten to you yet then."

"Gotten to me yet? What are you talking about?" She scooted back until she was against the window, putting as much space between them as she could.

"Lord Holiday. Or as you may know him, Lucas Holiday." He cast a pensive gaze out the window. "My nephew."

"Nephew?" Mary struggled to keep up with the bizarre series of events unfolding before her. Her sleep deprived mind must have heard that incorrectly. But now that he mentioned it, they did have the same dark hair. A five o'clock shadow of stubble dotted his chin. He couldn't be more than a few years older than Lucas. Mid-thirties at most. "But you look too young to be his uncle."

"My brother Luke, Lucas's father, was a great deal older than me. By the time I was born he was already studying abroad. Soon after he met his wife, and it wasn't long before they had their son." His face darkened, an eerie reflection of the grim expression Lucas always seemed to wear. "We were raised together. Grew up together. In truth, he's more like a brother to me than a nephew. Or rather, he was..." His nose wrinkled in agitated disgust and his hand squeezed the crucifix tightly. "I can't believe what he's become."

"Well you'll be happy to know that 'what he's become' is a perfect gentleman. I only met with him for tea to discuss business. Or is the business what this is about?" Mary's eyes widened as she contemplated the possibilities. What were the secrets that the young lord was hiding? Perhaps this priest claiming to be his uncle would have insights for him. "Has Lucas become a thief? An embezzler? Does Holiday Press have shady dealings I should be aware of? Hold on, let me get my notebook—"

"Holiday Press does not have shady dealings," he said, offense in his tone. "I had been overseeing the business after my brother's passing to make sure it would be waiting for Lucas. Holiday Printing Press is respectable and fair. I resent any accusations to the contrary." He finally pocketed his crucifix and slid away from her, putting a more comfortable and polite distance between them.

"Well I resent being followed and harassed."

He shook his head. "I merely wished to save you. And I wasn't following you. I tried to pay my nephew a visit today, but as you may have noticed, he's a bit reclusive." He kept his distance, but leaned closer, a dangerous glint in his eyes. "Did you notice anything strange while you visited him?"

More than a few things. But what did he count as strange? Martin Steepe was strange to her too with his mechanical hummingbirds and odd way of looking at the world, but Charlotte didn't seem to mind. "Growing mushrooms is an unusual hobby to be sure, but I don't see how it concerns me. Or you for that matter. A man deserves to enjoy his hobbies in peace."

The priest blinked at her. "Did you say mushrooms?"

"Yes." She crossed her arms. "He grows them in the cold cellar."

The priest gave her an incredulous look. "In a large wooden box? Full of soil from his homeland?"

"I suppose so. Just what are you insinuating anyway?" Suddenly she felt defensive. Lucas had saved her from falling down the stairs. He'd been nothing but gentlemanly and a good host, and so she'd forgive the possible ghost and possible blood in his teacup. She wouldn't let this stranger lambaste him in front of her. "If you must know, the mushrooms were delicious too."

He gave his head another slow shake as he straightened up. "I don't think we are understanding one another. Miss Hawke, I'm assuming my nephew has taken an interest in you seeing as how he invited you for tea. But my conscience won't stand by and let him harm you. You are aware of my brother's passing, the previous Lord Holiday, are you not?"

"I am. I was told that there was an accident. That he fell."

The priest let out a rueful chuckle. "Oh he certainly fell, but I assure you it was no accident."

"You mean to say he was murdered?" Not one to miss an opportunity to hear an incredible story, Mary flipped open her notebook and began writing.

"Oh yes," he said, "And the murderer is none other than his own son."

Mary dropped her quill as the words sank in. " Lucas? That's ridiculous! He's no murderer! He's a gentleman. Just what makes you think that?"

"Because one doesn't typically drive a wooden stake through one's heart by accident." He thumped his chest. "That's one of the best ways to kill vampires, you know."

Mary stood, swaying with the train car. "Do you really expect me to believe this madness? I barely know either of you, and yet here you are insisting he's a murderer." The man must know about her pen name. He was out to have a laugh on her behalf. She squinted at him. "Aren't you that priest who helped Roger?"

"If you are referring to the detective, yes. I hired him to investigate my brother's death. He's been invaluable in helping me uncover the truth."

"The truth as in him being a murderer? And what, a vampire too?"

"Yes!"

"What would ..." She searched her sparse knowledge of the Catholic Church. Who would a priest answer to? "Would the pope appreciate your baseless claims against a lord?"

"I can prove it to you. My nephew isn't an innocent man. I'm here because I don't want anyone else getting hurt."

She stared at him expectantly, curiosity getting the best of her. To hear someone else suspect him of being a vampire, well she wanted to hear him out. She already felt vindicated knowing she wasn't the only one to worry over the resemblance to Lord Hallow. When the priest didn't move or say anything else she dropped her arms. "And your proof?"

He blushed, a look of embarrassment causing him to glance away. "I don't have it at this exact moment, but I'm certain my brother left clues behind in his study in the tower. I plan to have the proof in my hands soon. And then I can make things right."

She slapped her thigh. "That was you poking around in the tower last night! I thought it would take a madman to go searching about in that storm."

"Me? No. I stayed elsewhere last night. I wouldn't dare get near my nephew at night. It is far too dangerous. That's when vampires are at their strongest."

Then who had it been? "But you don't have this proof on you?"

"No. I haven't been able to get into the tower yet."

Mary snorted. "Then your proof might not exist at all. Until I see it, I have no reason to believe you."

"My nephew is crafty at keeping me from obtaining it." His face wrinkled as if in pain, and he lifted a hand to clutch at his cross necklace. "You should stay far away from him and Holiday manor before he drains your blood or steals your soul to make you a vampire. There is no reason to risk your safety, even if you don't believe me. My brother died under mysterious circumstances. Who says it can't happen to you next? Nothing good can come from you gallivanting around with him."

Her fingers itched to write down his words. She reached for her quill. The drama of it all was perfect.

"Mister ... Holiday, I will take your warning into consideration. Although I assure you I have no relationship with Lord Holiday. My business plans have fallen through as it turns out. And so you see, I have no reason to visit him again. I wonder though, have you thought of his servants? They are in more danger than me, aren't they?" Like Alice in her story. Alice's position put her close to the hungry vampire, especially once too many other maids disappeared.

"I was too late to warn them. They're mostly gone, and his remaining butler is deep in his thrall. That poor man can barely function with how strong my nephew's grip is on him. You don't feel enthralled, do you? Do you feel compelled to return to the manor?"

"I feel compelled to sleep and not much else." And then write once she awoke. If she kept up this writing schedule she wouldn't have to miss any deadlines. Assuming Bertram allowed her to continue to publish. But that was a problem for another day. First she needed to deal with the priest.

He handed her a calling card. "My church is near Piccadilly Circus. If he comes around or you notice anything strange, please tell me. I will do everything within my power to keep you safe. I advise you to stay inside at night. And keep the rosary with you."

"I appreciate your concern for me, but I'm well versed in the ways of vampires. I've read plenty of vampire books."

His nose wrinkled. "Some make vampirism seem romantic. *The Vampyre*, *Varney*, and the worst offender of them all, *Twilight at Hallow Manor*. Too many young ladies have already been led astray by Lord Hallow. They are easy pickings for my nephew now."

She bristled. "I think it is a fine story. Have you bothered to read it?"

He looked out the window. "I wouldn't dare read such sinful litera-ture, but I've heard it gets a few points about vampires wrong."

"Like what?" She chewed on her bottom lip. She'd done her research and used her imagination when it suited the story.

He sighed. "Where do I start? That book is clearly designed to be a romance, and I doubt a vampire can love. People are food to them. Nothing more."

"You have no way of knowing that." She fisted her skirts in her hands. This priest would be lucky if she didn't drive a stake through his heart to stop him from insulting her story. She bet he didn't think anything but the Bible was good literature.

"Damned creatures who kill without mercy can't love."

The train slowed and she hopped up. "This is my stop." Her plan to make a quick escape failed when she stepped into the hallway and found it packed with everyone trying to get off at the same stop. She saw no choice but to wait at the back of the line with the priest behind her.

Her thoughts wandered while the line shuffled forward. Was it too late to reveal the vampire hunter in her story as a priest? Or maybe a monk who left the order to kill creatures of the night. It would be quite the reveal and make him seem more trustworthy. If she pitted them against each other with Alice caught in the center, she would have plenty of drama to play off. A love triangle would entangle Alice in both men further.

Outside the station she waited for Margaret as the crowd dissi-pated into hansom cabs and waiting carriages. Fifteen minutes later everyone else had left for The Great Exhibition and there was still no Margaret in sight. Home was too far away to walk, and a family climbed into the last available hansom cab. She wrung her hands. How long before the cab returned?

"Do you need a ride?" Mr. Holiday asked. "I have a hansom cab across the street. I can see you safely home."

She considered her options. She could accept the ride with a mad-man or wait who knew how long for another cab to appear. In the sunlight, the priest looked sane. And more handsome than any priest needed to be. The breeze tore a shiver from her, making up her mind. "If you don't mind, yes. But no more talk about ... you know." She glanced about before leaning toward him. "Murder and vampires."

"I'd be more than happy to recite some psalms for you during the ride instead." He looked far too eager at the idea.

She held in her groan. "Please don't."

They passed the ride in the hansom cab in awkward silence. When she climbed down at her house, he called out a cheerful "I'll pray for you!"

It felt more like a threat than a comfort.

Chapter 11

Margaret was still asleep when Mary swept into her room and ripped the covers off. Lack of sleep always left Mary grumpy, and her sister was the perfect target for her ire. Margaret had managed to climb into her nightgown whenever she returned home but left the previous night's trousers on. If Mary had waited at the station, she had a feeling she would have been left waiting all day.

"What do you think you're doing?" Margaret whined.

"It's time to wake up. You were supposed to meet me at the train station."

"Yesterday!" Margaret rolled over and curled up in a ball. "You didn't show."

"Because I missed the train. I caught the next one. You know, the morning train you slept through." Mary opened the curtains, sending bright light into Margaret's face. She groaned and rolled again.

"And since I didn't make that train, wouldn't you assume I'd be on the next one?"

Margaret's grumbled reply was incoherent as she pressed her face into the pillow.

"Margret!" Mary stomped around to the other side of the bed. "A priest had to drive me home. And he said he'd pray for me!"

"A priest praying for you, what a trial you had to endure." Margaret snorted. "Your soul has been saved at long last. Sounds like it worked out for you."

"But it may not have. What if I was stranded at the station? With The Great Exhibition open it's next to impossible to get a cab. Is it really more important for you to be gallivanting around?" If the priest had been a more dangerous madman, she would have been in real trouble.

"I was out with a friend," Margaret said as she sat up, her hair a mess. "I'm allowed to socialize, aren't I?"

"And who is she?"

"*His* name is John."

"John." The name took Mary by surprise. She knew her sister well enough to not expect her to be eager to court a man. Margaret feared marriage more than Mary did. "Out all night with some man? You...you didn't—"

"No! Who do you think I am?" Margaret threw her pillow at Mary who caught it. "Besides, we are friends, nothing more. Sometimes it is nice to have a friend who doesn't care to talk about marriage and other boring topics."

"Can you be certain he sees it that way? What if he is expecting more?"

Margaret glared as she climbed out of bed. "I don't think he is interested in women. If he wants more, it won't be from me." She yanked a dress out of her wardrobe. "What do you care anyway? I've been sneaking out for more than a year and you never cared until Mother left."

"Someone needs to look after you." Mary squared her shoulders. "And what do you mean you've been sneaking out that long?"

Margaret huffed. "See, you didn't even notice until it suited you. I can look after myself. I've been doing it for years while father poured all his pride onto you and Mother forgot about me unless she had something to criticize. I may not be the prodigy writer of the family, but I'm allowed to have my own friends."

"I never said you weren't."

"I'm glad we agree. So get out of my room." She pointed at the door, tapping her foot as she waited.

"Not until you apologize for leaving me at the train station. I almost got eaten by a vampire." She crossed her arms.

Margaret rolled her eyes. "Vampires aren't real. Are you that desperate to make everything about yourself?"

"I'm upset you didn't follow your promise to pick me up."

"I was there yesterday for half an hour waiting. You're the one who didn't show. I figured you could take a hansom cab whenever you finally arrived."

"Well, I couldn't because they were all taken!"

"Is this really what you want to focus on? Mother is gone, Papa sold the business, and you want to argue about having to ride with a priest?"

"You just don't understand."

"I'm sorry if I'm not willing to walk around acting like everything is okay like you while stewing over mild inconveniences. Because guess what?" She swept her arms out. "Everything isn't all right and neither are you."

"You don't know how I feel." Mary's nostrils flared. "We are okay."

"Then why do we no longer have Hawke? And why does father spend his days in his study staring out his window? He doesn't know what to do with himself. And you are getting obsessed with vampires to avoid facing reality."

"I am not! We will find our way. We still have the house and each other. Those are what matter."

Margaret slapped a hand against her wardrobe. "You sound like Mother. She never wanted to deal with our emotions either. She preferred to sweep them under the rug where she could ignore them."

The statement sucked the air right out of Mary. She leaned against the bedpost, clutching it to keep herself upright. "Take that back. I'm nothing like her."

"She was great at pretending she was fine until right before she ran off with Uncle. Are you going to remain in denial until Bertram runs Hawke into the ground? Or will you marry whoever Aunt Beth picks for you and continue to act like everything is fine like mother did?"

Mary shook the bed post. "I'm not her! I would never abandon you or Papa. And ... and I'm not okay either. There! Are you happy now?" She seethed, rounding her shoulders as she faced Margaret.

Margaret sniffed and looked away. "No. Stay out of my business, and then I'll be happy."

"And you're running around each night while pretending everything is normal during the day. That's just your way of acting like everything is fine when it isn't."

Margaret threw the dress in her hands onto the ground. "It isn't the same! I'm not trying to pretend about anything. I know how miserable I am and how scary the future is. I'm not avoiding it. All I want is time to enjoy myself before I have to wake up and face everything all over again."

"It is the same because you go out to avoid facing your fears. If you are so worried about a future you don't want, you should talk to Papa about it. Until then, you are no better than me." She marched out, slamming the door behind her.

She hadn't been in her parent's room in years. The door had remained shut ever since her mother left. Mary flung the door open and stomped into the room. Everything was exactly as her mother had left it, albeit with a covering of dust. Mary sneezed. Once and then twice. The small room would need to be cleaned and aired out before anyone used it again. Clearly Papa hadn't been sleeping in here.

Several dresses lay across the unmade bed as if her mother had decided they weren't worth packing. The jewelry Papa gave her remained on the vanity table, including the necklace depicting the Hawke logo. Her mother only wore it for important occasions associated with the family business. She'd always preferred her pearls.

Mary would be more than happy to take the jewelry her mother never appreciated enough for herself, but that wasn't why she was here. She opened the wardrobe. Two more dresses hung inside, both old. Of course, she'd taken the nice dresses with her, leaving the ones she didn't want any more behind. Mary flung the first dress onto the floor. The second, a faded peach dress with far too much lace, she yanked off its hanger and dragged it across the floor as she headed for the sitting room downstairs.

The dress caught on the railing of the stairs and she gave it a hard tug, ignoring the ripping sound as the dress came free. She chose the rocking chair beside the fireplace as her perch, dress splayed over her lap. She stopped by her desk, pulling a pair of spare fabric scissors out of the drawer.

"I'm nothing like her," she hissed under her breath as she jabbed at the air with the scissors. "I would never walk out on my family. I'd never leave my daughters behind wondering if I ever cared about them at all." Papa would never leave them, but it wasn't fair for him to lose the business. Or her. Mother and Uncle were selfish. They could have left without ruining the business too.

She turned the scissors on the dress and hacked away at the right sleeve. She'd always hated the gaudy lace on this dress. The years had turned the white lace into a dirty cream. A tea stain marred the sleeve. Once the sleeve was free she ripped it apart with her hands, letting her fury leech into the material. "Hawke should have been mine someday," she grumbled. She would have taken over her father's half of the business. She'd dreamed of it for years. Whatever it took to keep the business a success she would have done.

Writing was wonderful of course, but it was a lonely, solitary endeavor most days. With Hawke she loved interacting with the authors and curating the serials. There was no feeling that could compare to finding a surprise gem of a story and knowing everyone would get to see it soon too. She had her own ideas for stories, but she wanted to do far more with her time than write.

Once she'd ripped the sleeve in half, she tossed it onto the embers. Then she started on the left sleeve. Once it too had joined the first in the fireplace, she got to work hacking away at the body of the dress. She ripped the stands of lace off one by one. This dress had to be as old as Mary, if not older. It'd been modified more than once over the years, but the faded fabric and stains had reached the end of their life.

She fed each strip of lace into the fire, taking her time with her work. Each rip and tear of the stitches was music to her ears. It felt good. Like all those pent-up emotions were finally pouring through her fingers, into the fabric, and then burning up in the fire. Like the dress, they too would be ashes soon.

"Mary, when did you—" Her father stopped one step into the room, one hand resting on the doorway. His eyes widened as he took in her ripping apart the lace.

"Yes?" She didn't take her attention off the dress as she tugged the last of the lace off. She let out a cry of triumph before tossing it all onto the smoking sleeves. Then she attacked the rest of the dress, ripping, cutting, and tearing as best she could as the ugly peach fabric fought back. She managed a few small holes, but without fabric scissors she couldn't get far.

With a grunt of frustration, she heated up the fire poker and turned that on the dress next. She used the hot iron to singe the fabric and poke new holes. She laughed, the sound bouncing around the room.

"I-I'll come back later." Her father backed out. His footsteps pounded up the stairs as he rushed to his study.

After Mary tossed the dress into the fireplace with the rest of the mess, she sank back into the rocking chair and watched it all burn. Her emotions felt drained, like the cork had finally been released. But it felt good. Like she'd been waiting to release them. And never having to see that ugly dress ever again was a plus.

Margaret was right. She wasn't okay. No matter how much she tried to pretend she was. She was furious at her mother. Furious at losing Hawke. But what could she do about any of it? Absolutely nothing. She wasn't going to drag her mother home like she was a child. Nor did she want her to come home. And she didn't have enough money to buy Hawke back. All she had was *Twilight at Hallow Manor*.

Unless ... that was the answer. The story was hers. She owned the copyright. She could take it elsewhere. Hawke was no longer her Hawke, so why publish under it? There were enough printers in the city that she could have her serial printed herself. She couldn't run Hawke, but she could handle the business end of her own writing. There was no reason to let Bertram profit off her hard work.

Once the last of the fabric had burned up, she dug out her pages from the previous night and headed to her desk. It was time to finally make progress and save whatever she could from last night's scribblings. First she'd write the story, and then she'd talk to printers. Maybe Holiday. Vampire or not, Holiday did have the fastest presses.

Scuffling in the entryway drew her attention. She peeked out just as Margaret stepped outside. Her father peered down from the top of the stairs, looking at her in the same way Charlotte would when asking about dachshunds, afraid the Hammonds' dogs were coming to ruin her social life once more.

The rest of the week Margaret and Mary ignored each other. When they couldn't take their meals separately they didn't speak at the table while Papa read the newspaper. If Margaret caught Mary watching her, she'd look the other way.

Altogether Mary felt twelve years old again, and she'd hated being twelve. Back then, she was still on the cusp of being allowed to attend late night parties at long last, while being too old to play with the boys anymore. Like back then, she felt stuck.

Whenever she opened her mouth to apologize, the words got caught in her throat and her thoughts froze. Acting like this at her age was ridiculous, but as one week turned into two and the silence continued, breaking it felt harder and harder. Nothing she could think to say felt strong enough, didn't describe her feelings well enough.

Not that some aspects of their day changed much. Margaret continued to sleep in way too late while Mary retired early to wake up and get a head start on writing. And when she crept down the hall each morning she couldn't help but to peek in on Margaret to make sure she'd found her way home.

Mary pulled a fresh batch of scones out of the oven. Baking kept her hands busy when she needed a writing break. With Charlotte giving her tips, she found she could make passable scones for tea. Still, she refrained from serving them to Charlotte. If she kept torturing the poor woman with dry scones she wouldn't keep visiting. Even sweet Charlotte had to have a breaking point.

"There you are," her father said as he stepped into the kitchen with a sour-faced Margaret in tow. "I need to speak with you both."

Mary set the tray of scones down. Had he finally noticed her fight with Margaret? After all their fights growing up, he should be used to their silences and arguments. "Is everything all right?"

"I'm afraid I have grim news."

They both stared at him, Margaret's sour look turning to worry.

"What is it?" Mary asked.

He folded his hands in front of himself. "I plan to ask Parliament for a divorce. I understand you will both have strong feelings on this matter, but there is no other recourse. I'm sorry things have ended this way, but for my sake I can't keep looking back any longer. I need to think of what is best for me and you girls now."

Silence. He looked back and forth between them. Mary's mind froze like it had so often these past weeks. With her mother gone, she'd forgotten there were legal matters that would need to be looked after. Her mother's actions counted as adultery, and that made divorce possible. Yet even in a case this straightforward and even with the magicians pushing for more relaxed divorce laws, there would still be paperwork and hearings to deal with.

"And?" Margaret asked.

"She also sent a letter requesting the rest of her things."

Margaret snorted. "Don't tell me you are going to send them to her. She doesn't deserve any of them. She'll sell the jewelry for whatever money she can squeeze out of it."

"I want her Hawke necklace," Mary said. "Please don't send it to her."

"Send her an empty box," Margaret added. "That's what she deserves."

Their father frowned, his brow creasing as he considered them. "I understand if either of you are upset over this."

"Me," Margaret said, waving a hand in the air. "I'm upset you didn't divorce her the day after she walked out. She's made it clear how important we are to her. We don't owe her a single stitch of clothing."

Mary nodded. "She can look after herself. I already destroyed one of her dresses. The rest aren't worth sending." She lifted her dress and stuck a foot out, showing the boots off. "And I took her boots already. Her slippers too."

Their father didn't speak, stunned into silence. Mary gave his arm a sympathetic pat. "We support your decision. We aren't upset with you in the slightest, Papa."

"Won't you miss her?"

"She isn't worth it," Margaret grumbled before stomping out. "Good riddance."

Mary took a deep breath to calm her thoughts. "Of course, we will. But she betrayed all of us and that isn't an easy thing to get over. Maybe someday we will want to see her again, but until that day comes, please don't pester Margaret about it."

His eyes misted. "I was afraid you'd both be upset with me instead. I feel like I failed you both for not seeing it coming."

"We would never blame you." She hugged him, squeezing him tight.

He gave her a relieved smile.

A knock on the door echoed into the kitchen. "Could you get that?" he asked.

"I will." She headed for the door, glancing back as her father dabbed at his eyes. She opened the front door, finding a footman on their doorstep.

Chapter 12

"Letter from Miss Graham for Miss Hawke," the Steepe footman said as he held it out. The wax mark sealing the letter bore the Steepe Family crest.

"I'm Miss Hawke." She took the letter and the man bowed.

"Good day," he said as he turned to leave. She watched him go, not liking that he wasn't waiting for a response from her to return with. Bad news. It must be.

She headed for her desk and set the letter on it. Dread coiled in her stomach. Hawke was out of her grasp, and she loathed the reminder. At least it was better than facing the vampire hunting priest again. As good as her trip to Holiday manor had been for inspiration, the whole thing made her feel like she'd fallen into a world of madness. She didn't know how to begin to explain it to someone else without sounding mad herself.

And yes, it was a little thrilling. But it, on top of her family problems, felt like too much excitement at once. Oh, but Lord Holiday was handsome. Visiting him again might not be so bad ...

She opened the letter. Two tickets to The Great Exhibition fell out. She pulled the letter out. Charlotte's hurried writing asked her to come to The Great Exhibition as soon as she could. There was no explanation to be had, only instructions on how to get to the Steepe Tea booth. Did Charlotte have news? Or was she just sharing her good fortune? Either way a visit to The Great Exhibition would be a nice distraction. Time out of the house spent with a friend was exactly what she needed.

"Who was it?" her father asked as he stepped into the room.

"It was a footman with a note from my friend Charlotte. She wants me to come visit her. Her fiancé is selling his tea at The Great Exhibition and she is helping. She sent an extra ticket if you'd like to come along." She waved the tickets in the air. "I hear it is unbelievable inside."

He rubbed the back of his neck. "Take your sister. It will be a good day out for you two. I'll feel better knowing you two are having fun." He gave her a nervous smile. "That will be one less thing for me to worry about."

"I get the feeling Margaret finds me the opposite of fun these days, but I'll see if I can manage to drag her along with me. That's all I can promise." She reached for her cloak. "Are you going to send Mother the rest of her things?"

"No. But I'm speaking with my solicitor about the divorce."

"It is the right choice. Don't let anyone talk you out of it."

"I won't. And don't you worry about it. Have fun today."

"I'll try. Promise me you'll try to start having fun again too."

He smiled at her. "I'll try."

As with last week, Margaret continued to not speak to Mary. Or show up to go to The Great Exhibition. Mary went alone, disappointment tightening her chest. She'd thought the free ticket would lure Margaret out of her room, but she wasn't about to force her sister to go. That would only prolong their fight and lead to more hurt feelings. If Margaret wanted space, she'd give her space.

Doubts assailed her the whole ride to The Great Exhibition. Leaving Margaret alone to stew in her bitterness no longer felt like the right choice, but neither did dragging her out. They would need to speak again eventually. But Mary's feelings on the matter weren't wholly altruistic. Going alone felt pitiful. Everyone else would be going with their family, friends, or lovers. She didn't like the way loneliness beat against her chest.

As she stepped out of the carriage, her rehearsed apology speeches flew from her mind. The Crystal Palace looked like something out of a fairy tale. She bumped into the man in line in front of her because her attention kept flying this way and that as she entered. The Crystal Palace felt full of life with all the laughter and shouts of surprise surrounding her. The noise shook off the cobwebs of worry clinging to her.

The fog of magic along the floor made Mary feel like the building had been built in the sky. It reminded her of her dance with Lucas at Roquefort's party. Thinking of the party made her stomach squirm from all the butterflies. Dancing with Lucas shouldn't make her want to see him again. What could make her feel this way about a strange man who pokes around in dirt boxes at night in a dilapidated, possibly haunted manor? That's to say nothing of his raving mad uncle. Or the fact that in each of her encounters with Lucas, the man had never eaten around her. The only thing she ever saw him drink was that strange, sweet-smelling red tea. Maybe the priest wasn't so mad after all. No, it was just her nerves making her stomach upset. Probably.

Mary checked the directions Charlotte had written one last time before pocketing the letter and going in search of the Steepe booth. She paused at the displays along the way. Her gaze lingered on every dark-haired man she passed, searching for Lucas even though she knew he wasn't likely to be out. Not at this time of day. Still, that didn't stop her stomach from swooping when she spotted a dark-haired man of similar build admiring a display of cameras.

Two writers she recognized from their serials with Hawke stopped at a nearby display. Mary hurried on her way, wanting to avoid the inevitable awkward conversation if they noticed her. She wouldn't blame them if they were mad about Hawke being sold without any warning to the authors. Today she didn't feel like small talk about books or side-stepping questions about Hawke.

The closer she got to her destination, the thicker the fog grew until it was almost to her knees. She spotted Charlotte running a tray of scones to a family sitting at a table. She headed for the Steepe tea displays while Charlotte tended to the customers. Mr. Steepe restocked the tins of tea for sale as he chatted away with … no one. Behind the counter Arjun brewed tea, his back to Mr. Steepe as he paid the man no mind.

A laugh replied to him. She squinted, finally noticing the steam puffing from the teapot on the counter as it laughed.

"Mary! You made it," Charlotte said from behind.

"Yes, thank you for the tickets." She tilted her head toward Mr. Steepe. "Are you aware Mr. Steepe is talking to ... well, a teapot?"

"Oh, yes. That's Louie."

"...Louie?"

"Yes. The ancient teapot of Lu Yu." As Charlotte imitated the droning tone of the teapot, an exasperated smile crept across her face. "Apparently an ancient Chinese philosopher had him made. A thousand years later, and now Louie has found his way to the only other person in history who finds his jokes funny."

"Is that the same story-telling teapot from the party?"

"Yes. Thank goodness he only has the one." Charlotte wrapped an arm around her shoulders leaving Mary's mind rushing to make sense of Louie. "Oh but I'm so glad you are here!"

Charlotte led her toward the curtain hanging beside the counter.

"But it's a teapot," she said.

"One of his favorites."

Mr. Steepe turned and caught sight of them. He smiled. "Miss ..." His smile turned to uncertainty as his forehead scrunched in thought. "Hawthorne, no no ... Hawkins?"

"Hawke, dear," Charlotte corrected in a patient tone.

"Hawke, Miss Hawke," he rushed to say. "How do you do?"

"Um, well. And you?"

"I'm excellent, thank you." He turned his smile to Charlotte. "I think I'm getting better at remembering names."

"You are." Charlotte gave his arm an affectionate pat.

They were cute, Mary decided. Her parents had never been that adorable together.

Something bumped against Mary's legs, and she jumped. A snout popped out of the fog as a cloudy dachshund stared up at her, tongue lolling out of his mouth.

"Is that Oolong?" Mary asked.

"Oolong, how did you escape?" Martin reached down and picked the dog up. Whatever glamour he used on the dog made it look like he was holding a fluffy cloud shaped like a dog.

"You brought Oolong?" Charlotte asked in a hissing whisper. "He can't be here. We could get in trouble!"

"But my butler said he was getting lonely, and I couldn't bear to leave him behind today." His eyes made him look as innocent as Oolong as he rubbed the dog's head. "Besides, we'll both be leaving in a few minutes. I need to go outside to ship off a housewarming present to Bertram. He should have already arrived at our countryside retreat." He held a mechanical hummingbird in one hand. "I don't know why I never thought to try using them for more than honey earlier."

"I can't believe you are sending him a gift after he tried to ruin our engagement. And your reputation. And your business. And—" Charlotte did her best to keep her anger in check. With a deep breath, her tone turned a bit more gentle. "No one will fault you if you want time away from him."

"He is family and misguided is all. He'll come to his senses soon." Martin leaned closer to them, his gaze flicking about to make sure no one else was too close. "I made sure he would have plenty of time to think over what he has done. I got rid of all the coffee at the manor and have ordered the servants to not buy any." He smiled, clearly pleased with himself. The mere mention of Bertram's name made Mary clench her hands, but it was a small comfort to know that wherever he was he was being deprived of something he liked.

"I don't think—" Charlotte began, before shaking her head. "Never mind. You go handle that while I talk to Mary. And make sure Oolong doesn't trip up poor Arjun."

Mr. Steepe gave her a somber nod. "I'll keep him out of the way."

Mary turned back to Charlotte. "So your beau has you working for him now, does he?"

"As a matter of fact, I'm here on behalf of the bakery," corrected Charlotte, beaming. "The people are rather enjoying our pastries with their tea. Steepe cafés might just start selling more Clarke baked goods in the future."

"Well if this is how the courtship is going, I can't wait to hear about the honeymoon." teased Mary, "A trade meeting by the docks, perhaps?"

"Oh stop." Charlotte playfully patted Mary's arm. Her eyes sparkled as she spoke. "Anyway, you've arrived at the perfect time. The morning rush is over. Let's go have a seat and talk. I have news to share."

Mary's curiosity rose. "Good news?"

"Very." Charlotte poured them both a cup of tea and handed Mary's hers. Then she opened the second curtain and gestured for Mary to go through first. On the other side, a little table had been set up in front of the glass looking out over Hyde Park. A single folder rested atop it. "I wanted to discuss Hawke with you, but everything has been busy here since the opening. I've been helping Arjun out here and there. The poor man has to bring extra boxes of tea with him every day just to keep the shelves stocked. Martin has a new hire coming tomorrow to help out until The Great Exhibition closes"

"Sounds like everything is going well."

"Even better than I could have hoped." Charlotte brushed a stray strand of hair away from her face. Her content smile made her look lovesick. "Helping means I get to see Martin every day." She stared off into space.

Mary cleared her throat. "So what about Hawke did you want to talk about?"

The question pulled Charlotte back.

"Right. I asked you to come since I didn't know when I'd be able to find time to visit. Did you happen to read about any thefts here at The Great Exhibition in the papers?"

"No. All I've read are reviews and talk about the exhibits."

Charlotte stirred sugar into her tea. "Then the Steepes must have kept it out of the papers after all."

"Kept what out?" The conversation felt like a puzzle where Mary had only been given half the pieces.

"Never mind about the thefts. The short story of it all is Bertram got himself exiled to the countryside, and Martin has taken control over what remains of his businesses. He plans to look after them while Bertram is gone..." Charlotte took a long sip from her cup for dramatic effect. Before Mary could fully process and celebrate Bertram's exile, she put down her cup and continued, "...and we both thought you might like to have Hawke back."

The statement stole her breath away. It took a minute before she could find her voice. "You can do that? You can give Hawke back to us?!"

"We can. But legally, giving it to you will be a bit complicated, so we have to sell it to you."

"Name your price!" Barely able to contain her excitement, Mary reached across the table and grabbed Charlotte's hand, squeezing it tightly. She'd happily part with every last shilling Bertram had given her family if it meant getting the publishing house back.

"Half a penny." With her free hand, Charlotte opened the folder and slid the contract over to Mary. She then pried her other hand free from Mary's grip and curled a stray hair around her finger. "But there is one stipulation."

"Anything at all! I'll wipe down the tables and serve customers for you if that's what it takes."

"Nothing so drastic. I'd just like you to have a look at my next story." Charlotte laughed, adding coyly, "And maybe consider publishing it as well?"

"Even if it were the worst thing I'd ever read in my life I'd still consider publishing it. Every last chapter." Perhaps Mary was too excited. Under normal circumstances, her shrewd publisher senses would never be willing to agree to anything without seeing the story first. She took a deep breath, forcing her thoughts to calm. It would be prudent, she thought, to make sure she wasn't signing up to print out more garden gnome detective stories or the like. "So what's it about?"

"Well I'm still working on it. I want to write something completely different than my last one."

"I'd be happy to help you develop and edit your story."

"Even if it were the worst thing you'd ever read in your life?" Charlotte teased.

"Even if." Mary couldn't stop smiling.

Charlotte stood up, straightened her back, and put forth her best impression mocking a businessman. "Well Miss Hawke, do we have a deal?" She held her hand out stiffly.

"Why yes, Miss Graham," Mary replied, mimicking Charlotte's tone and expression and shaking her hand, "I believe we do." They gave one another an exaggerated handshake, trying their best to maintain a straight face before breaking down into delighted laughter.

"Oh wonderful. Everything is in the contract. We weren't sure if you or your father would want to be listed as the owner. We can make an appointment to go over everything with our solicitors once you decide." She rested her hand over her heart. "I'm going to feel much better once you have the company back."

Would her father want Hawke back? Mary didn't know. He could have been telling the truth about wanting more time outside of work. Or he could have faked his happiness for her and Margaret's sake. "Papa's out of town right now. I'll discuss this with him as soon as he gets back." Mary wasn't sure if she wanted to discuss it with her father just yet, but one way or another she'd see to it the publishing house was back where it belonged with her family.

"Martin has been looking over a few things. He said you are going to need a new printer soon. Bertram didn't have time to make any deals. He didn't have time to do much of anything with Hawke."

"Before Bertram got his hands on the company, I'd been looking into Holiday Press, but I suppose you already knew that."

"That reminds me. How did your tea with Lord Holiday go?" She rested her chin on the back of her hands as she peered at Mary. "Tell me everything. What is having tea with a lord like?"

"Delicious. And he has an enchanted library. But the visit was ... odd." She blew out a breath as she leaned back. "I don't know where to begin." Tea had been the least interesting part of her visit, but everything else was too unbelievable.

"Then begin with the library. Does it make it easy to find the exact book you want? That's the first enchantment I'd add to a library."

"No. The magic seems to do the opposite, but he is working on fixing it. The books fly about the room and are generally a nuisance. In fact, forget finding any book. But still, a library! The room would be a lovely space if the magic gets sorted out."

Charlotte hummed in thought. "I wish I could say I had a magical library. The books don't talk do they? All of Martin's boring business books would put me to sleep."

Mary snorted into her tea. "No, but that would be interesting." She set her teacup down. "You wouldn't believe what happened after the library. I barely still believe it."

"Let me guess, he flirted, didn't he." Charlotte whispered as she leaned forward."Wait, no. Even better. Did he kiss you?"

If only. A womanizer of a lord would be easier to deal with than whatever he was. "No. The railing on his stairs gave out under me and I fell. He caught me." Her stomach swooped at the memory, at the terror of the railing giving and then the warmth of the lord.

Charlotte gasped. "How exciting. What was it like when he caught you? Was it enough to make you swoon?" Her eyes sparkled with glee.

"It was warm. So warm." The embrace had almost made her forget how close she had come to falling onto one of those jagged railing posts. "But also terrifying. And he was very apologetic about the whole thing. I think he felt embarrassed about the state of his manor."

"Sounds like a gentleman. A real one." She topped off her cup of tea and stirred more sugar into it with more force than necessary, the tea sloshing onto the space. "Not like Bertram. That devil would let a poor woman fall rather than scuff his shoes to save her.."

"In Bertram's defense he is a serpent, not a man." That earned a new smile from Charlotte. "Lord Holiday does feel like a gentleman, but I feel terrible about everyone mistaking him for Lord Hallow. The poor man thought he was real. People are even sending him mail addressed to Lord Hallow. You should have seen how obscene some of those applications to be his 'maid' were."

Charlotte coughed as her tea went down wrong, taking another sip of tea before she spoke. "Are you serious? I knew your story was popular with women but not that popular." She cleared her throat and gathered herself. "And he hasn't taken up any of these young ladies on their offers?"

"I recognized some of those names.'Young lady' is a charitable term. But no. He seemed more embarrassed than enticed."

"...So he's still available," she sighed, that lovesick look she wore so often back on her face. "And it sounds to me like you rather fancy him. how romantic."

"I do, but well ... it's hard to explain."

"Why?"

"Because he's ... well he has a black cat and a strange butler and odd hobbies. He's eccentric." At the same time both of their gazes moved to the glass windows where Martin let go of a small mechanical hummingbird with a letter attached to its leg. Oolong sniffed at the grass. A grasshopper jumped away and the dog startled back, falling over in his haste.

Charlotte laughed. "Believe me, I understand 'eccentric' better than anyone else. In truth I wasn't sure if I could handle it, but a day with Martin is never boring. The way he sees the world makes me think in ways I never have before. There is no other man I'd rather be with, even if I do need to give him some help from time to time. He helps me too. I'm glad I didn't let my insecurities get the best of me and break off the engagement." There was nothing but adoration in her voice as she watched Martin and Oolong.

Mary sipped at her tea while she mulled over the advice. "You are right. I don't know if he feels the same about me, but I don't want to walk away. Not yet anyway." She felt a little lighter. The vampire business had to be a misunderstanding that would be cleared up soon enough. "His uncle is odd, but I suppose Holiday can handle him."

"Odd in what way?"

"He's a priest." Admitting the vampire accusation aloud felt too embarrassing. "He thinks his nephew murdered his own father. The man is taking his brother's death hard, although I suppose it is never easy to lose someone." Her pointer finger tapped the handle of her teacup from nerves while she waited for Charlotte's reaction.

Charlotte shook her head. "I don't believe for a second that man could be a murderer. He visited Martin just the other day, you know. He may not be one for remembering names, but Martin is a fairly good judge of character."

Mary snorted. "He can't be that good a judge if he hasn't gotten rid of Bertram yet."

"Well...nobody's perfect."

"Holiday mentioned that he and Martin were acquainted, but it seems a long way to go just to discuss repairing a magic library. Are they close?"

"They used to study magic together. They spoke a great deal about the future of Rune Press."

"The future of what?"

"Didn't he tell you? Holiday Press prints Martin's books about magic. The name Rune Press hides the true identity of the printer. Apparently they cooked up the scheme together a few years ago, and the late Lord Holiday agreed to it. Now that it's in his hands, I think your lord wanted to learn more about what was needed to continue their business. I refuse to believe someone that dedicated to helping the less fortunate learn magic could be a killer."

"He hadn't told me any of this."

Charlotte's eyes went wide and her hand clapped over her mouth as she realized her mistake. "You can't tell anyone! It's a secret." She waved her hands in a panic and paused to look about to make sure no one was listening. "Some of the nobility would ruin Holiday if they found out. Not only do they not want commoners to have magic, but for a lord to be spreading magical books about, I doubt they would treat him well for the betrayal."

"I won't tell a soul. I couldn't bear to see him ruined. Someone so..." Mary trailed off. She thought of the contemplative look his face always wore, and of the sadness behind his eyes.

"...So handsome?" chimed in Charlotte.

Mary snorted. "Oh stop. I'm not sure if I'm interested in him that way, but I'll consider it. Maybe if I get to know him better. I know for Papa's sake I should start thinking about marriage, but I don't know what I want in a man."

"I didn't know what I was looking for either. To be honest I still don't, but I do know that I like the way Martin makes me feel. You will figure it out. And when you do, be sure to give me every last detail." As she polished off the last of her tea, Charlotte glanced down at her cup. "Though I suppose if you needed a hint, you could always just read the leaves."

Mary squinted at the smattering of tea leaves floating in what remained of her tea. "I might if I could, though I doubt a teacup will be as useful in my lovelife as it was in yours."

"Don't be so sure. There is a fortune teller who does tea leaf readings of those who come here every day. She should be here by now."

"I hadn't considered that. Is she real?"

Charlotte pulled an ugly pair of glasses out of her pocket. The blue lenses didn't match her outfit. "I can check for you, but Martin said she has real magic about her."

"What are those spectacles for?"

Charlotte pushed them up her nose. "Martin got me a pair. They help you see magic. Want me to introduce you to the fortune teller? After I can tour you around. I still haven't seen all the exhibits yet."

She thought of the medium who'd interrupted her conversation with Holiday and all the previous fortunes she'd given her. "I have my doubts, but I see no harm in trying." Any guidance would be welcomed. With Hawke back in her hands that was one worry off the list, but she didn't think she could forget about the lord.

"Finish your tea and bring your cup." Charlotte stood, resting her hands on the small table. "Small warning. Don't be too quick to dismiss whatever she tells you."

"Why? I'm not sure I'll believe anything she says."

Charlotte lowered her voice. "The other day she warned Martin misfortune awaited him. Nothing happened until he prepared for bed. There'd been some mix up in the kitchen and he got a cold cup of tea. He was devastated."

If all Martin had to worry about was a bad cup of tea, she envied him. "I think he and I have different ideas on what counts as misfortune. I promise to not be rude, but I can't promise to believe her."

"Good enough." Charlotte led her past the tea booth and to the tables in front of it.

A woman who Mary wouldn't have looked twice at sat at a table for two. Whereas the annoying mediums who couldn't decide whether Mary was meant to be a spinster or not went for showmanship, the flashiest thing about the woman was her sign announcing her services. She reminded Mary a bit of one of her childhood teachers, a strict woman who'd had students convinced she had eyes on the back of her head.

A woman left the table with a big smile and one hand resting on her pregnant belly. The fortuneteller noticed Mary and crooked a finger, beckoning her to come.

"Good luck," Charlotte whispered.

Several rose-colored crystals shone against the woman's neck. What was with mediums and crystals? The woman wore large glasses that partially obscured her face. Mixed with the scarf she wore, the fortune teller could be anyone.

"Good tidings to you. I am Madame Fortuna. Set your cup down and we will see what fate has divined for you," the woman said, her tone theatrical with an accent that didn't sound like anything in particular. "Two pence to see what your future holds."

Mary sat down and slid her coin across the table, squinting at the woman as she did. "Mrs. Williams?"

"N-no. I am Madame Fortuna! Seer of the unseen." She tugged her scarf tighter. With each word, both her bravado and accent seemed to disappear. "Herald of the future."

"Mrs. Williams, I would know your voice anywhere." Mrs. Williams had been the strictest English teacher Mary ever had as a child. She was also certain the lady had a crush on Papa at one point once she found out who he was. That was something Mary didn't like to remind herself of. With her mother gone, now all manner of women could try to slide into Papa's good graces. Dinners with her past English teacher was not a future Mary wanted heralded.

"Keep your voice down," Mrs. Williams hissed. "I have to pretend to be exotic or people aren't interested. They want a show with their readings. If I appear too mundane they think me a fraud. Knowing I'm a boring school teacher ruins the mystique, don't you think?"

"Well, are you a fraud?"

"Young lady," the woman's voice turned severe. She couldn't completely keep her inner school teacher hidden. "Do you want your fortune read or don't you?"

A primal fear shot up through Mary's spine. A fear she hadn't felt since primary school. "Yes, ma'am," she said, sitting up straight. She quickly finished her tea and slid the cup across to Mrs. Williams.

"Good. Now then focus your mind and let's have a look, dearie," she said, having fully abandoned the persona of Madame Fortuna. As Mrs. Williams looked into the cup, Mary felt a nervous anxiety, as though her ability to drink tea was being evaluated and found wanting. She missed the phony accent.

"I see...." She pointed to the center of the cup. "Two triangles. Nearly symmetrical"

Mary craned her neck to look into the cup. "Is that good?"

"Why that's very good, my dear. The triangle denotes wisdom, and it is a sign of unexpected good fortune to come."

Wisdom and good fortune were a bit too simple an explanation to convince Mary that her former teacher had any real magic about her. Unexpected fortune could be anything. It could mean Hawke flourishing once more. It could mean finally finishing her story. It could even be referring to her and Lucas. Or it could be as mundane as not getting a cold cup of tea before bed. "Do you see anything more specific?"

Mrs. Williams looked again before leaning back. "The reading can only be as clear as the mind of the one who's being read. Your good fortune is clear, but everything else is muddled and undecided. Have you been having a lot of doubts lately?"

"Yes ma'am." Leave it to Mrs. Williams to see through her. Her writing had always given her emotions away to the woman. Now apparently so were her tea leaves.

"Then that is the problem. Your readings can't tell you the way if you don't even know which way you're going. If you are unsure of your next steps, there are too many possibilities for the leaves to divine."

"Oh." So not even the leaves could guide her.

Mrs. Williams contemplated a moment before returning the cup to Mary "Why don't you have a look? Tell me what it is you see."

Mary peered into the cup. Amidst the chaotic pattern the tea had left at the bottom, she saw two nearly identical triangular streaks of leaves. The way they curved slightly in the cup and came to sharp points made Mary recall her description of Lord Hallow. "They look a bit like fangs." The words slipped right out before she could catch herself.

"Oh for goodness' sake," The woman shook her head. "Have you been reading that dreadful *Twilight at Hallow Manor*? All the young ladies seem so desperate to find a bloodthirsty monster in their futures. Sorry to disappoint but there are no vampires out there ready to hunt you down. Or anyone else for that matter."

"Oh. Well erm..." Mary squeezed her thigh. Maybe this wasn't the best person to brag to about how much she'd grown as a writer since her days in school. Best to let her teacher think of her as merely a mere reader of "unladylike" literature.

Mrs. Williams waved a dismissive hand. "Rest assured that whatever your anxieties may be, you'll come out all right. We all go through times of doubt and indecision, but you clearly have the wisdom to make the right choice. You just need to focus that mind of yours," She shook her finger at Mary with all the conviction of a teacher quieting an unruly child. "...And I don't mean focusing on made-up monsters."

"Yes of course. Thank you, Mrs. Williams." Mary stood up and pushed in her chair.

Having completed her theatrics, Mrs. Williams shifted her scarf, letting her smile show. "So how is your father doing?"

"He is well, ma'am. As busy as ever. Good seeing you again. I don't want to hold up your business." She rushed off to where Charlotte waited at the Steepe booth to avoid telling her ex teacher about Papa's new future as a new bachelor. Eventually word would get out, but until then she was content not discussing the matter.

"What did she say?"

"Good fortune and wisdom," she murmured to Charlotte. "I don't feel very wise, but I'll never say no to good fortune." Mary felt much better about her reading today than any she had received on the streets by the train station. Mrs. Williams had never been one to lie. Then again Mary never knew the woman had a second persona as Madame Fortuna either.

She would find her way with Hawke and Hallow's story. Good fortune or no, she had no other choice. But Lucas? That remained foggy and uncertain.

Chapter 13

By the time she made it home, her mind spun with everything Charlotte had shown her from printing presses to jewels and artifacts. There had been plenty of displays that they still hadn't yet seen. She'd have to go again another day. Her father had been right. After spending the day out having fun she felt more ready to face the rest of her life, whatever that would entail. To start, she would need to address her fight with Margaret and talk to Papa about Hawke.

Thinking about the way Charlotte gushed about Martin made that familiar pang of loneliness creep up on her. Did she really want to consider a man whose uncle thought he was a vampire? Had her options become that grim? And yet she couldn't bring herself to write him off even while the odd experiences nagged at her. If anything, they made her want to know the full truth.

She climbed out of the Steepe carriage and waved the coachman off. Charlotte was going to spoil her with all the help. Mary would never be able to repay that favor of giving her Hawke back. No matter how much Charlotte blamed herself for letting Bertram buy it, Mary's father wouldn't have sold the business if they hadn't been in dire straits. She started toward the house, stopping when she spotted another carriage. A figure in black was nearly at her door.

Her eyes widened at the sight. She'd spent all day keeping an eye out for him, and yet here he was, Lord Holiday, once again out after dark.

He turned as the Steepe carriage pulled away. Feeling no choice but to continue on now that she'd been spotted, she headed up the walkway to him.

"Miss Hawke," he said in greeting as he tipped his hat to her.

She gaped at him in bewilderment. What would he be doing on her doorstep? And only once the last rays of sunset were disappearing over the buildings too. She didn't want to think of the "v" word, but his eccentricities were adding up in a direction she didn't like.With the darkness of night upon them, the idea felt unsettlingly possible. His uncle seemed a great deal more sensible with each odd occurrence. Her chat with Charlotte felt like a dream.

Strange dark spectacles that sat on his nose, and he carried an umbrella despite the clear sky.

"Are you lost?" she blurted out, her nerves making it too difficult to clear her mind. His handsome features made her heart race as he watched her.

"No, I was hoping to speak with you."

"I'm sorry, I didn't know you were looking for me. I spent the day at The Great Exhibition. I've read the accounts in the papers, but nothing quite compares to seeing it in person." Oh no, she was babbling. Her cheeks heated. "Were you at The Great Exhibition too?"

"No," he said.

She blinked. "Oh." She clasped her hands together, the awkward silence making her want to run away.

"I was checking on the printing press. May I come in and talk with you?"

Didn't vampires need to be invited inside? Otherwise, they couldn't cross the threshold. Therefore, as long as no one invited him inside, he couldn't eat anyone. "It's messy inside. I'd hate to offend your sensibilities."

"Miss Hawke, you speak as though you haven't been to my manor." He gave her the faintest of smiles.

That was an excellent point. "Well, I wouldn't want to make you uncomfortable."

The door swung open. "Is everything all right, Mary? Why are you dawdling outside?" her father asked.

Relief swept through her. He would know what to do. "We have a visitor, Papa."

He turned to Holiday, a smile lighting up his face. "Luke? Luke Holiday is that you? Why, you look exactly the same after all these years." He rubbed his eyes.

"I'm Lucas, his son. My father passed recently in an accident."

"Ah." he squinted at Lucas. "I'm sorry to hear that. You really are the spitting image of your father." He glanced between them, spotting Holiday's umbrella. "Come in and get out of the ... the rain." He frowned at the dry day before shaking himself back to attention. "Well, get in here and get some hot tea at least."

"Papa, are you su—"

"It is wonderful to see you again. Your father was a great man. I wish I'd gotten to publish him before he passed. He was a great writer, just never had enough time."

Mary shuffled out of the way as her father herded Lucas inside. Once inside, the man pocketed his dark spectacles. Mary chewed on her bottom lip, wondering if the priest was right or whether they were both going mad. She made her way back to the kitchen and busied herself with making tea while her father chatted with Lucas.

There'd been so few visitors lately that the thought of finding a way to rush Lucas out made her feel guilty. How could her father not be lonely without his brother and soon to be ex-wife around? Plus, all the writers who no longer came calling. And Lucas was already inside. What could it hurt to let him visit? Besides, it would give her time to puzzle out the truth. It wasn't that she wanted to look at his pretty eyes some more or listen to his soothing voice. Not at all. Hawke did need a new printing press after all, and this would be a step toward making that happen.

Oh, but those eyes of his. They made her feel like he could see right through her.

She took her time with the tea, brewing her favorite English Breakfast from Steepe Co. Once their new kettles were available, she'd have to get one. Half the time to boil? All the more time to write. Or take a walk. If she lived somewhere like the Holiday estate, she'd take a walk on the grounds every morning.

Catching a shadow in the doorway, she turned, but Margaret ducked back out of sight. Mary sighed. How much longer were they going to continue this immature argument? With Papa leaving they couldn't stay like this.

"Margaret."

No response except a creak of the floorboards. She sucked in a deep breath. "I'm sorry. I'll quit nagging at you about ... well, whatever it is you do at night." She didn't want to ponder all the options. Thank goodness the era of highwaymen was over. That meant the possibility of her sister moonlighting as a highwayman was one fear she could tick off the list. Gambling and illicit romances on the other hand ...

"I don't care who you court if you are courting. Just don't let yourself get taken advantage of. I don't want anyone hurting you." The magicians poking at the nobility brought new views on the freedom of magic and women, but a pregnancy outside of marriage would still ruin any woman's reputation.

The kettle whistled and she pulled it off the fire. She poured it into the teapot and carried the tea tray out. The men sat in the armchairs, her father talking while Lucas nodded along. Lucas's serious expression made her feel like she'd walked in on a business meeting.

"Making relationships with the booksellers is always the best way to get the latest information. They know better than anyone what is selling and what customers want. Holiday is already a well-known name. You shouldn't have any trouble getting meetings with them."

And so, she had walked in on a business meeting. She set the tray down. "Tea?" she asked as she set their cups out.

"I'll take mine in my study." Her father gave her a wink.

"Are you sure?" Her voice came out a note too high.

"I have letters to answer. I'll let you two chat in the meantime."

Oh no. Was he trying to play matchmaker?

"Good seeing you again, Lucas. Please stop by anytime. You are always welcome." He poured his cup and headed upstairs with it.

Mary squeezed her hands. She kept a close watch on his mouth, trying to discern its features in the fading light. Until she saw fangs, she refused to believe the invitation would become a problem. "I didn't mean to interrupt your meeting." She sat, her back stiff as she stayed on the edge of her seat.

"You didn't. He was giving me some advice. He knows a lot about publishing."

"That he does. Hawke Publishing was always his biggest love next to his family. You would be hard pressed to find an author in the city or a book seller he hasn't met."

"Then I would be a fool to not take his advice."

She spotted a dark smudge on the side of his hand. She offered him a linen napkin. "You have ash on your hand."

He turned his hand around, frowning at the smudge. He accepted the linen and wiped at the dark spot. "It is charcoal. I did some sketching on the train ride today."

She latched onto that tidbit. A normal hobby at long last. "I had no idea you were an artist."

The edge of his lips twitched. "Oh I wouldn't call myself an artist, but I find it relaxing. My uncle has more skill for it than I do. He always has."

"I've never had much talent for it myself." She poured his cup, feeling embarrassed they didn't have a butler or maid to pour his tea. At least the cook was due back next week. "Holiday Press isn't in trouble, is it?"

"Oh The press is fine. But I..." He took time to gather his thoughts, keeping his attention on his tea. "I, on the other hand, have found the transition difficult. I've been contemplating selling the press and the manor."

She gasped, and her hand knocked off the lid to the jar of honey. "Sell Holiday! Is the business not important to you?"

"It is, but returning home has been far lonelier than I expected. And my father, he was a better businessman than I." He looked down at his tea, his melancholy expression back. "I wish to do what is best for the press. I don't want to be the one who destroys the family legacy because of my incompetence."

"I would never call your knowledge of printing incompetent. Are you certain you aren't just overwhelmed at the moment? When I lost my mother, I struggled to write for a while." She turned her attention to her tea as well, not wanting to see his reaction to her pitiful problem.

Margaret stepped into the room, a fake smile plastered across her face. "Would anyone like some scones?" She set the plate of scones down. "Mary, I could use your help in the kitchen."

"I'm certain you can manage without me." Mary couldn't keep the ire from leaking into her tone. Margaret ignored her apology and now wanted to interrupt her time with Lucas? Margaret wasn't one to get jealous over a man, not even a lord, which meant she wasn't over their fight.

But this was too important to let her interrupt. She didn't have nearly enough money to buy Holiday, but if he planned to sell it then who would Hawke contract?

"Then have a scone." Margaret pushed the plate toward Lucas. "Please, they are fresh."

"I've already eaten, but thank you." He kept his voice perfectly polite.

Margaret's smile fell. Unwilling to back down, she sat in the seat by the window. The position put her too far away to comfortably join in the conversation, but close enough to remain a nuisance.

"I received interesting news today, and I was hoping to look into printing with Holiday soon." Mary smiled when she saw Margaret stiffen.

"Are you sure that's wise?" Margaret piped in.

"Yes. I will do what I think is best for my story." She turned her smile to Lucas. "That is as long as you are comfortable with me taking my writing to your press."

"I'd be honored for you to work with Holiday Press." His expression gave away nothing. Learning to read him was proving to be difficult.

"Excellent. I'll visit the press once I'm ready. I'll bring along Papa too. What does your press's schedule look like this year?"

They launched into business talk. It seemed Lucas had studied up on his press's time tables and pricing. He had an answer for all of her questions. Mary jotted down notes. Losing herself to the intricacies of printing serials made her forget Margaret was playing chaperone. And she found herself scooting closer to Lucas as they spoke. He became more animated as he spoke about his press. She felt as though she could listen to him talk about books and his press all night.

"Does he know what your story is about?" Margaret asked, pulling Mary out of her fog of printing costs and scheduling.

"I don't personally review everything we print," Lucas said, his voice gentle.

"But to take on Mary's pen name, you should know what you are getting yourself into."

Worry crossed his face. "Whatever do you mean? Is there something objectionable regarding your writing?"

Mary snapped her notebook shut. Might as well tell him before Margaret could. "I may have projects other than my own to print soon, but my *nom-de-plume* is M. H. Crane."

His brow furrowed in thought, but his blank look showed no recognition of the name. His cheeks turned pink. "I'm sorry, I don't believe I'm familiar with your work."

Margaret butted in again. "She's the writer of *Twilight at Hallow Manor*. Have you had a chance to read it yet?"

"No," Lucas admitted. "I haven't had much time to read since returning home." He picked up his teacup as if to take a sip, but stopped and set it down, bringing a hand to his chin. "Hallow Manor, you said?"

"Yes, as in Lord Hallow. The vampire," Margaret pushed. "Still getting his mail?"

Lucas coughed and cleared his throat. "I'm afraid the story sounds a little too bloody—" His voice went high on the word bloody "—for my tastes."

Margaret's eyes narrowed, and Mary jumped in before she could keep pushing. "I'm certain Holiday Press can handle any attention they get from the story. It is one of Hawke's most popular serials currently, and I bet it will do well for Holiday to have their name on it."

Returning to business talk seemed to calm the young lord back down. "My man in charge of the press is good at turning away anyone who is too nosy, assuming you wish to keep your name anonymous."

"Yes, I would. I'm afraid I don't handle that kind of attention well. It makes me nervous." And the pressure made it hard to write.

"I will let the press know to expect you. Once you are ready to start printing, take your first copy in and my workers will walk you through the process in detail and make sure everything is to your standards. You'll get a copy to approve before the press ships the copies out. Ask for Arthur. He knows the press better than anyone."

"Wonderful. The press Hawke was working with tended to be slow at times and late on delivery."

"Not Holiday." He started to reach for his tea, but in a smooth motion changed direction, grabbing his other hand instead. He folded his hands in his lap. "Holiday Press prides itself on timeliness. Always has. You won't have to worry about late deliveries with us."

Mary reached for a scone and dipped it in her tea. She bit into it, her toes curling in disgust. Garlic and rosemary overpowered her mouth.

The saltiness made her mouth dry. "What is wrong with these scones? I don't remember adding any seasoning." She dropped the scone onto her plate and gulped at her tea. Except all the garlic contaminated her tea too, the flavor seeping into everything it touched.

"I dressed them up," Margaret said. "Are you sure you don't want one, Lord Holiday?"

"I'm fine, thank you." He shifted in his seat. Mary cast a longing eye to Lucas's undefiled cup, but raised an eyebrow at how full it still was. Had he taken a single sip of it?

"Margaret, be a dear and get us some new scones. Ones without any of that ... seasoning of yours."

Margaret scowled as she pulled the plate of scones away. "I'll be right back, sister dear," she said, sarcasm dripping from her words. She made sure to waft the plate under Lucas's nose once more before leaving. The aroma seemed to make him wince.

"Forgive my sister's moodiness. My mother's absence has been hard on all of us."

"Grief is a difficult thing to process."

He had a way of carrying a conversation without giving anything away about himself when he didn't wish it. Mary would admire it if it didn't frustrate her. In fact, it occurred to her that they had been talking together for quite some time without her knowing the specific reason for his visit.

"I hope you'll forgive me for discussing my story. Had you come to talk business today? I'm sorry if I've gotten you off track."

"Not initially, no." He balanced his teacup saucer on his thigh, the thumb rubbing the rim of the saucer. "There is a play I would like to go see, *The String of Pearls*. I've heard it is very popular. Would you like to attend with me?"

She bit the inside of her cheek in shock. An invitation! "I didn't know there was a showing coming up. That sounds lovely." She couldn't ask Charlotte to go. The last thing she wanted to do was remind Charlotte that her last story never sold because it was too similar to *The String of Pearls*. She planned to read everything Charlotte sent to Hawke, but it would be hard for anyone to compete with Mr. Todd's story. Let alone a completely unknown author. "I would love to see it." To get asked to the theater by a lord!

"She can't," Margaret said as she plopped a plate of new scones down. By the looks of them, she'd done nothing but pour more garlic and rosemary on them. The scent was powerful enough to make both Mary and Lucas reel.

"I didn't say which night it was." Lucas shifted again, his discomfort seeping into Mary. If Margaret didn't have a good reason for her behavior today, she would make her eat all the garlic scones. Without any tea.

"We made promises to our aunt this week I'm afraid." Margaret's voice sounded as prickly as she looked.

"It is next week actually."

"Then yes!" Mary said in a rush before Margaret could come up with another excuse. "I would love to go next week."

Lucas's shoulders fell in relief. "I will escort you to the theater Tuesday night." He stood, his gaze straying toward the door. "Until then."

"Let me see you out."

Mary walked him to the door. Margaret hovered behind her, watching over her shoulder. Mary jabbed her with an elbow, but Margaret refused to back up.

Lucas tipped his hat to her once more before hurrying to his carriage, fumbling to put on his dark spectacles as he went. The silent driver climbed down to open the door for him. Overhead pink rays of sunset peeked through the gray clouds.

Mary shut the door and rounded on Margaret. "What was all that about? The poor man couldn't wait to get away from you."

"He's a vampire! That's what!"

Mary sighed. "You can't be serious. Didn't you laugh at me when I said the same?"

"I hadn't seen him being all vampire-y yet! You shouldn't have anything at all to do with him unless you want him to drink your blood."

"Oh, please." Margaret and the priest were making it difficult to keep her wits about her. "He is a little odd, but so is Martin Steepe, and he isn't a vampire. Everyone has their quirks."

"You don't understand." Margaret peered out the window beside the door. "I saw him in the cemetery the other night. He came out of a mausoleum."

"And what were you doing in the cemetery?" She rested her hands on her hips.

"Pretending mother was dead. But that doesn't matter! Who else would be coming out of a mausoleum but a vampire? And I mean just look at him. He is pale and clearly doesn't like the sun. That man is going to eat you. I don't mean that metaphorically, either, just to be clear."

"We're going into business together. I doubt even if he were a vampire that he would eat a customer."

"Maybe that is why he is thinking about selling, because he is eating too many of his own customers. Ever think about that?"

Mary considered the idea. "No," she said, voice going up a notch, "I haven't."

"Talk of blood made him uncomfortable. I bet he struggles to rein in his bloodthirsty nature." Margaret bit at the air in her imitation of a vampire, holding her hands up like claws.

"I didn't see any fangs."

"Doesn't mean they aren't there. He wouldn't touch the scones either because vampires loathe garlic. And maybe rosemary. I couldn't remember, so I put both on to be safe."

"That's ridiculous." She returned to her seat and finished her cup of tea. She peered into the bottom of the cup, staring at the two triangles of leaves. "Y-you're being ridiculous."

"What are you doing?"

"Trying to read my tea leaves." The pattern looked almost exactly the same as when Mrs. Williams read her fortune.

Margaret yanked the teacup away to get a closer look. "Looks like fangs to me."

"It's not fangs. They're just triangles. The fortune teller I saw earlier said that means good fortune."

"Or the leaves are trying to warn you about a vampire. There isn't any other leaf pattern that says 'watch out, a vampire is trying to eat you' is there?"

"Vampires aren't real," she said, voice quiet as her conviction bled out of her. "You said it yourself. I made up Lord Hallow."

"It wouldn't hurt to be extra careful going forward, would it? Don't you find it suspicious that Papa mistook him for his father? And that his father died in a mysterious accident and no one knows how. Trust me, I asked around."

"What are you trying to get at?" The taste of garlic wouldn't leave her mouth and she longed to wash it out with a cup of water.

"What if they are the same man? If he is a vampire he wouldn't age, right?" She waved her hands wildly as she spoke. "He might have left the country to explain his disappearance, giving him time to kill off his old identity before anyone could bring attention to him not aging. And then voilà, he comes back as his own son under a similar name. Everyone ignores the fact they look identical and almost have the same name because they are father and son, letting him get away with it."

"And here I was thinking I was the writer in the family. You could make a whole series out of that concept." Mary's tone got progressively less sarcastic as she spoke. She reached for her notebook on an end table and opened it up. "Actually, could you say that once more from the beginning? This might be just what the next chapters of my story need."

Margaret slapped the notebook shut. "Forget about your writing for a minute. Even if you don't want to believe he could be a vampire, what about his father's mysterious passing? It wouldn't hurt to be extra careful."

Mary considered Margaret's words. She had a good point. She barely knew the lord. "There is someone we can talk to about all this." Mary slouched. Either she was the only sane one left, or Lucas really was a vampire, and was expertly staking her out for his next meal. Of course. Why else would a lord take interest in her if not to eat her? She'd die an old maid at this rate. Or rather a young maid if he really did drain her. "There's a priest I met who might be willing to help." She could hear him out one last time...

"Holy water, great idea." Margaret snapped her fingers. "And crosses. Those help, don't they?" Mary reached for her cloak, but Margaret stopped her and pointed out the window. "We'll wait until morning. I'm not taking you out to wander in the darkness. That's how vampires get you."

"We're just going to talk with him. I'm still convinced there's a reasonable explanation for all of this." But there were a lot of oddities about him. The glasses, the supposed mushrooms, the wailing she'd heard in his manor, and the creepy tower. Now here he was poking around mausoleums at night. It all felt quite vampirish. "Would a vampire be a bookworm do you think? Enough to have an enchanted library?"

Margaret shrugged. "What else would there be to do but read if you're immortal and hate the sun?"

Mary hadn't thought of that. If she were an immortal vampire, she'd definitely have an enchanted library to pass the time. She wouldn't mind having one now too, but that wasn't the point. If there was something supernatural at work, then she may already have fallen right into Lucas's trap. She'd need help if she didn't want to wind up as his dinner come Tuesday.

Chapter 14

"I'm leaving to visit your mother at the end of the week." Mary's father announced over breakfast.

Mary froze, nearly dropping her spoon. She had woken up with a plan to visit the priest and see what he had to say. This unexpected announcement threw her emotions for a loop. Not a very auspicious start for the day.

"But Papa, I need to discuss Hawke with you." She pushed her plate away, the sudden pit in her stomach stealing away her appetite.

He waved a dismissive hand as he finished his morning cup of tea. "There's nothing to discuss, Mary dear. The business is sold. It's nothing we need to worry about."

"But there is! I spoke with Charlotte at the Great Exhibition. She told me that Mr. Martin Steepe is now in control of Hawke, and he plans to sell it back to us!"

"Mary," he sighed, "We can't afford—"

"For half a penny."

He paused. "Half a penny? Really?"

"Yes. As long as we publish Charlotte's next story that is, but I'm sure it will be good. Mr. Steppe's solicitor is going to need to know which of us is buying it back. If you don't want Hawke back, then..." Between the mention of her mother and the thought that Mary might lose Hawke a second time, Mary's heart was in her throat. She calmed her breathing and continued, "Then I will buy it. I can't stand to lose the company, and I want to have a bigger role. I've been helping you with the company for years and I think I've proven I can handle it."

He gave her a tired smile. "I never thought for a moment that you couldn't handle it." He rested a hand on her shoulder, giving it a gentle squeeze. "But you are still young. You shouldn't spend all your time working. You are a good writer and editor. Leave the rest to others. The last thing I want you to do is to make the same mistake I did. There's so much more to life than work. Don't let it trap you."

Her throat burned as tears threatened to fall. "I just wanted to make you proud, Papa. I wanted to follow in your footsteps."

"I am proud. I've always been proud of you. That's never been in question." He sat back in his chair. "And I'd like to be your accountant if you don't mind."

"My accountant?"

"Why yes. If you are going to buy Hawke, you will need to fill that position now that your uncle is gone. I was the accountant when we first opened up for business, you know."

She practically lept from her chair and hugged him. "You are allowed to do more than keep the books if you want."

He patted her back. "We can discuss it when I get home. I won't be gone long. Our solicitor can take care of anything you need."

"Do you really need to leave? Surely you could send her a letter about the divorce instead."

"Papa's leaving?" Margaret stumbled down the stairs, looking half asleep with her bleary eyes.

"Not for long. A week at the most. I thought you were still in bed," he said, standing and brushing the crumbs from his chest. He looked embarrassed to be caught making the announcement without her.

"Mary and I were going to go out this morning," said Margaret, glaring at Mary as she cleared her plate, "but I can see she was planning on leaving without me."

Mary threw her hands up in defense, palms out. "I didn't think you were going to get out of bed. I tried to wake you up twice before giving up."

"I told you I needed a minute."

"Yes, and a minute later you fell back asleep." She raised a finger, cutting off Margaret's protest. "And don't say you didn't. I heard you snoring."

Margaret's face flushed as she reached out to pull her hair into a bun. "Well, I'm here now. No need to keep complaining."

"You girls have a nice day," their father said as he slid toward the parlor.

"You should stay here." Margaret said, grabbing his arm to keep him from escaping. "There is no reason you need to give her any more of your time."

"I won't be gone long." He patted her hand. "And once I'm back we can finally put all this unpleasantness behind us."

"But what will we do while you're gone?"

He looked to Mary for help as he stammered. Margaret usually argued for her independence, not the opposite. "You'll be fine without me for a week or two. If you need anything, your sister can help you. Or Aunt Beth."

"Quite right. I'm certain we can handle ourselves without Aunt Beth needing to check in on us." Mary said as she tugged Margaret away. "Now come get some biscuits while they're still fresh. Then we can get going."

Their father nodded so fast she feared he'd hurt his neck. "And I'll bring you back some candy." That'd been his go-to gift since they were girls. Books and candy. As an adult Mary continued to enjoy the tradition. When he worked long hours, there was no better feeling than discovering a small bag of candy he left on her desk.

After a quick bite to eat, the girls made their way out the front door, waving to their father. "It's too early to go out," Margaret grumbled as they reached the street.

"The walk will wake you up," she said as she took a moment to figure out which direction to go.

"Are you really going to buy Hawke back?"

"Yes. Charlotte is practically giving it back to me as long as I publish one of her stories. I will need to hurry up and find a new printing press for Hawke. "

"Well it's good to have the company back, but find someone other than Holiday to print. You don't need to make it any easier for him to snatch you up and eat you."

"No one's getting eaten. And I'll get Hawke figured out. I'm more worried about what you plan to do next. If you don't want to marry, you should have some other plan for the future."

"I'd much rather work than marry. Maybe I can start helping with Hawke more."

"That would be a good start."

"But enough about all that. You are distracting me from what we need to focus on today." Margaret fished out a crumpled list from her pocket. The list contained all of two items, crosses and holy water with the water underlined twice. She looked over the list and nodded, her mind seeming to wander before letting slip, "I just don't see why Papa feels the need to go."

"What was that about distractions?" Mary elbowed.

"Well I can't ignore it. Even if there is a bloodthirsty monster stalking you," protested Mary, crossing her arms."There's no reason to go in person. He should stay home."

"Well, she is his wife. This way she will know she isn't welcomed back. If she is with Uncle, maybe he can get some of Hawke's money back."

"And give him a swift punch to the chin too." Margaret punched her own hand, and both girls smiled at the thought of their uncle's come uppance."The timing is awful. He can't go when there is a vampire on the loose."

"I don't think he would know how to protect us from a vampire. Besides, I think going will be good for him. It is time he faces the truth as well and moves on without her. It will give him closure."

"Do you think she ever loved him back?"

"I don't know, but he loved her."

"That makes it worse. Better to be in a loveless relationship than to love and not be loved back." Margaret checked her list again before sliding it back into her pocket. The church's bell tower appeared on the horizon from behind a row of townhouses. "I don't want to get married and be miserable," Margaret whispered.

Mary linked their arms together. "Papa would never force you."

"That wouldn't stop Aunt Beth from trying."

They rounded a corner, and the church came into view. The gray stone matched the bell tower. "Be careful. If you start talking about Holiday being a vampire, Papa will think Mother leaving has taken too much of a toll on you. He will question your sanity. Aunt Beth would tell him to send you to Bedlam."

Margaret rolled her eyes. "As if I'd want to worry him like that."

"Do you think a vampire will get him if he leaves?" Had she been worrying over him too?

"Papa won't be in any danger, but his presence might help protect you. Vampires prefer to drink the blood of pretty, young women. Everyone knows that! He'll be safe when he leaves, but you won't be."

"What about women vampires? If I were a vampire, I'd pick a handsome young man to feed from instead."

"Well, I wouldn't." Margaret stopped in front of the large wooden door of the church. "How do you know this priest?"

"He's Lord Holiday's uncle. He also knows a lot about vampires. He's quite the critic of my story, however. Don't you dare tell him I'm the writer or he might ban us from his church."

"If he is Lord Holiday's uncle, how can we trust him? He could be working for his nephew."

"Believe me, he isn't," she said as they headed for the front door.

"Good morning, ladies," a deep voice said from behind.

They both jumped, Margaret letting out a squeal as she turned and flapped her list at him. He backed up a step, eyebrows arching.

"Are you a vampire too?" Margaret demanded.

"No." Father Holiday looked about, hands twitching. "Please don't say that word out in the open. You'll worry my congregation."

"Can you help us deal with a vam—" Margaret stopped herself and cleared her throat. "With one of those?"

"If that is the issue you are here to talk about, we should go to my office where we won't be overheard."

Mary and Margaret exchanged a look. "Fine," they replied in unison.

He heaved the heavy door open for them. They stepped inside. The light pouring in through the stained-glass windows lit up the inside of the church. All the light made the space feel inviting. An elderly woman shuffled out into the entryway.

"Father Holiday," the woman said as she passed him.

"Mrs. Greene." He bowed his head. "I'll see you Sunday." He held the door open for her. Once the woman was down the stairs and out of earshot, he nodded to Mary and Margaret. "This way to the back."

He turned to the right and into a short hallway that opened into the main room of the church.

People dotted the pews, their heads bowed in prayer. The sight looked serene until she spotted the woman with tears streaming down her face. The woman sniffled into a handkerchief. Mary looked away, not wanting to intrude on the woman's grief.

At the end of the hallway on the left side a little room sat across from what looked like a classroom. Mary and Margaret hung back a few steps.

"He looks a lot like his nephew," Margaret whispered. "Are you sure about this?"

"Yes. He's the one who gave me a ride home from the train station, and he is probably the only person who won't think we've taken leave of our senses. "

The little office smelled of incense. Papers covered the desk. Two plain chairs sat on the other side with another tucked into the corner. A lone potted rosebush sat on the windowsill. It all looked normal. Mary felt a mix of relief and disappointment at that.

"I like your rosebush," Margaret said, her voice soft.

"Thanks," Father Holiday said. "It was a gift from my mother years ago. It is originally from Holiday Manor. There is a large garden behind the manor that she adored and designed.."

A branch of the rose slithered away from an empty teacup on the desk.

"Did your plant just drink tea?" Margaret asked, aghast. "That can't be good for it."

"I don't advise leaving any drinks unattended." He made a face as he scooted his teacup away from the bush. "On the other hand, I should have learned better by now." He pulled a piece of taffy from his pocket. "And the bush should already know that bad roses don't get candy."

The bush shook as though a wind rattled the branches. He pocketed the candy.

Mary ignored the accusatory look from Margaret. No doubt she itched to complain about Mary dragging her from one odd man to the next. "Did you grow up at the manor?" Mary settled into one of the chairs while he gathered up the papers on his desk, tidying the space. A few sketches littered the letters. They were all excellent. One included a perfect sketch of the church. Another depicted a lone man praying in a pew.

"Yes, right up until I went away for school. From then on I only spent the Christmas season there." He paused, frowning. "I suppose Christmas this year will have to be spent elsewhere." He sat down with a sigh. "Excuse the mess."

"That's a lot of letters," Margaret said as she leaned over the desk.

He slid them away from her. "They aren't mine. I help members of my congregation who can't read or write."

"Very priestly of you." Margaret sat down beside Mary.

"Erm," he said, looking unsure of what to make of her comment. "I try?"

"Do you write to anyone?" Margaret leaned forward, snooping on the letters again. "With this many letters one of them has to be yours."

His hand stopped on one letter. "All right, one of them is mine. I wrote to the Vatican asking for advice on dealing with vampires and no one bothered to respond. I plan to follow up on my inquiry." He slid the letter into the desk drawer. "I assume you are here about my nephew."

"Yes. He visited us last night, and Margaret says she saw him in the cemetery."

"I saw him coming out of a mausoleum in the middle of the night. That isn't normal."

"Agreed." He leaned back. "Though you shouldn't be at the cemetery at night either. It isn't safe for a young lady."

"I was grieving," Margaret snapped back. "I didn't want to be bothered, but when he visited us, he was far too interested in my sister."

"You didn't let him come into your house, did you?"

"I wasn't going to," Mary said, "but Papa wound up inviting him in. He went to university with your brother and was excited to see Lucas."

"Clever play on Lucas's end to choose a victim he can get easy access to."

Mary wrinkled her nose. "Please don't call me a victim. It makes me feel like I should be dead."

"Has your father shown any strange behavior since my nephew visited?" He folded his hands on top of his desk. "Perhaps anything out of the ordinary for him?

"Yes!" Margaret slapped a hand down onto the desk, explaining frantically, "Papa decided he wants to leave to visit our mother all of a sudden this morning. They are divorcing, and I don't see why he feels he has to talk to her in person when she walked out and abandoned us. Plus, Lord Holiday asked Mary to go to a play with him and now Papa will be gone that day. I find it too much of a coincidence."

Father Holiday nodded gravely. "Lucas has enthralled your father. He has hypnotized him to get him out of his way."

"I don't see why he'd go to the trouble," Mary said.

"Because you're a beautiful young lady, Miss Hawke."

That was unexpectedly sweet of him. She opened her mouth to thank him.

"To a vampire, nothing is more delicious."

Changing her mind, she shut her mouth.

"She can't go to the play with him. He'll drain her in the alleyway after." Margaret did her vampire impression.

"He's already had a chance to eat me, and he did nothing."

Father Holiday rubbed the stubble on his chin. "He may have already recently fed. Once he gets hungry, you'll be his next pick. A chimney sweep in my congregation passed away last night from a mysterious disease. He'd been sick for a few weeks. I believe a vampire may have been feeding on him."

Mary fisted her hands, her blood freezing.

"I've long been afraid he'd target my congregation. When is the play?"

"In two weeks."

"Two weeks. Plenty of time to take care of this issue before the play. First, we should get you some protection against vampires." He crossed the room to the single set of bookshelves. He reached between two books to a hidden knob and pulled the door open. He moved the door slowly to keep any books from sliding off.

Mary and Margaret jumped up, eager to see inside the hidden room. He stepped inside and they followed. One step later, Mary discovered there was nowhere else to go. The space was more of a closet than a room. Margaret bumped into Mary's back, and she in turn bumped against the priest's side. The contact gave her the urge to blush like a schoolgirl. The priest was handsome like his nephew, and she would have guessed them to be brothers if she didn't already know the truth.

She would enjoy attending church if she got to listen to someone as comely as him every Sunday. Instead, she'd grown up listening to a reverend who had likely been an old man since the day of his birth. His droning voice had always made it difficult to stay awake.

Father Holiday cleared his throat. "I think you ladies should wait in my office. There isn't enough space for all of us."

They backed out of the room, but Margaret hovered in the doorway. At the back, a short set of shelves was full of vampire books and serials. *Twilight at Hallow Manor* poked out from between *Varney the Vampire* and *The Vampyre*. Above them, wooden stakes were stacked in a neat pile. On the left wall hung a crossbow and across from it a set of pistols.

"I'll never look at a priest the same way again," Margaret murmured. "I'll always wonder what they have hidden away in their secret rooms."

"Most of them probably don't have secret rooms," Mary said. "This is just a closet hidden behind a bookcase."

"That still counts as a secret room."

"Here we are." He handed Mary a silver flask emblazoned with a cross. "Holy Water. If he attacks you, toss it in his face." He leaned back into the room. "You should protect your neck as well. Here, wear this." He handed her what looked like a tall clerical collar, but the white cloth felt much stiffer and heavier than it appeared. "He'll think twice about biting you if he has to go through this first." He smirked, tapping his own collar with a metallic *clink*.

She pocketed the flask and slid the collar on. With a little effort, it could nearly pass for a choker necklace. Still, neither felt like enough against a vampire. "Will any of this protect me from being enthralled?"

"Do you suspect he's enthralled you?"

"I don't know." She adjusted the collar. Lucas's visit hadn't felt dangerous once she started talking to him. He'd been a perfectly polite guest. If not for the possibility of vampirism, she would have been thrilled to have him visit again. He didn't wave off her questions about printing and publishing the way her uncle always had when she tried to learn more. And he didn't try to discourage her like Mother had.

"You were staring at him like a prized Christmas goose at one point when he was giving you the press's prices," Margaret said.

"That doesn't mean I was enthralled. It just means he is handsome, is all." And a lord. And knowledgeable about books. And strong. He'd caught her without a second thought on the stairs with his quick reflexes.

"She's definitely enthralled. Or smitten."

"Seduction is a common weapon for a vampire to find his next victim," Father Holiday said, his voice somber. "If she's already become his thrall, it will be harder to keep her safe. She won't be able to control her own actions if he comes looking for her."

"Hold on, I never said I'd been seduced." Mary crossed her arms over her chest. "I enjoyed discussing business with him. That isn't the same."

"Denial," Margaret said. "You want to kiss him until you can't remember your own name."

"What? No!" Although she wouldn't mind testing the waters with one kiss ...

Margaret gave a grim nod. "Father, how do we stop the vampire?"

"He can't be bargained with or reasoned with. There's no way to reverse the curse. Believe me. I've searched." His gaze lingered on the stakes, before he slowly reached out and grabbed hold of one. "There's only one way to stop a vampire."

"You're going to kill your own nephew?" Mary clapped a hand over her mouth in horror. "You're a priest. Priests are supposed to be against killing."

"Kill? No. I'm afraid my dear nephew died a long time ago." Stake in hand, he shuffled out of his vampire room. He set the stake down on his desk. "I have spent weeks mulling over this problem. It pains me to turn against my own family, but it has to be done. It is because he is family that I should be the one to stop him before he can harm anyone else."

"But what if you're wrong about him?" Mary took a step back toward the door. "I won't help you kill an innocent man."

"Innocent?" he scoffed, "Once I find the proof, you'll see for yourself how 'innocent' that monster is. Then there will be no other choice."

"But you haven't found your definite proof yet, have you?"

He shut the door to the vampire room, turning it into an innocuous bookshelf once more. "No, but I know where to find it."

"Then I want to help you find it. I won't help you take any action against him until I have irrefutable evidence."

Father Holiday balked. "It is far too dangerous for you to get mixed up in this further. Although ... you could be useful. The manor gates won't open for me, but they'll open for you. That has been my main hurdle in getting the proof I need."

Margaret threw up her hands. "That silly little gate is all that's keeping you out? I won't let you put my sister in harm's way just because you haven't thought of cutting through the bushes."

Father Holiday gave Margaret an exasperated expression. He grabbed the stake from his desk and stabbed down at the rosebush. Before it found its mark, the bush's tendrils caught the stake and after a short struggle ripped it from the priest's hand. The beautiful red rose opened its maw at the center of the flower and gnawed on the weapon. Content with his explanation, Holiday returned his attention to Margaret.

"I see." She shuddered.

Father Holiday wagged a finger at the rose. "Drop it."

The bush shook the stake at him.

His voice deepened in warning. "I said drop it."

The rose gave the stake one last shake before throwing it onto the desk.

"Good." He finally handed over the taffy.

"Where do you think this proof of yours is?" Mary asked.

"In the tower on the manor grounds. My brother kept his study at the top. If he knew something, he'd have hidden it there."

"And do you have a plan to find it?"

"Not exactly, but I do have some idea. I just need to get to the tower before the play. I can't stand by and let you offer yourself up to him, Miss Hawke."

"Great," Margaret mumbled. "I can already tell this will go wonderfully. No way am I letting you handle everything or it will be a race between whether the vampire or the roses can gobble us up first."

Chapter 15

With the people heading for The Great Exhibition gone, the train station was deserted. Father Holiday escorted the sisters off the train and onto the platform, the sounds of their footfalls echoing in the hall after the train departed. The quiet of the station felt foreboding, as if they were walking right into danger and there would be no one else around to help them.

Mary still didn't want to believe Lucas wanted to feed on her, but every new detail she learned needled at her, and it was getting to be too much to ignore. Maybe he really was a vampire using the popularity of Lord Hallow to find victims. And if he wasn't, well what kind of lord kept hardly any staff on hand, kept a mysterious box of dirt from his homeland in his basement, and only ventured out at night?

Father Holiday loaded a suspicious bag into their hansom cab. He'd borrowed the cab from someone he knew. Apparently there were plenty of people willing to do a favor for a handsome priest in need. Mary forced her attention back to his bag.

"Why do I have to be the carriage driver?" Margaret whined as Mary finished adjusting her clothes. With Margaret's glamour in place, they might get away with their plan. Just as long as the young lord didn't look too closely at her. It would take all three of them, but by the end of the day they would have proof over whether or not Lucas was a vampire.

"Because he doesn't know you well. Glamour and clothes won't be enough for me to hide in plain sight. Plus, you know how to drive."

Margaret puckered her lips in a pout. "Isn't it dangerous for me to be all alone with a vampire?"

"They are predictable creatures. While he's out stalking his prey, he's unlikely to take any interest in you." Father Holiday handed her a small satchel. "But if he tries anything, use this."

She opened it. "Rice? Is this his appetizer before he eats me?" She closed the satchel and tightened her grip on it, looking as though she were ready to lob it at the priest's head.

"Vampires are compelled to count such things. He won't be able to stop until he counts every grain. Since there are hundreds in there, that should give you plenty of time to make your escape."

The train pulled away from the station, clanking along the rails. Until the next train, there'd be no fast way back to the city.

"That's mad if you ask me. I don't see why a vampire would want to stop and count anything."

"Maybe immortality is that boring?" Mary offered.

"Madness is the norm for these monsters," he reminded Margaret before turning back to Mary. "Now, I know the perfect spot to hide the cab. We'll go on foot from there. It'll be easier to sneak in that way. We'll get your sister in place, and as soon as my nephew is gone, we'll make our way to the tower. We will be right in and out. No dallying. Then back here to catch the train into London."

"Don't you dare let her get eaten, or I'll feed you to that devil myself," Margaret warned as she poked him in the chest with the blunt end of her stake.

"And I told you I can't guarantee either of you will stay safe." He slapped the stake away. His brow furrowed as his frustration with Margaret grew. "Don't forget that you demanded to come along on this mission. This is no time to be getting cold feet."

"What's in your bag, Father?" Mary asked, trying to change the other two came to blows. They climbed into the cab and Father Holiday set the bag on his lap. Margaret stepped into the role of driver. At least this time she didn't try to push the horses into a run.

"Just some emergency supplies in case we run into any trouble. Nothing for you to worry about." He hugged the bag to his chest. "And Please. Call me Matthew."

"Why not Matt?" Margaret called out.

Matthew took a deep breath before responding, as if calming his impatience with her. "Because Matt is for close friends and family only."

They rode in silence as he watched out the window, looking for his spot to hide the horse and hansom cab. He guided Margaret into a small clearing beside the road. The two girls set to the work of hiding the cab. Despite their mother's insistence, neither of them cared much for flower arranging. However, the glamour spells they had learned came in handy for filling in the clearing with twigs and vines to obscure the cab. Then they walked the last few minutes to the manor. As soon as they hit the property line, a row of tall hedges lined the road, giving way to pink and red rose bushes at the gate.

"Stay clear of the bushes."

Mary stepped away from a bush as a branch caught on her hair. She untangled herself while Matthew watched the closed gate. "If you'll step up to the gate, Miss Hawke, opening it now shouldn't cause suspicion when he is about to leave."

"Please," she said, "call me Mary. You might as well call me by name if we are going to risk our necks together." She crept up to the gate, hiding behind the right pillar. The gate slid open far enough for them to pass through.

"Perfect. We need to be fast so no one spots us going through it."

"Why not climb over the bushes or hedges?" Margaret asked.

He shook his head. "Can't. They're the same enchanted rose bushes as the one in my office. It'll be a fight to get through them, and we don't have the time. On the count of three we run to the stables. One!"

"But—" Mary tried, but he was already counting.

"Two!"

"What if—"

"Three!" There was no time to argue before he sprinted off. The sisters looked at one another before taking off after him. Mary found herself at the back of their group, Father Holiday too fast for her to keep up with. Margaret lagged only a few steps behind him, but the gap between them and Mary grew with each step. Clearly Margaret didn't sneak out just to spend her nights at illicit tea parties. Perhaps Mary ought to start taking late night walks about the cemetery too.

By the time she reached the stables, her breath came in great wheezing gasps. Father Holiday breathed heavier than before, but was no worse for the wear. Margaret leaned against the stable as she caught her breath. Mary refused to let herself look at the pile of hay in the corner, knowing she'd be too weak to resist falling onto it.

If they had to run, it was good to know she'd be the first one eaten. Maybe she should have asked for one of those stakes too.

Father Holiday checked his pocket watch. "Ten minutes before he leaves. We are cutting it close."

"Where is he going anyway?" Mary asked in a hushed whisper.

He shrugged. "It changes based on the week, but he leaves at the same time every week. He visits a lot of mediums and spiritualists."

"You've been watching him that much?"

"Through the detective I hired, yes. I wanted to find out the truth and get evidence since Scotland Yard seemed content to rule my brother's death an accident, but I find that hard to believe." Frustration clung to his words. "Unfortunately, the detective hasn't been able to get onto the property."

"How can you be sure it was murder if he hasn't found evidence? Maybe the police are right."

Matthew only barely managed to contain his indignation. "Do you really think my brother staked himself in the heart? He was not a man who savored violence."

"What? A stake through the heart? But Lucas told me that his father died in an accident. F-from a fall." Mary's confidence wavered. She suddenly felt a pang of shame for having taken Lucas at his word. A handsome enough face and she'd fall for any lie.

"Is that so?" The priest gave a rueful laugh. He reached for his crucifix necklace, breathing deep to calm himself. He dropped his voice to a whisper. "I can't just sit by while this murderer walks free. Not merely for my brother's sake, but for the sake of all the other lives that have already been lost. And for those we can still save. Like you." He closed his eyes, lips moving in a silent prayer.

Margaret tugged on his arm. "We have a problem." She waved toward the front of the stables. There near the far corner snoozed the driver in the shade of a tree. He sat on a wooden chair missing a leg that he'd propped against the tree trunk.

"Over there," Father Holiday said, pointing at Margaret and then the carriage. "I'll take care of the driver, but my nephew will be here any minute."

"What should I do?" Mary asked, still huffing to catch her breath.

He frowned at her. "Just stay right there out of sight."

Margaret took one last look at the sleeping driver, adjusting her glamour a bit to more accurately look like him. She snickered before turning, shoving her hands into her pockets and strolling toward the carriage waiting in front of the manor. Meanwhile Matthew grabbed the back of the driver's chair and pulled him across the lawn to the thick row of hedges lining the road. Not once did the man wake up. The priest leaned the chair against the bushes and then ran back to the stables.

The branches of the hedges reached for the driver, snaking around him and the chair. Once they had a tight enough grip, they dragged him deeper into the hedge line until they completely gobbled him up.

"Did they just eat him?" Mary gaped at the hedges. She'd thought them a mere nuisance before, not a genuine danger.

"I'm sure he'll be fine. By the time the roses spit him out, Margaret will have driven away with Lucas, and we will already be at the tower."

"Then what precisely are they going to do to that poor man?"

Father Holiday dragged her behind the stable. "Let's just say if you go into the bushes, you won't come out the same." He shivered.

Mary hugged herself, regretting coming along with him. She'd wanted to ensure she found out the truth, but this trip felt more dangerous than she'd imagined it. The more she found herself willing to believe Lucas a vampire, the more her stomach cramped.

As if on cue, the door of the manor burst open, the butler stoically holding it ajar. Out strode the shadowy black figure of Lord Holiday. Mary held her breath. Surely he'd recognize their deception. He'd see that Margaret had replaced his usual driver, wouldn't he? Yet he seemed to pay no mind to Margaret as she opened the door of the carriage for him. Nor did he seem to notice her exaggerated, trance-like movements as she hobbled to the driver's seat. With a crack of the reins, the carriage rolled down the driveway. The gates opened further to let the carriage pass. Once the carriage was through, the gates slid closed with a clang, sealing the property off again.

Mary wrung her hands as she craned her head to catch sight of her sister's figure as the carriage drove off down the road. "I'm not sure leaving Margaret alone with the vampire was a good idea."

"She'll be fine. She isn't his type. I've found he tends to prefer older prey. And you."

She scowled as his words kicked her confidence in the teeth.

Father Holiday took a deep breath. "Are you ready?"

"Yes." That was a lie. She didn't think she'd ever be, but she wasn't going to back out now. As Matthew had said, this was not time to be getting cold feet.

He headed for the manor as she rushed to catch up. "What do you think you are doing? The tower is behind the manor."

"Exactly. The bushes are overgrown and surround the rest of the property line. The rose bushes separate the back of the property from the front too. The only way to skip them is to go through the manor and garden, and the garden opens right up to the tower. I'm not risking the grasping branches ever again." He started forward again.

"We'll be seen!"

He waved his hand in dismissal at her. "You must have noticed that he only has that butler. Ever since my nephew's return the man has been just as enthralled and overworked as the driver. One man shouldn't be hard to avoid." Instead of heading to the front door, he scooted around the decorative rose bushes to the open dining room window to their left. After a quick inspection through the window he hefted himself over the windowsill.

Mary tried to follow his path. With her skirts getting in the way, she couldn't manage half of his graceful slide inside. Halfway in with her feet off the ground, she flopped like a fish as she tried to get herself through the window.

Noticing her predicament, Matthew crept over from the doorway and grabbed her by the arms to pull her inside. Her left knee banged against the windowsill, and she hissed from the pain. She regretted not changing into a disguise like Margaret. Skirts were not a good outfit for espionage. But then she'd never considered the ease or comfort of sneaking into someone's house before. Stories always made it seem easy. Fun even. Well, they were all liars. Every last one of them.

"The butler is the hallway. We'll have to wait for him to move on." He crept back to the doorway.

Mary rubbed her knee before joining him. She'd have a bruise by morning. In the hallway, an enchanted broom swept the floor. The butler leaned against the wall, one shoulder and his head pressed against it, arms crossed over his chest. A drop of drool clung to the left corner of his mouth.

"Dreadful. He is too enthralled to act under his own power. We need to save his soul before that monster can destroy it."

"I think he's just sleeping."

A duster floated out of the parlor and swept the paintings along the wall. When it reached the butler it paused to dust the top of his head before moving to the next painting. The butler jerked awake, eyes wide as he looked about.

Mary and Matthew ducked back into the dining room. The butler sneezed. Mary pressed her back against the wall, staying as still as she could. Her pulse raced. Across the doorway from her Matthew's hand wrapped around a candlestick sitting on the cabinet beside him.

"Need a maid or two is what," the butler muttered as he approached the dining room. They both slid farther from the doorway. The butler stopped in front of the doorway, grumbling incoherently under his breath. Then he turned for the parlor. He snapped his fingers and the broom followed, sweeping the floor as it went.

"Hurry," Matthew whispered as he crept out and down the hallway. Thumps from the library drowned out the creaking of the floorboards.

Once they made it to the back door that opened into the garden, he picked up the pace into a jog. He made his way through the labyrinth of winding paths, never hesitating at a turn. Mary stuck close, afraid of getting lost if he left her line of sight. If not for the tower growing closer, she would have been convinced they'd gone in circles.

Unease twisted in her gut every time she thought of Margaret. Lucas didn't have any hope of seducing Margaret. Sometimes she wondered if any man stood a chance. But if Lucas was a vampire, then Margaret had better behave lest he catch on to what was happening. She would be as vulnerable to being enthralled as anyone else.

They passed through the back entrance of the garden. The path ended abruptly at two stone pillars on either side of the path. Beyond were the moors and the tower. The stone path continued to the tower, bordered on either side by grass and the trees dotting the grassy hillside.

At the base of the tower Matthew stopped, staring up at the tower with the mournful look of a man drowning in grief. He bowed his head and prayed, ending by crossing himself.

Mary opened her mouth to say something, but no words came out. How could she offer any words of comfort to this man who, despite having lost his brother and nephew, was risking his life just to help her? Instead, she looked down and tried to repeat the crossing motion. It was unfamiliar to her, and she strained to recall how he'd done it.

The priest noticed Mary's flailing arm and winced. "You did that backwards. You should use your right hand..." He glanced back up at the tower. "You know what, never mind. We have more important matters at hand." He gestured to the base of the door. "This is where my brother was found. He'd been staked through the heart and drained of blood."

"Which means you suspect a vampire of having done the deed."

"Exactly. My brother had been acting strangely the past year. He had been drawn into vampire novels, spent more and more of his time in the tower, and wouldn't say what it was he was doing in there. I hadn't realized my nephew had become something else entirely. I didn't put the pieces together until I found out about Luke's death." He swallowed, his Adam's apple bobbing. "My nephew has acted oddly since his return from staying with his mother's family, confirming my fears."

"I'm sorry about your losses."

"I will pray for them," he said as he pushed the heavy door open. "And I will stop my nephew from killing anyone else. It's all I can do now." The small windows along the tower let dim light into the spiral stairwell. At the base behind the stairs was a small sitting room arranged around the fireplace. The old wooden furniture felt like it was from the medieval period. Candelabras hung from the walls.

To the right of the room was a wooden door to nowhere. It hung open a hand width, letting them see the bricks on the other side that separated them from the rest of the ruins.

"Why is the tower in use but not the rest of the ruins?" she asked as he started up the stairs. "Is it safe to be in the tower?"

"Yes. My brother was able to restore the tower, but the rest of the ruins required too much work. The manor needed too many updates for him to be able to do both, but he'd always hoped to get around to the rest of the ruins one day."

"Not enough work on the updates. The banister on the main staircase broke off when I visited."

"At least you didn't fall through the stairs like one of my cousins did. Before my brother inherited it, the manor suffered from neglect for many years."

"But I thought Holiday Press had always done well. Was the family in dire straits?"

"Yes, for over a decade before our grandfather rebuilt the family fortune by going into the printing trade. And by being a miser. He passed his ways onto our father. I remember once my bedroom roof leaked every time it rained for a whole summer. Several generations of neglect take a while to fix."

"That explains the state of the manor." The spiraling climb up the tower stairs made her head swim. She focused on the views outside the slitted windows to chase the dizziness away. The staircase opened to a single round room at the top. A desk sat across from the largest window. Beside the desk rested a low bookcase. A plush armchair sat beside the fireplace. Two tapestries hung across from one another. The right one depicted the manor. The second, a knight.

Matthew lingered in front of the knight tapestry. "My brother always loved medieval history and stories of knights and dragons. I think that is why he took on this tower project, to have his own medieval room." His hand brushed over the tassels. "Lucas and I picked this one out for him as a Christmas gift. That was several years ago before Lucas left to travel abroad. I can't help but to wonder if things would have gone differently if he'd stayed home. I hardly recognized him when he came back."

"You mean that metaphorically, right?"

"What?"

"To recognize him all you need to do is look in the mirror."

He stared at her, his nose twitching from dust. "We look nothing alike."

"You look similar enough to be brothers. You even have the same eyebrows."

He reached up to cover his right eyebrow. "Stop looking at my eyebrows."

"It was just an example." She had no idea he'd be touchy about his eyebrows of all things.

"I singed one off as a child. And it took ages to grow back. I don't like anyone looking at them."

"Is that how you got that small scar in the middle of your right eyebrow?" It was becoming on him, and added character to his face.

"Stop looking at it!" He turned around, keeping his hand clamped over his eyebrow. "Start looking for proof instead.."

"And what exactly is it we're looking for?"

"Evidence. You know..." He gestured towards nothing in particular. "Letters. Diaries. Written confessions. You'll know it when you see it."

A stack of papers fell from the desk. Mary jumped at the sudden movement. The papers fluttered across the floor, one bumping into her boot. She jumped for Matthew, grabbing his arm. She sucked in a deep breath, holding in her scream.

Two green eyes stared back at her from the desk.

Chapter 16

"Meow," George said from where he sat on the desk. He stretched, backside and tail sticking up in the air. His front paws clawed at the desk.

"Careful," Matthew warned. "Lucas may have enthralled the cat too. Or they might even be connected. That could be his familiar."

"I thought witches were the ones with familiars?" More than a few scary old stories made references to covens of witches living in the woods performing elaborate spells and hexes. These days no self-respecting female magician would dare call herself a "witch," opting for a far more practical lifestyle. It did however occur to Mary that nearly every one she'd met had some manner of animal with her. Usually a cat or a raven, though she once met a magician's daughter at a party who would not be separated from an eel she carried in a fishbowl. Perhaps, as Charlotte once suggested, Mrs. Hammond's dachshunds truly were instruments of magical destruction.

He huffed. "Well if a witch can make a cat do her bidding, is it so ridiculous for a vampire to do the same?"

"Oh, I doubt anyone can make a cat do their bidding."

Matthew considered her words as he finally dropped his hand from his eyebrow. "I don't know," he conceded. "Cats are wicked by nature. They make the perfect pets for bloodthirsty killers."

George jumped from the desk into the chair and then to the floor. He strolled over to them, rubbing once against the front of Matthew's legs before moving on to Mary's. She bent down and scratched his head, earning a purr for her efforts.

"Don't pet it!" Matthew hissed.

"Why not?"

"I told you they're wicked. He could be warning Lucas about our intrusion as we speak."

George butted his head against her hand. "I think he's just a normal cat. If he saw us as a threat, he wouldn't be this friendly."

"Try to pet his belly and see how friendly he is," Matthew said, exasperated. "Either way, there is no time for him. We need to search the room. See if my brother left a letter or anything unusual somewhere." He headed for the desk.

Mary gathered up the fallen papers, all of them blank. George followed her, butting his head against her hand every chance he got. He meowed each time she didn't pet him. "How demanding," she muttered as he sat down on the last piece of paper.

Matthew opened every drawer in the desk. He ran his hand over the bottom of each one. "No hidden compartments."

"Should there be one?"

"Well everyone's desk should have at least one hidden compartment." He shrugged. "It's where I hide my whiskey. Sometimes brandy whenever Luke managed to get his hands on a good bottle for me."

She didn't have a hidden compartment. If she did, she'd hide candy in it, far from her sister's grabby hands. Margaret had a nasty habit of devouring her candy in a matter of days while Mary preferred to take her time. "But you're a priest. You're not supposed to drink, right?" She always saw priests as aiming to be more holy than everyone else.

"Of course we're allowed to drink! The best beer in the world is brewed by monks."

"I'll take your word for it. Never much cared for beer." She rubbed George, distracting him while she pulled the paper out from under him. George's pupils widened, and he pounced on the paper. "Do you think Margaret is all right?"

"I'm sure your sister is fine." He moved on to the tapestries, lifting both of them and feeling the stone walls behind them. "There has to be something here."

Mary tugged the paper away from the cat. Having lost his prey, George lay down in the middle of the room, watching both of them. He soon grew bored of them and moved to perch at the top of the stairs. There he groomed himself as they continued their search.

Matthew made a noise of frustration in the back of his throat as his search behind the tapestries proved fruitless. He stopped in front of the tapestry of the manor. "He's had this one fixed. It used to hang in a forgotten corner of the library. Last time I saw it, the tapestry had holes in it. My father told me it was as old as the manor." He gave the tapestry a sad smile. "Lucas and I used to hide in the same corner of the library during boring family parties and play games."

"Were you close before he ...turned?" It made her consider what she would do if Margaret became a vampire. She would never have the strength to hurt her. Or Papa. But she wasn't a priest with faith on her side.

"Yes. I'm only three years older than him." He stepped away from the tapestry. "He was shy as a child, and eager to please his father." His voice cracked. "He lived to make him proud."

"I know how betrayal from someone close to you feels. My mother recently ran off. For weeks after, the first thing I thought every morning was that she had abandoned me." Those mornings left her feeling empty and guilty, as if her mother's decision was somehow her fault. Having breakfast with Papa and Margaret while they all acted like their lives were carrying on as normal only made the emptiness grow.

"It is not an easy thing to come to terms with. I'd like to one day hunt down the monster who cursed my family and mete out the Lord's judgment upon it. Maybe that will bring peace to the souls of Lucas and my brother." He whirled around and eyed up the room before he stomped over to the bookshelf.

She gathered up the few pages that hadn't fallen from the desk and added them to her neat stack, revealing a little leather book. She shoved aside the papers and opened the book. Neat lines of handwriting filled the pages. "Is this what you're looking for?"

Matthew paused in his search of the bookshelf. "What is it?"

"A diary. It's dated in days of the month, but no years are listed." She pulled out the desk chair and sat down. The window beyond the desk gave her a beautiful view of the moors. No wonder he'd been intent on having the tower as his study. Nowhere else on the grounds could beat the view. She flipped to the last page and began reading aloud.

"Another maid is gone. My son, it seems, cannot resist them. I regret letting him go on his travels. If he had stayed home he would not have returned a bloodthirsty creature. Sometimes I wonder if he is still my son at all, or simply a monster wearing his face. I cannot stand by any longer and allow him to continue on as he has, but I do not know what to do. How to stop him."

Ink drops marred the beginning of the next paragraph. "He is coming. I can hear him on the stairs. He can be as quiet as a mouse if he wishes, which means he wants me to hear him. I see now the fate that awaits me, and I am helpless to change it. He is at my door now. Dear God, someone please—"

She sucked in a deep breath, her heart hammering. "Th-that's how it ends." She flipped through the last few pages of the book, all of them blank. What a tragic ending, one she wouldn't be able to forget. If she could come up with an ending for Lord Hallow that was half as memorable, she'd be pleased.

Matthew's wide eyes stared at the knight tapestry. "That is worse than I expected," he said, voice hoarse from grief.

"I'm so sorry, I..." Mary trailed off.

"It's all right. I've had time to come to terms with losing my brother. And my nephew." Matthew placed a hand on her shoulder. "I know this can't be easy for you to see for yourself. You truly cared for him, didn't you?"

"I'm fine." Mary exhaled. She didn't like the way he said "cared" as though she no longer felt anything for Lucas. As though he were already gone. And yet, all of the awful things she feared about him were true. The evidence was right there in front of her. But there was no time to be upset. She flipped through the diary, steadying herself by focusing on her work. "This book is full. It will take hours to read everything." She stopped on a page with dried red splotches. Her hand recoiled from the page. "That looks like blood."

"This has to be our proof. It could be the key in finding out who cursed him."

She cleared her throat and began to read the next page. "Without my wife I have become a wanderer with no destination. A ship with no harbor in a colorless world. I do not know what I am to do next, save for simply surviving until tomorrow." She shivered and shut the book. "I had no idea your brother had lost his wife." She dreaded to think that Lucas was so heartless as to devour his own mother.

"She is very much alive. I suspect Luke had her sent away to keep her out of harm's way. Or she wanted to visit her sister." He turned his gaze out the window. "It must have pained him terribly, but he managed to save her."

Until now, sneaking into the mansion had been frightful, thrilling, and at times bordering on fun. It was like reading a good horror story. The danger was exciting. But as Mary sat there in the tower, suddenly that danger felt all too real. The dust coating the tower gave the room the air of a forgotten place, one that had once been well loved, but no longer. As she read, the loneliness from the pages coated the room. This last testament of Lucas's father made it seem like a horrible creature of the night could swoop down on them at any moment. She shuddered.

"No time to dally. We'll bring the diary with us and read the rest in my office. We'll be safe within the church." Matthew stood, the chair scraping across the floor and startling George. The cat hissed his disatisfaction. "The sun will set soon. We need to go now before he returns. He'll be at his strongest at night." He grabbed the book and tucked it inside his jacket. Mary stared at the lumps in his coat, wondering what all he'd brought. In comparison, she felt unprepared.

He pushed the chair back to its original position, and then they made their way down the stairs. Going down proved more dizzying than going up. It didn't help that George sped ahead of them, winding through their legs as he passed by. She worried she would trip over him if she wasn't careful. He waited at the bottom in front of the door, tail swishing.

They all left the tower and headed for the gardens, George punctuating each few steps with a meow.

"He is spying on us," Matthew said, peering at the cat over his shoulder. "Watching our every move."

"I think he just wants attention."

George stopped, head dipping and rear end wiggling as he spotted a pink flower swaying in the breeze. He pounced on it, back legs kicking as he twisted onto his back and chewed on the pink petals. He sneezed, letting the flower go and making a face of disgust as he spat out a petal.

Matthew turned left instead of right like she'd expected at the next turn. "Stay down." He pointed ahead. "There. He might be a thrall too." The gardener headed into the garden, whistling a merry tune as he went.

Matthew led them away from the man. Their path headed alongside the manor before curving back toward it. The twists and turns of the garden made little sense to her. George ran to catch up with them.

"Get rid of the cat," Matthew whispered.

"I don't know how. Do you have any food we could distract him with?"

"Of course I don't. Do you think I walk around with table scraps in my pockets?"

"Well you did have a whole bag of rice." With how weighed down his pockets looked, nothing seemed out of the question. Each one looked about ready to burst. What all could he possibly have shoved into them? She only hoped that if the need arose, he'd be able to find what it was he was looking for before it was too late. She'd try to remember to make the vampire hunter in *Twilight at Hallow Manor* a bit more well organized.

The priest huffed. "I don't have anything for the cat. Now let's go!"

As they reached the main path, Matthew stopped without warning. Mary bumped into his back. He kneeled on the path, and she followed his lead. The snip-snip of garden shears warned them of the gardener coming closer and closer.

George ran past them. Matthew tried to grab the cat but was too slow. George's tail slipped right through his hands.

"George, ol' boy!" the gardener greeted as he bent down to pet the cat. As soon as the man stood George headed for Mary. She froze as her eyes connected with the gardener's.

The gardener tipped his hat to her. "Miss Hawke. Father. Beautiful afternoon for a walk." Mary couldn't quite place the man's accent, settling on some sort of Welsh. Whatever it was, it wasn't at all how she expected a thrall to talk.

Matthew cleared his throat. "Good evening." George turned from Mary to rub on Matthew's legs. Matthew put on a strained smile as he reached for the cat, panic shining in his eyes.

The gardener carried on until he reached a tree farther down the path. A broken branch hung from it. His whistling returned as he worked.

"Inside. Before he realizes we shouldn't be here." Matthew ran for the back door. Mary stumbled as she struggled to keep up. George ran ahead of her. Inside they stopped, listening for the butler. He appeared from the parlor, heading for the front door.

Matthew grabbed her by the arm, hauling her into the kitchen. The room was empty of servants, but clean. After the tower she couldn't ignore how devoid of life the manor felt. There should be servants bustling about the kitchen. So where was everyone? How was the manor getting by with so little help? She bumped into something and jumped. Turning, she found an easel set up with a charcoal sketch of the kitchen sitting on it. On the nearby counter sat a sketch of George.

The drawings weren't particularly well done, but they were much better than she could draw. The image of George was a somewhat accurate depiction, though something was off about the eyes. The same went for the kitchen drawing. The perspective was off and the windows looked much too small, and the George in this drawing was little more than a black blob with eyes.

In the hallway George meowed as he walked in circles.

"The cat used to do that when my brother arrived. No..." He stared down the hallway, a hushed panic in his voice. "Lucas is back. He wasn't supposed to be home for another half an hour." Matthew checked his pocket watch to confirm his suspicions. "George must have alerted him somehow."

"Do you see Margaret?" She wrung her hands.

He peered back into the hallway. "No. She's probably still with the carriage."

The floorboards creaked as footsteps approached the kitchen. They ducked behind the open door. Matthew tensed as his hand slid into his jacket. Lucas paused in the hallway. Matthew pulled a stake from a pocket inside his jacket. Mary grabbed his arm, shaking her head at him. Even having read the diary, she couldn't bear to see such brutal harm come to Lucas. There had to be another way out.

"Ah, there you are," he said, his voice carrying that accent he seemed to hide around Mary. Matthew tightened his grip on the stake, pulling his arm free of Mary's grasp. As much as she wanted to choose mercy, she was out of options now. As quietly as she could, she grabbed her flask of holy water, then she and the priest nodded at one another, preparing their ambush. They began to step out from the door.

"Meow," the cat interjected, stepping forward to greet Lucas. Mary and Matthew held their breath.

"Bonjour Georgie. Look at what I brought you. A new toy."

Matthew slid back behind the door. Mary peered through the crack. Lucas tossed a ball onto the floor. It rolled down the hallway, and George pounced on it. The ball glowed and wiggled its way free of the cat's grasp, rolling away on its own power. George reared up before pouncing again.

"What a fearsome little hunter you are." Lucas laughed. Warm affection filled his voice.

If not for the fear freezing her face in place, the nickname would make Mary smile. Hearing his voice made it tempting to reveal herself to get some of his attention for herself. She dug her nails into her arm to snap herself out of it. Perhaps Matthew was right, and she really had been enthralled by Lord Holiday. Fighting his spell grew harder by the minute.

"May I get you anything, my lord?" the butler asked, his voice slow as he drew out the words.

"Nothing for me. I just came for Mrs. Bettle's wedding ring. I seem to have forgotten it."

"It's in the library I believe."

"Ah, good. I bet the ring will get her talking. It is far too sentimental for her to ignore." Lucas headed for the stairs, the enchanted ball keeping George occupied as he chased it down the hallway.

As soon as the hallway was clear, they tiptoed to the front door. The creaking of floorboards overhead made her heart race. Outside they made a break for the waiting carriage. As soon as she spotted them Margaret climbed down.

"You need to hide. He's coming right back."

"You weren't supposed to be back yet," Matthew said.

Margaret rested her hands on her hips. "Don't blame me. I took the longest route I could, but that is hard when there are only two roads out here."

"Are you all right?" Mary searched her neck for any puncture marks. It was mercifully clean.

"Yes, unless you count the terrible jokes I had to listen to him tell. And he laughs at his own jokes. Who does that?" Disgust dripped from her words.

"Jokes?" Mary blinked at her. If not for Margaret's visible distaste, she would have thought she was joking. "That doesn't seem like him." He'd always been too stiff and formal.

"Believe me, it's true. He enjoys puns far more than any man has a right to. Thank goodness I'm supposed to be mute. I never would have been able to laugh."

Behind them, the hedges spat out the real driver. "Jesus Christ!" Matthew blurted out, jumping in surprise. The driver's once loose locks were now in an elaborate plait dotted with roses. It flowed elegantly in the wind as he fell flat on his face. Slowly, the man shambled to his feet, stretching and yawning. With half-opened eyes, he looked around bewildered for a moment before stumbling toward the front door.

Matthew turned, catching Mary and Margaret staring at him. "...be praised! Jesus Christ be praised, the man is all right!" He rushed toward the gate. "Now we can leave without worrying about him."

"The bushes, again?" Lucas's voice drifted to them. "You need to find a new spot to nap."

"Run!" Matthew and the sisters ran through the gate and turned down the road for their hansom cab. By the time they reached the small clearing Mary collapsed onto her knees, sucking air in through big wheezing gasps.

"Did you find anything?" Margaret asked as she leaned against the hansom cab, catching her breath.

"We found plenty," Matthew said in a somber voice. He pulled the diary out, turning it over with gentle care. "Everything we need is in here."

"My God, Margaret, it's all true." Mary wrapped her arms around her sister. Her voice wavered as the gravity of it all began to set in. "He truly is a vampire. I'm so sorry I ever doubted you."

Margaret squeezed back. "It's ok. I'm just glad you're safe."

"For now," chimed in the priest. He put his hand on Mary's shoulder, his face grim. "But I'm afraid it's even worse than I thought. You heard him looking for Mrs. Bettle's wedding ring, didn't you?"

Margaret tapped on her chin. "Bettle...I swear I know that name from somewhere. One of the authors you keep passing on?" She turned to Mary who, still catching her breath, could only shrug her shoulders.

"However you know her, you ought to know that she died a few months ago."

"What?" Mary wheezed out, "But he said the ring would make her talk!"

"Yes. He's not content to merely prey on the living, but it seems he's communing with the dead as well. I shudder to think of how he's planning on tormenting that poor old woman's soul." His hand balled into a fist, slamming it against the cab. "I need to stop him before he can hurt anyone else. Where did you drive him?"

"We didn't get very far, but he did tell me to make my way to the cemetery near...wait..." Realization dawned on Margaret's face as she snapped her fingers. "The mausoleum! That's how I know the name! It was the Bettle mausoleum he was coming out of."

"Oh no. I thought he might only be seeking shelter there during the day." He ran his fingers through his hair, grabbing the back of his head. "If he's raising the dead to serve him, he could have a whole army at his disposal."

"You can still...stop him, can't you?" Mary couldn't bring herself to say the word "kill."

"I plan to find out during the train ride." He clutched the book to his chest. "This is the record of my brother's final months. I'm going to find out everything I can about that beast. Then I will give him the justice he deserves."

"You need to promise you'll stop him before he comes for my sister." Margaret gripped Mary's hand tightly.

"I don't know if I can." Matthew paused, taking his time before answering. "But I'll try. You have my word."

Mary patted her sister's hand. "Well I'm not waiting around to be eaten. I want to help."

"I admire your courage," he said with a sad smile, "but it's just too dangerous. I've been training for this. Crucifixes and holy water will help you to escape his clutches, but I don't think I can get you ready to really fight that monster."

"You won't need to." Mary kept coming back to how she had originally planned for Alice and the hunter to defeat Lord Hallow. Just as it seemed the vampire would finally sink his teeth into the young maid's neck, the hunter would swoop in to rescue her from his clutches and deliver the coup-de-grace to the villain. Of course it was all just fiction. She had no experience hunting anything bigger than a fly. Still, it had to be better than doing nothing, right? She twiddled her thumbs as she tried to convince herself. "You just need to set up a trap. And I...I'll be the bait."

"Bait? You can't go fishing for a vampire!" Margaret stomped her foot and turned to the priest. "Tell her how awful a plan this is."

"He is rather taken with you. It could work," Matthew said, rubbing the stubble on his chin. "But how will we draw him out?"

"Well, he is supposed to take me to see *The String of Pearls.*" Mary smiled, gaining confidence with each word she spoke. "It would be a waste to miss the play. It's one of my favorites." A fire burned in Mary's blood. She refused to let herself become another of Lord Holiday's victims, but there was more. After hearing his voice, she couldn't let go of her feverish desire to talk to him again.

"Even he wouldn't dare risk being caught feeding in a crowded theater. Very clever."

"Clever? Have you two gone mad? You might as well serve yourself up to him on a platter if you get lost in the crowd!"

"Don't worry. I will keep your sister safe. We'll corner him before he gets the chance to harm anyone, and I will do what needs to be done." He checked his watch. "But we need to hurry. If we miss the train we'll be stuck here until morning." He climbed into the hansom cab.

After the tension of the night, it was all such a relief to feel like they had a fighting chance now. As her mind relaxed, Mary asked, "By the way, what happened with those bushes? I could have sworn they were going to eat the driver alive."

"Ah yes. That." He blew out a long breath. "When the manor was first constructed, the rose bushes around the property were enchanted to 'do great harm' to trespassers. To an extent, they still do."

"How awful! What have we done to that poor man..."

"Oh but that was a long time ago. They've become a bit more tame ever since my grandfather tinkered with the enchantments. He was apparently quite the dandy in his youth, and being the height of fashion was everything to him." He seemed to gather his thoughts, but his voice spoke more with embarrassment than with terror. "So now the bushes 'do great hair' instead. My brother had been trying to fix the enchantments. Clearly he had no success."

"That's all?" Mary deflated. She was almost disappointed that the bushes hadn't been more wickedly brutal. At least then she wouldn't have felt so silly for being afraid of them. "You had us all worked up and terrified over a hairdressing rosebush?"

"Believe me it's not as pleasant as it sounds. I would know. My brother knocked me into them once when I was a child. I was too small to fight off the branches." His eyes stared blankly out the window as a shudder escaped his lips. " It was awful."

"Better than being eaten by a vampire," Margaret grumbled before snapping the reins.

Chapter 17

"D on't forget your choker!" Margaret said as she crammed the metal monstrosity around Mary's throat. Rose engravings decorated the metal with a red crystal in the center. The cold bite of the choker made her shiver. "There. That ought to chip a tooth."

"Yes it's very pretty, but a little tight," she choked out. She was already wearing the sturdy clerical collar that Matthew had given her. Layering another choker on top of it made it difficult to turn her head, and nearly impossible to look down. Still, the delicate metal engravings were much prettier than the plain white cloth around her neck. Much more appropriate for a young lady to be wearing to the theater as well. "Where did you find this thing anyway?"

"I saw it in the window of a shop and knew it would be perfect. I was even able to talk the shopkeeper down to a much better price. I doubt he'd be selling something that clunky to anyone else."

Mary tugged at the layers of armor around her neck, trying to loosen them. "Is this truly necessary?"

"I'm not taking any chances. Better to be a bit stiff in the neck than to become a vampire's feast."

"It's just...it still doesn't feel right. Don't you think it is wrong for his own uncle to kill him? Of all people, a priest shouldn't be breaking one of the 'thou shalt nots.'" If anyone were to try to find a way to prevent Lucas's death, it should be Matthew.

"He's already dead, Mary. That priest said so himself. No matter how you feel about him, you have to remember that," Margaret said, her matter-of-fact tone leaving no room for emotion. "And remember that he's a bloodsucking monster. Just think of all the lives you'll be saving by doing this." She placed a hand on her sister's shoulder, her concern warming her tone. "Most of all your own."

A knock at the door startled them both. She hadn't even left her house yet and already her nerves were getting the best of her. This would be a long night if she couldn't stay calm.

Mary moved to answer the door, Margaret hovering a few steps behind her.

The tall figure looked down on the sisters, dark and imposing against the light of the early evening sky. "Good evening," he greeted with a bow. He dressed fashionably in a black top hat and tailcoat, the outfit reminding her of the first time they met. The tension in Mary's stomach nearly evaporated when Lucas gave her a shy smile. Warmth rushed through her chest.

"Good evening." She hated the way her heart skipped a beat when he smiled. She shouldn't appreciate the smile of someone wanting to drink her blood.

"Is your father home? I had a few questions about some local book-sellers I wanted to ask him."

"He's currently unavailable." Margaret jumped forward. She squeezed between Mary and the wall. She held a bag of rice behind her back. "Now, I expect you to have my sister back at a reasonable hour and unharmed. Is that clear?"

His smile fell and he gave Margaret a somber nod. "Of course. I will have her back after the play."

"Good." Margaret moved out of the way.

"We should get going. I'd hate to be late." Mary stepped out, for a moment feeling eager to escape Margaret's attention. She wondered if this was how it felt to be Margaret. Mary promised herself she'd hover over her less in the future. Then again, it would be reassuring to know that Margaret would be watching over her tonight as she blithely marched into the lion's den.

His smile returned. "Martin let me borrow his private box. He assured me it has an excellent view of the stage."

"How lovely. I can't wait to see who is playing Mr. Todd. Did you ever read the book?"

"No. But I've heard rave reviews about the play. I'm curious to see what all the talk is about."

Their driver held the door open. The well-dressed man was a far cry from the usual mute driver. What had those bushes done to him? Great harm and great hair indeed.

"New driver?" she asked as she climbed in.

"No, this is my usual driver in the city. I took the train to avoid the long carriage ride. I'm staying in the Holiday townhouse tonight."

"I didn't realize you had a townhouse. Why don't you stay more often?"

"I much prefer the countryside. The manor is where I grew up, and it holds many fond memories for me. I'm afraid I can only handle the city in short bursts."

"I would choose the manor as well if I were you. The countryside is beautiful. Except for the unfortunate accident with your stairs, I thought the manor was a lovely home."

"I enjoy how peaceful the manor is, even if it is still in need of some more upkeep." He slid in across from her. His dark spectacles peeked out of his pocket. The sky was already growing darker, and by the end of the play night would be fully upon them. Matthew had warned her to lure him out before intermission lest they be forced to face him at his full strength.

She'd read pieces of the diary as they prepared for today. It was a long heartbreaking tale of the man's son devolving into a monster that couldn't be stopped. It all seemed to take a toll on the elder Lord Holiday. At times in his entries, it seemed he was grieving the passing of his wife despite her still being very much alive. Perhaps he knew it was only a matter of time before his own son turned his brutality onto him. But even with this damning first-hand account, she still couldn't see the monster in the man sitting across from her.

Margaret was right. She had been enthralled. His nice clothes and handsome features made her want to get closer, not farther away. It didn't make any sense to her. How could a man who'd been so quick to save her on the stairs murder his own father? It had to be a trick. That had to be the reason she could only see him as the polite young lord and not the bloodthirsty son the diaries had shown him to be.

He rubbed his arm and shifted in his seat. "How is your writing going?"

"Very well." Some business talk. That would stop her mind from racing. "Though I'm far more excited about getting back to publishing once more."

"You've found a new employer?"

"Oh, hadn't I told you? I'm buying Hawke Publishing back."

"Congratulations!" He smiled and politely applauded.

His support tickled the inside of her stomach. "Thank you." She looked away. Gaze too long at that smile and she might just melt. "I think the first few months will be bumpy, but we have enough popular stories that I'm certain I can get us back on track soon. I'd like to consider doing business with your press, if that is all right."

"It would be an honor to do business with you and Hawke. Arthur will love getting his hands on more serials. The man simply loves reading them, and I'm certain he'll go out of his way to see yours printed."

"You sound more confident today. Does that mean you aren't going to sell the press after all?"

He leaned against the window. "I haven't decided yet. I'm considering my options. I suppose much of it will depend on whether I decide to stay at Holiday Manor or return to stay with my mother. There is a lot to be decided." His cheeks turned pink. "I apologize, I don't mean to be a rain cloud."

"No need to apologize. You have a lot on your mind, I understand. I admit I do too with Hawke. It is a little nerve-racking to be taking the company over. I've always wanted to, but I worry that I won't be as good as Papa."

"You should ask him if you need help. It is the one thing I regret, not getting to learn more about the press from my father before he passed. His lessons feel old and dusty after my years away from home."

Mary had lost herself in the conversation before the mention of Lucas's father. Remembering the man's lamentations snapped her out of her trance. She chewed her bottom lip, trying her hardest to maintain her focus. "I'm sure he would be proud of you for stepping up."

"And yours is as well I imagine."

They each gave each other a soft, shy smile. It felt as though he understood her worries in a way even Margaret couldn't. The last thing she wanted to do was disappoint Papa. Despite all that she had read in the diary, seeing him now she couldn't stop feeling as though Lucas felt the same way about his father.

The carriage pulled up to the theater and reality crashed back down around her. Once the vampire was gone for good, what would happen to Holiday Press? If Hawke had the money, she'd consider buying it, but she couldn't afford it. And Lucas ... she didn't want to lose him either. This was the closest thing she'd ever had to her own romance.

The driver opened the door and Lucas gestured for her to go first. The theater buzzed with people. Carriages came and went while a steady river of people streamed inside. She looked about, spotting the carriage Margaret drove. Father Holiday peered out the window at them. She forced her attention forward to keep from drawing Lucas's attention to them.

"With this many people, the play has to be sold out," she said as Lucas joined her.

"Yes. I'm glad Martin offered his private box. Apparently he had an urgent matter at the Great Exhibition to attend to. Something about a ruckus caused by that little dog of his." He offered her his arm. She accepted, enjoying how she felt being on his arm. His presence felt steady beside her despite the situation.

She'd never been one for stories about broken hearts and passionate vows of love that withered away as quickly as the autumn leaves. She'd always preferred the stories about trust that weathered all. She wanted a man she could always depend on, even when others weren't looking.

The lobby proved to be packed with theater goers milling about chatting with one another. As they went, women turned to watch Lucas. His arm tensed from all the attention. She scooted closer to him.

"Is that Lord Hallow?" A woman from behind them whispered.

"Do you think he's hiring a maid?" said another, a gloved hand covering her mouth as she giggled.

They ascended the staircase to the balconies. When they reached the top, a gaggle of women stepped aside. The leader of the group curtsied to him. "Good evening, Lord Hallow." She batted her eyelashes at him. "I've heard so much about you."

Mary's grip on him tightened. Part of her felt ready to fight the woman and put an end to her flirtations to say, "Excuse me, but this is my vampire, not yours." But that wouldn't go well. And more importantly, she shouldn't be getting attached. A murderer couldn't be left on the loose, no matter how handsome and polite.

"Holiday," Lucas murmured, his voice quiet.

"Pardon?" the woman said, looking bewildered.

"My name is Holiday. Not Hallow." He stepped around the group of women. "Please enjoy the show."

"I understand now why you thought Lord Hallow was a real person," Mary said. "Especially if you get that manner of treatment anywhere you go."

"Since my return, I have been called Lord Hallow far more often than my real name."

"You do realize that woman was trying to flirt with you, don't you?"

He glanced over his shoulder. The women hadn't gone down the stairs. Instead, they stood at the top, watching him. "She is only flirting because she hopes I'll be like Lord Hallow, but that is not who I am, nor someone I wish to pretend to be." He turned back and smiled down at Mary. "...Though I mean no offense to his creator."

She giggled. "None taken." Damn his charms. He was more like Hallow than she wanted to believe, but here she was giggling like a schoolgirl over him.

He stopped at their box and opened the curtains for her to step inside. She entered the little balcony. Their spot was just to the left of the center of stage, providing them with an uninterrupted view of everything. Any minute Margaret would be finding a spot in the gallery seating with Matthew. She searched the crowd below but couldn't spot them yet. There were too many people moving up and down the aisles.

"This is a great view." She'd never sat in a private box before. As good as the view was, the private box also meant he'd have an easier time snacking on her. She doubted he'd attempt to drink her blood somewhere as public as the theater, but she couldn't help but to run a finger over her choker. "Can I tell you a secret about my writing?"

"Of course," he said as he settled in beside her. "You have my confidence."

"My story wasn't meant to be a romance. It was supposed to be a dark horror story with Lord Hallow as the tragic villain. Then for whatever reason my readers started swooning over him. I didn't understand Hallow's appeal at first, and I struggled with how to turn him into a romantic lead."

"You seem to have managed those struggles quite well," he said, gesturing in the general direction of the ladies in the next box over staring at him. "Clearly the character is very compelling."

"Yes, and once I met you, I...I felt like I finally understood Lord Hallow's appeal." Her face blazed red. Might as well get her confession out of the way. If he turned her down, she wouldn't have to live with the embarrassment for long. And neither would he. "You are a gentleman and I feel comfortable talking with you. I'm grateful to you for taking my writing and publishing aspirations seriously. And you are handsome," she said, speaking the last of her confession fast enough the words blended together.

He tilted his head as he regarded her, surprise raising his eyebrows. "You are one of the most popular writers in London right now. Your talents in that regard were never in question for me. I admit I'm embarrassed for not having read your work, but I've had no time for pleasure reading lately. You've also lent me a kind ear with my troubles, and I'm appreciative. It has been nice speaking to you."

As she gazed out at the theater goers below, she finally spotted Margaret. Margaret lifted a hand to let her know she was watching.

"I never knew much about the printing side of things. I've always wanted to know about how publishing works at all steps, and I've enjoyed learning from you"

He smiled, the warmth of his expression softening his edges. "That is the first time someone has ever thanked me after listening to the boring intricacies of printing presses. Most are relieved for it to be over."

She laughed. "I enjoy the boring intricacies. It makes me appreciate the books and serials I read more knowing all the work that goes into them."

When the play finally began, she grudgingly turned her attention to the stage. Lucas's presence kept trying to distract her from the play, tempting her to watch him instead. However, the dramatic flair of the man playing Mr. Todd was an excellent competitor for her attention. She found herself absorbed by the performance as he descended further into madness and killed more and more customers.

Instead of pulling a lever to send his victim down into the basement in his usual style, Mr. Todd slit a man's throat with a razor. From her vantage point in the box, she caught a glimpse of two stage hands just off stage wearing gloves emblazoned with glowing runes. Moving in unison with practiced gestures, they waved their gloved hands towards the victim in the barber's chair. A gratuitous amount of blood erupted from the man's throat, splashing unrealistically high into the air. Even so, the illusion was compelling, blood flying above the heads of the audience and onto Mr. Todd's face. It wasn't the way Mary remembered it happening in the serial, but she had to admit the effect was great for the play. Deliciously gruesome.

Lucas gagged and leaned forward, staring at the floor of the box instead of the play. Mary's hands tightened on her arm rests. The blood had to be triggering his bloodlust, she thought. At this rate he would pounce upon her and drain her dry.

Lucas looked up as Sweeney Todd cackled on stage. Blood marred the floor at his feet. Lucas jerked up. "I'm sorry, I need some fresh air." He headed out of the box. Mary stood. Margaret appeared entranced with the play, but Matthew watched the box. She waved at him before turning to follow Lucas. A lead weight sat in her belly at the thought of what was to come next. Tears stung the corners of her eyes. Poor Lucas. She hoped Matthew caught whoever was responsible for turning him into a monster.

She caught up to Lucas near the stairs. "Wait for me!"

He paused as he turned toward her, panting. "Please don't miss the play on my account."

"I've already read the book and watched an earlier play adaptation. I can miss a few minutes." They still had twenty minutes until intermission. If she couldn't get him in place by then, the plan would be done for. "Do you feel unwell?"

"I know it's fake, but even so, it...it stirs something in me. All that blo—" his voice cracked on the last word, apparently unable to even say it. He cleared his throat. "All I need is a few minutes of fresh air to clear my head."

"I'll come with you. If you aren't feeling well you shouldn't be alone." Best not to work up his appetite and then let him loose on the theater. She smiled and took his arm.

"Very well." His muscles relaxed under her grip as he gave her an embarrassed smile. A bead of sweat rolled down the side of his face. "I welcome the company."

"There is a pretty spot behind the theater with benches on the lawn. It would be a quiet place to sit." And it was on the local church's grounds, but he didn't need to know that. Not yet.

The lobby was deserted. By intermission it would fill back up, but for now their footsteps tapped through the empty space, making her feel all too alone with him. To chase away the silence, she babbled at him.

"The rest of the play is just as grisly. You might want to skip it."

"I should have looked into what the play was about. I remember my father loving the book, but I never knew anything about it." He rubbed the back of his neck. " I should have waited until the *Romeo and Juliet* performance started next month."

"Plenty of brutish violence in that one too, I'm afraid," Mary said with a soft chuckle, "I imagine it would be every bit as gruesome."

"I suppose that is true." He smiled weakly as he held the front door open for her. "I appreciate you accepting my invitation, and I'm sorry to have ruined the play."

What kind of vampire didn't like bloody stories? "You haven't ruined anything. I'm happy to have a reason to go out, is all. If I may be honest with you, I don't much care for *Romeo and Juliet* anyhow."

He sucked in a deep breath of air. "I don't either. People take it to be a great and powerful love story. I believe it was written more as a warning that shouldn't be romanticized."

"Yes. The foolish and rash things young people do when they're in..." Mary trailed off, unable to say the word "love." Her task still weighed heavily on her mind. She swallowed, her throat pressing uncomfortably against her layers of chokers. Could she really go through with this? No words came out as she noticed the silence going on for a bit too long.

Lucas glanced down at her, seeming to regain control of his nerves. "...When they're in lo—"

"When they're in their youth!" She interrupted, clearing her throat. "Oh yes, growing up I was full of rash ideas. I'd hate to be stuck with some of the decisions I would have made in my teen years without my Papa's guidance. Thankfully, I've learned to apply my more unusual ideas to stories rather than my own life." As she nervously rambled, she began to sorely wish that last statement were true. She would much rather have preferred to write about her current predicament than live through it. At least it might help break her writer's block.

He slid on his dark spectacles as the sun slid out from behind a cloud. "Not what I expected to hear from a writer. Many writers I've met have lived with their heads in the clouds and bring ideas for their books to my press that are too ambitious to work."

Once more, Lucas's calm demeanor when talking about writing managed to calm her down. "Writing is an art, but publishing is a business. Without Hawke Publishing, I don't know if I would have learned to think in those terms. Learning to think like a businesswoman was good for grounding me."

"I always understood the business side of things much more than the writing side. Running a press is more a matter of numbers than anything else. Sometimes it can be easy to forget that I'm talking about books when I'm looking at publishing times and print run numbers." He looked up and down the street. "Which way are we going?"

"This way." She turned to the right. Their plan would have to be a little ahead of schedule. The thought sent a pang through her heart. She was having such a lovely night, she had nearly forgotten that it was a vampire whose arm she clung to. Human Lucas was a man she would have loved to get to know better. She could listen to him talk for hours, conversing and losing herself in those eyes. And those lips. Her fingers impulsively grazed her own lips.

She pinched herself. She had to focus. At the alleyway beside the theater, she paused at the entrance. "What if we take a shortcut through here? It's dark and no one will see us." That ought to tempt him. There'd be no one around to witness him drinking her blood.

"Are you certain?" His brow creased as he peered into the alley.

"Yes. It will get us there in no time." She ran a hand through her hair, tilting her head back to bare her neck as best as the collars would allow, repeating slowly, "And no one will see us."

His head tilted as he watched her, his eyes fixated on her neck. Despite his calm exterior, Mary heard the excitement creep into his voice. "If you insist."

The tall buildings on either side plunged the alleyway into deep shadows. Sunset would start any minute now. They had no time to waste. All she could do was hope Matthew understood enough to get into place.

The alleyway led to a narrow intersection, each path barely wide enough for the two of them to walk side by side. As they walked forward, a man crouching in the alley stood up, blocking their path.

"Pardon us, sir," Lucas offered politely.

"Beg-pardon, yer grace.'Fraid I can't do that." Strands of Maragaret's hair peeked out from under the glamour. Mary was relieved to see her sister had gotten into position in time. The look of a street urchin was rather convincing on her. The accent, however, needed some work. A lot of work.

"Why is that?" Lucas asked, seemingly unaware of the trap being sprung. "Are you hurt?"

Margaret laughed and pointed to their left. "Ask 'im."

Out of the alleyway, Matthew marched forward, crucifix in hand. The flow of his cassock made him look like a vengeful spirit as he emerged from the darkness, calling out, "This ends tonight, monster! Hellfire awaits you!."

"Run!" Lucas hissed. He grabbed Mary by the hand and led her around a stack of barrels down the path to their right. Mary followed, being sure to hit the hidden tripwire lying in wait a few steps later.

"Ah!" she yelled as the barrels came crashing down behind her. "My ankle!" She faked a fall that she knew couldn't have been any better than Charlotte's fake faint at Mr. Steepe's tea party. But Lucas was looking forward, too distracted to notice her poor acting. All too late he noticed that he had run into a dead end, with the barrels trapping him in the alleyway.

Lucas stopped and turned. Mary and Matthew climbed around the barrels. Matthew reached down to help Mary up.

"Don't you touch her!" Lucas yelled as he sprinted back. He punched Matthew square in the nose, sending him sprawling backward onto a barrel that rolled right into Margaret, knocking her down too.

Lucas reached down and grabbed Mary's hand. He pulled her back up. Once she was on her feet she stumbled. He caught her with his other arm and pulled her off her feet altogether. She gasped as she found herself in his arms, being held like a princess.

"Hang on," he said as he climbed onto a crate. She wrapped her arms around his neck as he jumped right over a barrel. He hit the ground running, returning to the front of the theater.

Mary gaped over Lucas's shoulder as Matthew and Margaret pulled themselves off the ground. Lucas's breath quickened as he ran for their hansom cab.

"To the train station! As fast as you can go!" he called out to the driver as he yanked the door open. He climbed inside, depositing Mary on the seat opposite him. "Go!" he cried as he pulled the door shut. The carriage pulled away as Matthew came limping out of the alleyway.

"What was that?" Mary asked. She hadn't expected him to run. Quite the opposite. When she lay awake last night, she'd imagined his thirst for blood taking over as he attacked them with bared fangs and too much snarling. In person, she couldn't imagine him snarling at all.

"I'm sorry," he said as he offered her the pillow leaning against the far door. "Please put your ankle up. I take full responsibility. I had no idea my uncle would be here."

"Oh, your uncle?" She did her best to feign ignorance. Her right ankle did twinge a touch, but it was already fading as she propped it up.

"Yes. I didn't want him to hurt you. You see, I...I haven't been completely honest with you." He fidgeted.

That much was obvious. "Whatever do you mean?"

"Before, I told you that my father had died in an accident. A fall." His look of heart wrenching sorrow matched his somber tone perfectly. "But in truth, I believe he was murdered."

"Murdered?" she asked, the shock and curiosity in her voice was much more genuine. He ought to know it was he who killed his own father, right?

"Yes. And I believe it was my uncle who did it."

Mary gaped at him in shock. "Him?" she finally got out. "But he's a priest."

"I know. That's why I don't expect anyone to believe me. Who in this entire country would trust my word against a so-called 'man of God?"

"I don't understand. Why would you think he was murdered? Didn't he fall from the tower?"

"He did fall, but he was found with a piece of sharp wood through his heart," he said, his hand clutching his own chest. "My uncle had always had some ... peculiar beliefs regarding the occult."

He most certainly did. "That's awful," said Mary, her head spinning. Suddenly the facts didn't quite add up. A stake through the heart would make sense if Luke had been a vampire, but Matthew had said it was Lucas who did the killing. Why would he lie about that? And hadn't he said Lucas's father had been drained of blood? Which version was right? Who was telling the truth?

"I've seen him poking around the manor, and I fear he may be after me next. That's why I've been so hesitant to return home to my mother or let her come back to England. I can't let him harm anyone else I care about." His eyes turned to Mary, full of concern, as he patted the ankle he thought to be broken. "I've already failed in that regard."

Suddenly the carriage felt very hot. Her heart raced and her palms sweat. Was the killer sitting across from her, or was he with unsuspecting Margaret?

Chapter 18

She made sure to limp onto and off the train. Best to keep up appearances rather than admit she'd faked her fall. At least until she figured out who the true villain of this story was. Then if she needed to run, she could take him by surprise. Lucas remained as polite as ever through her plotting, letting her lean against him for support.

She waited on a bench while he fetched the carriage, her head craning to see better as the last of the passengers filtered out of the station. No sight of Matthew or Margaret. And that was the last train until morning. If they weren't hiding out of sight, she'd be stuck alone for hours with Lucas, and Margaret with Matthew.

Her stomach cramped from all the worrying. Next time she'd know better than to let Margaret get involved in her mess. What if Lucas wasn't a vampire at all and she'd only been fed lies by a priest searching to gain the family inheritance for himself? Or what if Lucas really was a vampire and now she was trapped with him with no stakes or rice or other weapons to fend him off? Her stomach gave another pang and she groaned.

Lucas's carriage pulled up in front of her. He climbed out and offered her his arm. "Please allow me to help you in." A gentleman to the very end.

She limped toward the carriage on her left ankle, hating how good the warmth of his arm felt. Why couldn't he stop being handsome and charming until she figured out whether he was evil or not? His good manners made everything all the more confusing.

"Oh no, did you hurt your left ankle too?" He wrapped an arm around her back to help hold her up.

Drat. She'd forgotten she was faking a hurt right ankle, not left.

"I think I favored it too much earlier. Now they both ache."

"Do you want me to carry you?"

She gave him a strained smile. "That isn't necessary. A good night's rest, and I'll be fine in the morning." As if she would get any sleep tonight.

They passed the ride to the manor in silence. She could practically feel him brooding beside her as he stared out the window at the dark countryside. Even with nothing but the moonlight lighting up his frame, he was still handsome. She'd never understood the appeal of brooding romantic leads before, and yet the temptation to draw him close rose up in her. To touch those soft lips to her own...

The carriage pulled through the gates, distracting her as she spotted the tower out her window. Lucas climbed out first, walking to the front of the manor and pressing his hand against a rune near the front door. After a brief incantation, the rune glowed brightly and the sound of the front gates shuddered. He then returned to the cab and offered her his hand. She accepted.

A light flickered in the highest tower window over his shoulder. She blinked and the light was gone. "Is someone in the tower?" Surely Matthew couldn't have beaten them here. Impossible.

Lucas turned. "No. The gate will only open for me now. No one else can get onto the grounds unless I'm with them."

She was as good as trapped then. Even if Matthew did come, he wouldn't be able to get in. Maybe Lucas would be kind enough to throw her body over the bushes for him to find.

He took her to the parlor. With a wave of his free hand the fireplace flared to life, casting the room in a cozy glow as the runes on the mantle flickered in time with the flames. He sat her in an armchair and dragged an ottoman over for her ankles. "Would you like some tea?"

"Yes, please."

"I'll be right back."

He left. The open curtains to the large window showed nothing but darkness on the grounds. No other carriage came to the gate. She shifted her chokers, wishing for the first time that night that she had more around her neck. Something brushed the underside of her legs and she jumped, pressing a hand to her mouth to silence her scream.

"Meow." George's head popped out from under her skirts.

"You are good at scaring me, aren't you?"

George meowed in response. He circled once around the ottoman before deciding to jump up on her lap instead. The cat sprawled across her lap, purring as she petted him. A yawn escaped her. Here in front of a fireplace with a cat on her, the theater felt like a world away. Coming down from the rush of their flight left her exhausted.

Lucas's footsteps approached the room, and she perked back up.

"I'm sorry. My stores are rather low on tea. All I have now is this." He set the tea tray down on the stand beside her. He poured the tea, the red color bright against the white porcelain of the teacups. " It's my favorite blend, but I'm afraid it is a bit of an acquired taste. It may not be to your liking."

A shaky hand accepted the cup of what she was certain had to be blood. An acquired taste indeed. Even so, best not to refuse her host's hospitality, lest her own blood end up in the pot next. "I'm certain it's fine. Thank you." She balanced the saucer on George. Uncharacteristically, the cat remained perfectly still. He didn't even bother to open his eyes.

"Do you want something to eat? I can make you a sandwich or fetch you some leftover soup."

"I'm fine," she said, still eyeing up her cup. The tea was not as opaque or thick as she had expected, but rather a clear ruby red. Perhaps the blood was watered down to make it go farther? The dilapidated state of the manor would suggest that money was tight. As she pondered the frugality of her vampiric host, she realized the peculiar way in which he had phrased his offer to have food brought to her. "But surely you don't mean to say you'd be making the food yourself?"

"Indeed I would. I may not look it, but I am actually quite capable in the kitchen. I've done plenty of my own cooking lately to avoid anyone getting a chance to tamper with my food."

"Oh I wouldn't want to be a bother to you at this hour," she said. If he did plan on feasting on her, she wouldn't just sit there and let herself be fattened up like a Christmas goose. Though it did strike Mary as peculiar that he didn't have anyone enthralled to do the task for him. "Don't you have kitchen staff to handle your food?"

He sat down across from her, taking his teacup with him. "It has been difficult for me to trust anyone to handle my food. I'm afraid my uncle is a far more capable manipulator than one might think. I believe he would have my meals tampered with if he could get to my food. After all, I won't give him the chance to stake me. My butler and I handle what we can ourselves, even if it means sticking to simpler fare most of the time."

She sniffed at her tea. A citrusy scent drifted off her cup. Her dry mouth pressured her to try the blood red liquid. Her curiosity was rewarded with light notes of vanilla mixed with a tea she couldn't identify. It left a far more pleasant taste on her tongue than she had expected. "What is this?"

"Red rooibos tea. I've always found it relaxing. Martin introduced me to it the summer we studied and traveled together. He sent me several tins of this blend as a welcome home gift."

She kept her head down to hide the way her cheeks flamed. She felt ridiculous for thinking his tea could have been blood. Had she been wrong about everything? Too eager to believe Father Holiday because the allure of a vampire was too hard to resist? She took another sip of the tea.

"This...rooibos was it? It's rather nice. I don't think it will replace Steepe English Breakfast as my favorite, but it is very refreshing. I wouldn't have ever known how lovely it is had you not shared it with me." She took one last sip before setting it down on the tray. "I don't know how you manage in a house this big without more servants."

"Magic mostly. Although I fear I have overworked my butler. In truth it wasn't until I invited you over for tea that I realized how paranoid I'd become."

"You didn't eat any of the tea tray with me. Did you think I'd poison you?"

"I ate before to make sure you couldn't tamper with my food. And yet you never mentioned it until now. I can't imagine what you must have thought. Looking back on it... oh it's quite embarrassing." He shifted from unease.

She laughed. "I did think it odd, but I thought it'd be much more rude to comment on it. May I ask about your glasses?"

"They are for the sun." He pulled them out of his pocket and held them up. "I've always had sensitive eyes. Some sort of disorder that afflicted my grandmother as well."

"And that is why you have a tendency to appear out at night, I take it."

He nodded. "With the glasses on I am fine going out, it's more the embarrassment of wearing them that keeps me home. I'd grown used to my mother's family knowing about my condition that returning here has made me feel like a fish out of water every time someone stares."

"Isolation is never good for anyone. It is no wonder you've grown paranoid living out here on the moors."

George meowed, the end of the meow cutting off into a yawn as he stretched.

"That is why I invited you to the play. I enjoyed your visit despite my stairs falling apart under you. I wanted to see you again. I thought a play would be a good way to get out of the house as well."

"I appreciated the invitation. And I appreciate George not stealing my charm bracelet this time."

Lucas cracked a smile. "I hadn't realized George hitched a ride with me to the party until he brought me your bracelet. His gift was far better than the stockings and dead mice he typically brings me."

"I went searching for you when you left our dance, but you'd disappeared."

"I wasn't feeling well." He looked down at his tea. wincing at the memory. "Roquefort let me borrow one of the spare bedrooms to lie down." He took a deep breath before meeting her eyes. "Are you promised to anyone or have any suitors?"

Her heart skipped a beat. Sure, like any other lady wishing for love she'd fantasized about this moment. Except it never included a black cat asleep on her lap or a vampire sitting across from her. A handsome vampire with title who also worked in publishing.

"I don't."

"Once I take care of this problem with my uncle, I would like to see you again. But you deserve to know I'm not the English gentleman you deserve. In fact, I'm—"

Her heart pounded. "You don't need to tell me. I already know. Your uncle told me when he told me to stay away from you. Even so, I'd very much like for you to come visit me again." Maybe she'd gone mad for her pulse to race in excitement at the thought. He'd been nothing but a gentleman to her. As long as he didn't start biting her neck she was willing to keep an open mind. Unless....unless he'd enthralled her to think that way. Her thoughts got muddled up again, her fears and desires warring with each other.

He put his teacup down and moved to the edge of the ottoman. He took her hand in his. His fingers weren't cold this time, but warm. "Are you sure? What I am makes some people uncomfortable. Frightened even. Some would go as far as to call me a ... well, a monster." His fingers twitched.

"As long as you are an honorable man, I don't mind." Her foggy mind struggled to think. Whatever cologne he wore made her feel like she was lost in the moors. "Are you an honorable man?"

"I do my best." He leaned closer and their eyes met. She tilted her head up, raising her lips to meet his. Her pulse fluttered in anticipation.

Then a great crash sent glass scattering to the floor as a figure clad in black burst through the window.

Chapter 19

George jumped off her lap with a yowl and ran from the room. The figure rolled through his leap, seamlessly hefting a crossbow and pointing it at the couple, his priestly robes now tattered from the broken glass. "Unhand her you fiend!" Matthew cried out as he steadied his aim.

Mary sighed at the interruption. Couldn't he have let her have one kiss first?

Lucas jumped to his feet. "What are you doing, you madman?"

"Stopping you from taking another innocent life." He circled around the armchair, each step as careful as a hunter stalking his prey. Behind him by the road, a hansom cab had been driven directly into the bushes. The lanterns hanging from it swayed. "Don't worry, Miss Hawke. This ends tonight."

"You are quite right," Lucas said as he stepped in front of Mary. "This has gone on for long enough. I'm done running from you." In one fluid motion almost too quick to see, he grabbed a pillow off the sofa and tossed it at his uncle's head. Matthew fired, his bolt pinning the pillow to a painting of the manor.

Lucas dove across the room and tackled his uncle. The men crashed to the ground, wrestling as they both fought for the upper hand. The crossbow went skittering across the floor.

The priest's stiff collar did little to stop Lucas's hands as they closed around his neck. Choking gasps escaped his lips as Matthew strained to reach into the bag slung across his back. He pulled out a bulb of garlic and, grabbing Lucas by his waistcoat with his free hand, shoved it into his nephew's mouth.

Lucas pulled away, gagging and spluttering. "Was that garlic? What is wrong with you?"

"I have plenty more." He threw a clump of garlic at Lucas, whacking him in the forehead with it. Then he was back on his feet, darting toward the crossbow. Lucas grabbed his leg, tripping him.

The butler stepped into the doorway, blinking the sleep out of his eyes. He took in the scene in front of him as Lucas threw a punch at his uncle, catching him in the side of the jaw. The butler shook his head. "Not paid enough," he grumbled as he turned to wander away.

Matthew rolled away and hopped back onto his feet. He pulled a stake out from under his coat, and as he turned to dodge another punch, Mary caught sight of the bandolier of stakes across his chest.

She backed up until she hit the wall. Indecision tormented her. Who could she believe? Which man could she trust? If only she could get them to sit down and interview each over a cup of tea, maybe she could find out who was lying. But the teapot had long since been tossed to the floor in the scuffle. Time was up, and she had to make a decision now. Glancing to her side, she noticed the crossbow was within reach.

Matthew ran at his nephew, stake held high. Lucas blocked his arm and swept his feet out from under him. He hit the ground with a thud which knocked picture frames and curiosities in the room to the floor, a whoosh of breath leaving him. Lucas ripped off the bandolier and tossed it out the window. Then he was back on his uncle, their prior wrestling match resuming as they fought for control of the last wooden stake tightly clenched in the priest's fist.

They both panted from exertion, their faces red.

"You've been trying to kill me since I returned," Lucas grunted.

"I'll avenge my brother's death. I won't rest until I do."

"What does this—" Lucas stopped to catch his breath "—have to do with my father's death?"

"Everything!" A vein in Matthew's head throbbed as he fought to keep Lucas from pinning him down.

"It was you, wasn't it? You've been after my inheritance this whole time."

"I don't care about your petty inheritance. I care about justice!" He rammed his knee into Lucas's stomach. The surprise loosened Lucas's grip enough for Matthew to break free. A punch to the cheek put Lucas on the ground, and now the priest pressed his advantage. He climbed atop his nephew and stabbed down at his heart with the stake. Lucas's quick hands grabbed his uncle's wrists, only barely keeping the stake from being driven home. Grunting and straining, their arms shook, the deadly stake held precariously between them.

"Stop fighting now or I'll shoot you both!" cried out Mary, taking aim with the crossbow at the men. She worried it was too bold a lie. It had taken Mary a minute to figure out how to load the crossbow as they fought. Even if she could figure out how to shoot it, she wasn't confident her bolt would find its mark, and reloading would be out of the question. Her bluff seemed to work however as both of them scurried apart, eyes wide as they tried to console her.

"Mary? What are you doing?" Lucas said, voice softening even as he strained to breathe.

"Run, Mary!" Matthew yelled, his voice haggard. "I'll stop him. Get out now before he eats you."

"No. I'm not letting you two kill each other. Not until I know the truth."

"You know the truth," Matthew snapped. "You know what he is! Death is the only salvation for him and his wicked kind."

Lucas's nostrils flared and his hands balled. " Damn you. You would smile to my face. To my mother's face. You acted like our family, and only now do you show yourself for what you are with my father gone. Despicable. Even for you!"

"Your mother?" Matthew's brow furrowed. "I love Antoinette. She always felt like a big sister to me. Wait..." He trailed off, eyes darting back and forth across his nephew. Horror dawned on his face as he demanded, "What have you done with her?"

"Don't you dare say her name, you dogmatic oaf. I won't let you hurt her." Lucas looked ready to spring on his uncle again. "This is the last time you harm our family."

"Our family?" He pointed the stake he'd managed to keep at Lucas. "You're no family of mine, filthy vampire!"

"V-vampire?" Lucas stammered, gaping at him. "Have you truly gone mad?"

"What do you mean? You admitted to it," Mary chimed in. "You said some people would call you a monster for what you are."

"What? I'm not a vampire." He balked. "I was telling you that I'm French."

"French?" She lowered the crossbow. "Since when?"

"Since I was born! My mother is French, and I've been away in France these last few years at her family's vineyard. What lies has Matt been feeding you?"

"Be quiet! All I've done is protect a vulnerable young lady from you. Your lies might work on her, but they won't keep me from avenging my brother's death." He jabbed the stake in Lucas's direction to punctuate his words. His nose began bleeding again, and he pulled his handkerchief out to press it to his nose.

"Hold on...who killed the former Lord Holiday?" The crossbow was heavier than she'd expected. Her muscles ached from holding it. If this continued much longer, she'd drop it.

"He did," both men said at the same time, pointing at each other.

"Even your trickery cannot counter cold hard facts." Matthew scoffed as he set the stake on a table, well within arm's reach. He then reached into his coat, producing the book and holding it up in triumph. "I have your father's diary. It proves you are a murderous creature of the night. Every page chronicles your descent into damnation."

"His diary?" Lucas's mouth opened and then closed in shock. Finally, he gathered his thoughts. "Where did you find it? I've searched the manor top and bottom to find something of great importance to him."

"Miss Hawke and I found this in his study."

Lucas reached out slowly towards the book before balling his hand into a fist. "If that is from his study, it must be what he told me he was working on. He wouldn't tell me what it was."

"I'm sorry. I only went along with him to find out the truth," Mary said, feeling the urge to apologize. "I had to know for certain if you were just a vampire trying to feed on me."

"Of course I'm not a vampire." Lucas swallowed hard as he spoke the last word, dread making his muscles tense. "Those creatures don't exist. And I would never ever dream of harming you!"

Matthew tossed the book at him. "Then what is this all about?"

Lucas fumbled to catch it. "I don't know what this is. He never told me." He quickly flipped through the pages, looking over sketches of bats and blood-spattered entries about vampires. He then looked up and narrowed his eyes. "Wait...is this book how you justified killing him? Is that why you staked him in the heart? You're completely insane!"

Mary cast Matthew a dubious look. "He has a point. Staking him through the heart is something you'd do to stop a vampire, not something you'd do if you were one. How do we know Lucas was the murderer?"

Matthew puffed his chest out. "How much more proof do you need? Watch! I'll prove it by triggering his bloodlust." He yanked his handkerchief away from his nose and held it out toward Lucas. "What do you think of this blood, hmm? Do you want to drink it?" He shook the handkerchief.

All color drained from Lucas's face and his eyes fluttered. "I—" was all he got out before he tipped forward onto the rug, his stiff body landing with a thud as he dropped the book. Mary flinched at the sound of his face hitting the rug.

Matthew stared in disbelief, arm still held out. "Did you really just pretend to faint? Do you expect me to fall for it?"

Lucas didn't respond.

"Believe me, I've seen a fake faint and that one was real." She'd have to give Charlotte a few notes next time she wanted to faint her way out of an awkward situation. "Is he alive?" She set the crossbow down.

"Of course not," he said, sounding less sure of the notion than he'd been before the theater. "A vampire is a walking corpse. The living dead."

"Well I don't think vampires usually faint at the sight of blood."

Matthew knelt down and felt for a pulse in Lucas's neck. Matthew paled as his nephew let out a groggy groan. "His pulse is strong. I don't understand."

"Aha! I've got you now, vampire," Margaret cried as she bolted in through the broken window. In one hand she held a stake, in the other a pouch of rice. She wore her hair in a fancy braided updo covered in a crown of roses. Mary was certain her sister's hair was far more plain at the theater, and this most certainly hadn't been a part of her street urchin glamour. She tossed the rice across the room, pelting Matthew and Mary with little white grains. "Count that, you fiend!"

The two of them stared at her.

"You already got him?" Margaret lowered her stake with a disappointed scowl. "Aww. I wanted to do the staking."

"I've made a grave mistake," Matthew declared. "He isn't a vampire at all, and you aren't going to be staking anyone." He reached down to help Lucas onto the sofa.

"What do you mean he isn't a vampire?" Margaret demanded.

"It was a misunderstanding," Mary said.

The enchanted broom drifted into the room and got to work sweeping up the rice into a neat pile.

"Please quit talking about vampires. I can't stand the thought of them," Lucas whispered. He kept his eyes squeezed shut.

"Do you want your tea?" Mary offered. Her face turned red as embarrassment washed over her. She couldn't think of a worse way to ruin a blossoming courtship. Already she missed the soft warmth of his lips, and it burned all the more deeply thinking she'd never again feel them pressed against hers. This would be a hard one to explain to Papa.

"In a minute. Once the room quits spinning."

"Are you all right? What happened?" She held a hand to his forehead.

"The bl—" He swallowed, the word "blood" caught in his throat. His eyes flitted open a moment to point at the handkerchief in Matthew's hand before closing them again. "That. I don't do well with it."

"When did this start?" Matthew demanded. "You were never so squeamish when we were children. We'd be covered in cuts and bruises whenever we climbed trees together."

Lucas nodded, clearing his throat. "And you remember whenever my mother would bandage us up?"

"Of course. You would close your eyes and pray intently that we'd be safe from the..." Matthew trailed off, his epiphany smacking of disappointment. "You weren't praying at all, were you?"

Margaret sighed, twirling a finger around a delicate curl hanging from the side of her hair. "I thought this would be a big adventure."

Mary finally turned her attention from Lucas to her sister. "What happened to your hair?"

"The bushes got me." Margaret walked over to the mirror near the doorway and stopped to admire herself. "Great hairstyle. I like it. I didn't like being unable to fight the bushes though. Not when I thought I had some staking to do." She stabbed her stake into the chest of an invisible vampire.

"Why on Earth did you think I was a vampire?" Lucas opened one eye.

Mary sat down on the edge of the sofa by his legs. "Well, for lots and lots of reasons. For one thing your own father's diary said so. And I only ever saw you out around nighttime. Plus, I never saw you eat, and you only ever drank red tea. And then I thought I had caught you sleeping in a coffin full of dirt from your homeland in the cold cellar..." Mary realized she was rambling and cut herself off there.

He groaned and sat up, looking a little woozy but stable. "To think I was worried about you finding out I'm half French..."

A shy laugh escaped Mary's lips. "Oh it all sounds so silly now." The tension she had been holding in the past week had finally started to subside. It was reassuring to finally have explanations for all of Lucas's peculiarities and to know that she hadn't fallen for an actual bloodsucking monster. Looking around at the state of the parlor in the aftermath of the scuffle, she only regretted that she had let it get so far. Picture frames and broken bits of pottery littered the corners of the room.

Mary's eyes glanced around, landing on a small, ornately decorated mirror. The sheet covering it must have fallen off at some point during their fight. Just like the mirror she had seen in the library. Suspicion dawned on Mary's face as she realized it was in fact the very same mirror as before. She could have sworn that mirror had shown no reflection for Lucas. Surely there was an explanation for this too. She tilted her head slightly to look at the mirror. The angle perfectly reflected an image of the sofa Lucas was in. But not Lucas.

Mary grabbed and hefted the crossbow. "Where's your reflection?" She demanded.

"My what?" asked a groggy Lucas. He recoiled away from the tip of the crossbow bolt as best as he could.

"In the mirror." She pointed, looking at the reflection once more. She watched the crossbow's reflection in the glass. It floated in mid air, with no one holding it.

Matthew caught sight of the reflection and blanched. He didn't appear in the mirror either. "Oh God, where's my reflection? What have you done to me?" He circled around the mirror, eying it as though he expected it to bite him. "Care to explain to your guests what this is? Hmm?"

Lucas gave a nervous laugh. The flush in his cheeks made him seem more afraid of another embarrassing secret being revealed than the crossbow bolt aimed at his chest. "Just an enchanted mirror. Nothing exceptional."

"Don't you lie to me. That is a scrying mirror, isn't it?" The priest stepped forward and gently pushed the crossbow down, replacing it with his wagging finger. "Now why oh why would you need a mirror that can only reflect the images of the dead? You're trying to become a medium again, aren't you?"

Lucas rubbed the back of his head. "I've been dabbling. When I thought you were the murderer, I knew no one would take my word over yours. I thought maybe I could hold a séance to contact Father to see if he knew who killed him. When that didn't work, I tried scrying."

"Those séances channel dark and terrible energies. They're an affront to the lord. You ought to let the dead rest," Matthew said, crossing himself.

Lucas scoffed. "I assure you he's not resting. He has been haunting the manor, and I haven't been able to speak with him. My attempts at a séance failed. Nothing of his I've used has been strong enough to let me speak to him. But this book of his, it might do." He weighed it in his hands. "He must care about something so strongly that he wishes to linger in this world. Maybe this will tell us what it is."

Matthew's face turned worried. "And you're positive it's him? That he's haunting this manor? It has always been old and drafty. Could be the wind. Or George." The cat peered in through the doorway.

"I believe something is haunting this manor," Mary said, drawing both men's attention. "The time I spent the night I saw...something out the window. A face. It looked just like you, Lucas. He scared me and I ran into my room before he could say more."

"That sounds like him. I've heard him asking for help and wailing, but I haven't been able to communicate. Sometimes I catch glimpses of him, but no more. The butler hears him too."

Matthew sighed as he ran a hand through his hair. "I suppose if it's to help the deceased find their rest, then I can let the seance go this one time. For my brother's sake." Matthew extended a hand to Lucas, pulling him to his feet. He maintained the handshake, staring down his nephew, adding, "Get the truth from him so he can finally find peace. Someone killed him, and if it wasn't you, I want to know who."

"If you wish, we can do it tonight while we are all here. It won't take long to set up."

"We should do it in the tower," Mary suggested. "I've seen a light in there several times. And that's where we found the book."

"He loved his study," Matthew said in agreement. "He was holed up in there for months before his death. Let's try. It's time the truth is revealed."

Chapter 20

"I'm sorry," Mary said as she waited at the base of the tower with Lucas. Margaret was busy petting George near the garden entrance. Matthew had wandered off, requesting a minute to clean the blood from his face. She suspected he was gathering up his stakes again. "I didn't want to believe your uncle at first, but he was so certain you'd killed your father. I already had my suspicions, but then to hear him echoing all of my very worst fears..." She rubbed her arm as she stared at her feet. "I feel like such a fool."

"It's all right. I would have been worried as well in your shoes. I just hope tonight proves my innocence to you. I was so focused on hiding my heritage from you that I never considered how some of my more eccentric actions would look."

"Mushroom growing struck me as too unusual to be true."

He smiled. "I learned it from my mother. We used to forage through the woods collecting mushrooms when I was a child. She's always loved good food. " His smile fell. "Can you forgive me for getting you caught up in this feud?"

"Forgive you?" Mary asked, bewildered. "Please, I should be begging for your forgiveness. I can't begin to explain how embarrassed and sorry I am."

"Even if I did feel you had truly wronged me, I'd forgive you in an instant."

"Really? Even though I destroyed your parlor? And conspired to have you, erm... killed?"

"Oh the manor is already in shambles. A broken window here or there won't make too much of a difference." Lucas laughed. "And even as an assassin's helper, you were very good company. Up until we were attacked in the alleyway, that was the most pleasant evening I've had in quite some time."

"I'm truly flattered." Mary brought her hand to her lips to hide her grin.

"At the very least you had a good reason to fear me. Or rather, you thought you did. I was afraid you would loathe me when you discovered my heritage like others have."

"Who could possibly hate you? Even if you didn't have all the ladies in London fawning over you, you're still so kind and gentlemanly." She had to stop herself from adding "and handsome." And that was to say nothing of his soft, tender lips...

"I'm glad you think so." He adjusted the lantern in his hand. "But my family has made its fair share of enemies, and not merely because of my heritage. The other nobles see us as a shameful stain because we work for our money. It was my grandfather who started the press, all to cover his massive gambling debts. He poured what little remained of the Holiday fortune into creating the press, and it seems that was the only gamble he ever made that paid off." He turned his gaze to the top of the tower. "I think what really upsets the nobility is that our family is doing so well now. Much better than some of them in fact. Don't let the state of the manor fool you. My father made a few careful investments of his own, so we're not quite as destitute as some of them would wish to believe."

"I never thought you were. You don't owe me any explanations either. It was foolish of me to jump to such wild conclusions about you. It's not all Matthew's fault either. I just haven't been thinking clearly since my mother ran off." It felt like nothing had gone right since then.

"Ran off? I thought you said she had passed."

"No. She ..." She took a deep breath to steady herself. "She and my uncle stole all the money they could from our family and ran off to God-knows-where. That was why my father felt he had no choice but to sell the publishing house. I'd always wanted to take over Hawke one day and then suddenly it was all gone. And then I met you. And you were so enchanting I just..." Mary hadn't realized just how much tension she'd been keeping bottled up, and finally letting the truth out in front of Lucas threatened to overwhelm her. She held strong, not wanting to appear pitiful in front of him. "I wasn't ready to be betrayed again and I overreacted. Badly."

"What happened to you is simply awful. I can't blame you for feeling that way." He smiled, turning and gesturing towards the manor. "And I know a thing or two about overreacting."

She giggled. It helped her beat back her tears. "I can't possibly thank you enough for being so understanding. I don't know if I could do the same were I in your position."

"Well it's not often I am told I am 'enchanting.' I confess I was a bit...enchanted myself," he said, slowly turning back to Mary. "When you brought me to the alleyway out of everyone's sight, I thought perhaps you had more romantic intentions. Another overreaction I suppose."

Her head jerked up as she met his eyes. "No, not at all. It hadn't been my intention at the time, but it certainly wouldn't have been unwelcome. A kiss I mean." Her face blazed with heat. "I mean, you didn't have to. That is to say—" She stopped, feeling like anything she said would only make her situation worse. She might as well go bury herself in the mushroom bin.

He considered her words, the minute seeming to drag on forever to her. She eyed up the rose bushes debating whether or not to step into them and disappear for the night.

"Let us wait until after the séance. I want to make sure my name is cleared and that there are no other misunderstandings between us first." He smiled, amusement softening the heavy air about him, and highlighted his bruises.

"Your bruises look fierce. Are you all right?" A dark ring around his left eye marred his face.

"Oh I've had much worse. Matt and I used to fight as children all the time. I just hope we can put all of this behind us after tonight," he said, adding with a smile, "and I think he got the worse end of the beating tonight."

Matthew stalked through the garden gate with a pained expression, a hand holding his side. Perhaps he had indeed gotten the worse end of it. George ran ahead of him, stopping in front of the tower door. He scratched at the door and gave Lucas an expectant look.

The tower felt menacing in the dark with the moon behind it. With nothing but lanterns guiding their way, the spiral stairs seemed to go on forever. George led the way, his meow echoing down the staircase whenever they fell too far behind. Mary and Margaret hung several steps behind the men.

"A Frenchman isn't much better than a vampire," Margaret whispered to Mary.

"You sound like Aunt Beth," she snipped, lightly smacking her sister's arm. "He saved me twice when he thought I was in danger. And he's only half French anyway."

"And he's into contacting the dead. Don't forget that. Maybe Aunt Beth was right about the French. Is that something they all do?"

Mary shrugged. "Everyone has their hobbies. Like growing mushrooms. Or charcoal sketching. Or communing with the dead."

"A real catch," Margaret agreed with a giggle. "And here I always imagined you'd wind up with some pretentious writer or critic."

Mary elbowed her in the side. "Don't make fun. You don't want me to start making snide remarks when you bring one of your 'friends' home, do you?"

That quieted Margaret down. "You'd better not."

At the top of the tower, she almost tripped over George who'd decided to lay across the top stair.

Lucas got to work lighting candles and arranging them in a circle in the center of the room.

"Do you know how séances work?" Margaret whispered.

"Erm, I think we hold hands and the dead come and talk to us?"

"You should have listened to me when I warned you this place looked haunted. Now we have to deal with ghosts too." She clutched a flask of holy water, eyeing the corners of the room with suspicion. "I hope you never court someone else because I can't handle another. You'd better just settle for the Frenchman."

"Settle, you say." Mary rolled her eyes. "Thanks for your vote of confidence."

Lucas pulled out his father's book. "Well it doesn't seem to be his diary, but what is this anyway?" He opened to a random page, reading in silence. He paled and slammed the book shut. "I see why he didn't give me any details." He leaned against the desk for support.

"It was certainly written like a diary. Specific dates and everything. We thought it had to be about you. The son kills the father in that story," Mary said. "It was well done too. I didn't want to put it down until I finished."

"Very convincing," Matthew agreed, "But why would he write such a thing?"

Lucas placed the book in front of him and sat down on the rug. "Let us find out." He gestured for the others to join him. "Please sit in a circle. We are nearing midnight. That will be the best time to hold the séance."

They got into place around a small table, Lucas sitting across from Margaret, flanked by Matthew and Mary. George lay by the cold fireplace, tail swishing as he watched the window.

"And you're certain you know what you're doing? Ghosts are dangerous, you know," said Margaret. Her nervousness suddenly turned accusatory. "Unless of course you're just another fake. Have you ever even done this before?"

"Of course I have," replied an offended Lucas, "I'm no charlatan. Why not long ago I helped an old spirit haunting a mausoleum to find her rest."

"Oh, Mrs. Bettle?" asked Margaret

Lucas was taken aback. "How did you—"

"Looks like you're something of a psychic medium yourself, Margaret!" interrupted Mary, laughing nervously as she stepped on her sister's foot, "But if you helped her I'm sure we'll help your father as well."

"Yes we will." His sad smile faded as he set out and lit four candles, their flickering light doing little to beat back the oppressive, heavy darkness of the study. "I still can't believe I won't be spending Christmas with him. I can't imagine how much I missed during my time in France."

"You didn't miss much. Your father spent too much time cooped up in here. Once I visited and had dinner with your mother, but never saw him at all," Matthew said as he folded his legs. "How is Antoinette, by the way?"

"She is staying with her sister who is taking good care of her. I get a letter from her every week. She's been taking this about as well as can be expected."

"I was worried about her when she left. This didn't feel like her usual summer trips to France. I was so used to her being around that it feels..." Matthew's morose look was not that of a killer, Mary thought. A killer of vampires maybe, but not his own brother. She started to think neither of them could be guilty. "It's as though I lost both my older sister and brother at the same time."

Lucas reached for his uncle's shoulder, stopping short as he changed his mind. "We will find out the truth tonight."

The more Mary listened to him, the more she could pick out the slightest hint of a French accent. It wasn't quite strong enough to make him sound like a foreigner, but enough to add an alluring veil of charm to his speech.

Margaret nudged her, leaning over and whispering "You're staring."

Mary glared. "Is that what you are worried about right now?"

"No. I'm more excited about seeing the ghost."

"You?" Mary smirked. "And here I thought you were scared of ghosts."

"Absolutely terrified, but If there's no vampire and no ghost, then what was the point of tonight? We could have stayed and finished the play. That would have been a much easier way to get a good fright."

"There are far more important things at stake here. We'll finish the play another day."

Lucas opened the book, positioning it in the center of the circle. On top of it, he placed the scrying mirror. In the darkness, only the light of the candles was visible on its surface. "If everyone is ready, let's begin. We will need to hold hands to focus the magic on calling him." They all clasped hands, Mary holding onto both Lucas and her sister. In any other instance, she might have been lost in the warmth and strength of his hand. Instead, she did her best to focus on the séance. Margaret's eyes glazed over in boredom as Lucas began murmuring in Latin. Matthew on the other hand mouthed a silent prayer. He squinted at the book, a stake peeking out of his coat sleeve.

The candles flickered and Mary shivered as a chill passed through her. She'd never given much thought to séances before. There'd been none she'd wanted to participate in or any dead she wished to disturb.

Perhaps that was why her attention kept falling to Lucas and the way the candlelight played across his features. He was far more fascinating than contacting ghosts she didn't know. He and Matthew really did have the same eyebrows, although Lucas's left one was marred by the darkening bruise around his swollen eye.

The wind groaned through the window. She squeezed Lucas's hand. Another chilly draft tickled her shoulders, this one spreading goosebumps across her skin. As if awakening from its rest, the mirror rose from atop the book, slowly spinning and tilting forwards in midair. It was eerie to see the light of the candles reflected in its surface, but none of their faces. It continued to twirl about at a gentle pace, sending candlelight about the room like a lighthouse.

"Father, are you here? Can you hear me?" He called out to the room. The candles wavered again, but no response came. He reached down, resting his and Mary's hand on the vampire book. "Father, I wish to speak with you. If you can hear us, please let us hear your voice." With that, the mirror froze in place, pointing at the fireplace, the light of the gentle fire dancing across its surface. Mary craned her neck to get a better view of the image in its reflection.

"Who's my good boy?" a voice said. It sounded similar to Lucas's, but deeper and without that hint of an accent. Everyone at the table turned to look at one another.

Lucas frowned. "What?"

Matthew squinted at the candles. "Is that you, Luke?"

"There," Mary said, pointing at the mirror. She leaned towards Lucas, catching a glimpse of something in its surface. It looked to be a pair of boots moving back and forth. "Do you see that?"

"See what?" Matthew asked, leaning over to look into the mirror. The three of them shifted back and forth, jockeying for a better view. Only Margaret remained in place, eyes forward and as wide as saucers. Her mouth hung agape as she jerked her head towards the fireplace.

"Behind you," she whispered.

The three of them turned. In front of the fireplace a spectral figure lay on his stomach, head resting in his hands as he cooed to George. George's tail swished as he watched the ghost.

"That's a good little Georgie," the voice cooed.

"Father?" Lucas said, letting go of Mary and Matthew's hands "Father is it really you?"

"Of course it's me," his father grumbled as he pet George. The cat seemed to nuzzle into the pale, translucent hands of the specter. "Who else does he think could be haunting this place?"

Lucas stood, drawing his father's attention at last. Lucas's eyes glistened as he blinked back tears. "I've finally done it, Papa! I've finally managed to contact you. I've been trying for months to speak with you."

His father finally looked up, meeting his son's eyes. "You can see me?" Lucas could only manage a nod in response.

"Ahem," said the ghost as he scrambled to stand up, dusting himself off as he straightened his shoulders. His form appeared to solidify, even casting a shadow of its own. It was as though his whole body had come into focus. If not for being able to see the fireplace through the hole in his chest, Mary wouldn't have taken him for a ghost at all. "How much of that did you hear?"

"My God," said Matthew, stepping forward and laughing as he embraced his brother. The ghost had form enough to hug back. "It really is you!"

"It's good to see you, Matty old boy." He stepped back from the hug and poked at the hole in his chest."I think I may be in need of my last rites."

The priest wiped tears from the corners of his eyes."Finally ready to convert, are you? You certainly took your time."

"It's dreadfully boring stalking about the manor grounds. Quite exhausting to venture much further beyond the tower as well. I think I'll take my chances. If I'm wrong, at least Hell will be interesting." The brothers chuckled and embraced once more.

Lucas stepped forward, reaching his arms up to join in, but stopped himself short, clenching his fists. "Our time may be limited. Father, If you're here, it means you had some unfinished business left on this Earth. Help us find your killer so that we might set your soul at ease."

"He's right," said Matthew, turning to face his nephew. "I've been trying to find out the truth since you died. Did you see who your attacker was?"

Luke shook his head."I'm afraid I only got a brief look at his eyes as I tumbled down the stairs. I had been drinking that night, you know."

"Surely you must have seen something, Father," Lucas implored. "Please try to remember."

The ghost turned his back, facing the fire and stroked his chin. "Oh, I remember who did it, but I don't know if I should say. He doesn't deserve the blame."

"Don't cover for your own killer. He needs to be brought to justice," said Matthew. His gaze drifted to Lucas before returning to the ghost. "It was Arthur, wasn't it? He's coveted the printing press from the start.Without you or Lucas, the press would be his."

"Arthur? No, no." The ghost paused before continuing. "No, my killer is in this very room."

Chapter 21

Mary and Margaret both gasped and grabbed each other's arms, clinging to each other. Mary's chest tightened as she struggled to draw a breath in. Which of the men had deceived her?

Matthew and Lucas waited in mirrored images of each other, their jaws clenched, shoulders taut. They both looked ready to spring on the other once more.

The elder Lord Holiday gave a heavy sigh. "I never saw it coming either. I was such a fool to drink in the tower."

"It doesn't matter if he's family, Father. He won't get away with it. Let the truth be known."

Mary and Margaret squeezed each other.

"It was..." The ghost turned around with a dramatic flourish. "George."

Mary's breath left her in a relieved whoosh.

"Who's George?" Margaret asked in a hushed whisper.

"The cat," she whispered back. "Now hush."

"What? How is that possible?" Matthew asked, waving his hands in frustration. "Are you sure it wasn't a vampire?"

"Vampires?" The ghost laughed, doubling over at the waist. He reached out to support himself against a wall, but passed through the solid stone, nearly falling over before steadying himself. "All those old stories I used to tell you about vampires were made up. Don't tell me you still believe them!"

Matthew gave his brother an incredulous look. "Well the cat most certainly didn't stake you through the heart and drain your blood, now did he?"

"Let me explain." He gestured toward the book. "I was celebrating finally finishing my vampire story, *The Shade of Greymoor*. I'd been meaning to finish writing it for years, but seeing the success of *Twilight at Hallow Manor* inspired me to finally get it done. It was a long year of hard work practically locked in this tower, so when it was done I may have had a few too many cups of brandy to celebrate." He pointed to an empty bottle beside his desk. A thin layer of dust covered it, as well as the pile of empty bottles behind it.

"As I had exhausted all of my refreshments, I stumbled back towards the manor," he continued, "Unfortunately, partway down the stairs I tripped over George. I never saw him in the darkness. I fell and crashed into the railing, and the newel post at the bottom splintered. It pierced me clean through the heart. All of my bl—" He stopped himself, seeing Lucas turn pale. The story was rather gruesome, but it was even more unnerving to see more color in the cheeks of a ghost than in that of a living breathing man. "All of that ...stuff must have drained into a crack in the flooring."

"That pain," said Lucas, clutching his chest. "That's why you've been wailing. Oh Father, I'm so sorry to have made you suffer for so long."

"Suffer? No, no. Honestly, I barely felt the thing. You probably heard me yawning. As I said, it's dreadfully boring in here. But I'm afraid the only thing that's wounded is my pride. To meet such an undignified end...and to have the culprit running free!" He pointed an accusatory finger at George. As if blissfully unaware of his crimes, the cat wound around the ghost's legs. "Oh, but I can't stay mad at you, can I?" The old lord bent down to pet the cat.

Mary stepped forward. "So you mean to say that Lucas is innocent, right?" She tried her best to give this moment the solemnity it deserved, but she couldn't stop a smile from creeping across her face.

"Yes of course," said Luke as he squinted at her. "Pardon me miss, but have we met before?"

"In a manner of speaking." The image of the face in the window still made Mary shudder, even though the very same face was before he now, looking like a cheerful old man. "My name is Mary Hawke. I believe you haunted me when I stayed here a few weeks ago."

"Ah yes! You're that lovely young lady who was staying in the guest room. I'm terribly sorry if I frightened you." He drifted towards his son as he spoke, placing a hand on his shoulder and adding with a wink. "It's not often my boy brings a pretty girl to the manor. You can't blame an old man for making sure he acts like a gentleman."

"Father..." sighed Lucas, rolling his eyes. Mary held a hand to her mouth to stifle a giggle.

"Only kidding, Lucas," he said with a chuckle. A sudden bolt of realization then seemed to shoot through the ghost. "You said 'Hawke,' correct? As in Hawke Publishing?"

"Yes. My father said he knew you in university."

"Oh yes. Nathaniel!" The elder Lord Holiday laughed. "Your father always had his nose buried in a book back in our school days. I had to drag him out all the time to have any fun. Is he well?"

"Father, please!" Lucas interrupted. "We need to figure out what is binding your soul to this world. If it wasn't your murder, what could it have been?"

"Of course." Matthew snapped his fingers. "Don't you see Lucas? The suspicious nature of his death. The distance and mistrust between us. The fate of the printing press. We nearly killed one another over a simple accident."

Luke looked up to the priest. "You nearly what?"

Lucas nodded in agreement with his cousin, seemingly oblivious to his Father. "Of course. In your final moments, you knew how we would react. You knew we'd each suspect the other of murder, and we'd both try to avenge you in our own way, so you stayed here to keep us from fighting. To lead us to the truth."

The elder lord blinked. He took a moment before finally smiling. "Of course. Family always comes first, right?" He nervously patted each man on the shoulder. "No more suspicion and no more fighting, all right?"

Matthew slung an arm around his nephew's shoulders, blinking away tears as he did so. They murmured their apologies to one another. While the two were occupied with one another, the ghost drifted over towards Mary.

"Were they actually trying to kill each other?" He asked her in a hushed voice, eyes fixed on the men as they continued to embrace.

Mary nodded sheepishly. "I'm afraid so. I'm afraid your story had Matthew convinced Lucas was a vampire. I confess I was rather convinced as well."

"What? Preposterous!" Luke let out in hushed indignation. There was a sparkle in his eye as he turned back to Mary. "Was the story really that compelling?"

"Oh absolutely! I thought it was brilliant. The diary format made the story so intimate and convincing. I couldn't stop thinking about the ending. It made me shudder in horror."

"Forgive my impertinence." The elder Lord Holiday dropped his voice as he leaned toward Mary. "But Miss Hawke, is there any chance you would consider publishing *The Shade of Greymoor*? I can't bear to leave it behind to collect dust. I'd planned to send it to your father the next day before my ... erm ... untimely demise happened. It's been tormenting me since."

"... Is that what's been keeping you from moving on? Really?"

"Well I don't know. Just because I'm dead doesn't mean I know how this works exactly."

Mary sighed. "I'll see what I can do. It might be tough to publish two vampire serials simultaneously though." She brought a finger to her chin. "I suppose it might work if we change him from a vampire to some sort of fabulously wealth businessman."

"It's a bit too late for me to make such a drastic change," Luke said, shaking his head. "But there is one person I do wish to entrust my story with: M. H. Crane."

Mary coughed. "Is that so?" she choked out.

"I know it may be unprofessional to ask you to bring my story to him, but please. I beg you to fulfill the wish of a deceased old man. I think I could finally be at rest knowing that the author who so inspired me had seen my work."

"Well it's just that the author....is rather reclusive."

The ghost's shoulders sank. "I understand. Please forgive me for making such a bold request of you after having only met you this evening." He started to drift back to his brother and son.

"Wait," she said, reaching out to grab the ghost's arm. "Can I entrust you with a secret?"

"I won't tell a soul," said Luke with a smile.

"Well, M.H.Crane has already seen your work." She gave the starstruck ghost a moment to gather himself "Because I... I am M. H. Crane."

"You?" Luke's mouth hung agape. "Oh my word it is such an honor to meet you Miste— Miss Crane— I mean Miss Hawke." He stumbled through every word like an eager schoolboy. " I'm just so thrilled to finally meet you. I simply adore your work. It's so incredibly inspiring that I—"

Luke's rambling was cut off as a wave of light seemed to emanate from within his chest. A look of serenity washed over his face. "I feel it now. It is time. Miss Hawke? Thank you. I can rest easy knowing my book is in your capable hands." His smile fell. "I suppose I should go say my goodbyes now. I only wish my dear Antoinette were here. I should have liked to have seen her one last time." Already his form was fading, turning clearer and clearer by the minute. Soon he'd be gone completely.

"Great show," Margaret whispered as the elder Lord Holiday drifted over to his son and brother.

"Let's give them some privacy." Mary moved over to the door.

Margaret let out a long yawn. "As exciting as this night has been, please tell me your vampire lord is going to give us rooms for the rest of the night. I'd love a good nap right about now."

"Stop calling him a vampire. We'll see about the rooms once he's had time to say his goodbyes."

Margaret leaned against the wall, glancing back at the men. "Do you regret not getting a chance to tell mother goodbye?"

Mary considered the question. "I don't think so. Not anymore. I don't think she could have said anything that would have changed how I felt. Her leaving still would have hurt the same. And no apologies can make up for all her harsh words."

"I feel the same. I feel better than I used to, I think, but I'm worried about Papa."

"You can tell him that when he comes home. Make him some of those garlic rosemary scones of yours. He can't think about mother if he is too busy focusing on the awful taste."

Margaret tried to pinch Mary who dodged her attempt. "I was trying to save you."

"I appreciate the attempt. Since his innocence has been proven, promise you will never serve scones ever again."

"Fine, but you are going to feel silly when you get home and realize all we have to eat are those scones."

"I'll stop and get groceries on the way home. Maybe we'll get better scones from Charlotte's bakery."

Across the room, Matthew embraced his brother. For a long moment, he said nothing. He finally stepped back, saying, "Give mum a hug for me." With that he patted his nephew on the shoulder and walked to the doorway.

"Father, wait," Lucas said. His father was rapidly fading, his solid form giving way to a glowing silhouette of a man. "I still need your advice. I can't fill your shoes. There's so much I don't know about being a lord and running a business." He glanced toward Mary. "So much I don't know about life."

"My son." The ghost wrapped his arms around Lucas. "You know all you need to. You've already made me a proud father. The only shoes you need to fill are your own."

"But I don't know enough about the printing press. Can't you stay a while longer and teach me?"

The ghost laughed, now little more than a glowing orb, his form nearly transparent. "Don't ask me, ask Arthur. That man always knows what he is doing and never fails. He certainly knows more than I ever did. Give him space to run the press, and he will handle everything."

Lucas's mouth hung open as he watched the fading light of his father.

"You'll do great. Remember to never drink in the tower. And watch out for George on the stairs."

Lucas's mouth snapped shut. He nodded. The elder lord finished fading away. The candles went out with him. Lucas relit the lantern, his forlorn gaze drifting back to where his father had been. "I think I would like to sit for a while. Alone."

"I'll show the ladies to a guest room," Matthew offered.

"Thank you," Lucas murmured as he got to work cleaning up the candles.

Matthew led Mary and Margaret back to the manor in silence. When they reached the back door, Mary dared to put a hand on his shoulder. "Are you going to be all right?"

The priest nodded. "My brother was a good man. Temperance was not one of his virtues but...he was still a good man." He looked up to the twinkling stars of the night sky, smiling as he wiped the corners of his eyes. "I'll see him again soon enough."

He guided them down the hall to the same room Mary had stayed in at her last visit. This time when she peered out from her bedroom window, the light in the tower comforted her.

Epilogue

Letters from readers were pouring in for *The Shade of Greymoor*. They wanted more chapters. And more of Lord Hallow's story too. Hawke's readers couldn't get enough of the macabre it seemed. And those craving a much cozier adventure were praising a new book of Charlotte's that Mary was testing out, *Calamity in a Coffee Pot*.

She leaned back in her seat, surveying the small pile of mail. Pride filled her. Hawke had rebounded better than she'd imagined, and with Holiday Press printing them, there had been no issues in getting the serials out to their readers.

Her father hadn't been able to let go of Hawke after all. Despite his title of accountant, he had taken over some of his old work of reviewing submissions, but she liked that. Having the business in common gave them plenty to discuss over dinners together and even more to bond over.

"Your tea, Miss Hawke," the butler said as he set the tea tray down with a smile. Clean shaven and with a well coiffed head of hair, the man looked a decade younger than when she first met him. It was amazing what a good night's sleep could do to a man. Not to mention all the new maids and other servants Lucas had hired recently.

"Thank you. I want to be alerted as soon as the guests start arriving." A Halloween party had felt like the perfect time for Lucas to step into his role as lord. This first party was a small one. She'd invited Papa and Margaret as well as the Steepes, Roqueforts, and Matthew.

"Shall I add a log to the fire?"

"Yes, please." Now that it had been cleaned up the library made for a cozy room to read the mail in. When she stayed the night during her visits, she would sit in here and read with Lucas before bed, each of them lost in different books while they sipped on tea. She relished those nights and the comfort of being near him.

She returned to the papers in front of her. Visiting the manor gave her some time alone in the morning to look over business before Lucas arose. Lately he'd embraced his more esoteric talents and taken to helping other families who, like him, had lost a family member with unfinished business. Matthew helped and prayed for the deceased. Unfortunately, that meant plenty of late night seances with grieving families and spiritualists that kept him in bed late.

At the sound of a thump, she looked up. The library had been behaving more lately, the books staying in their proper spots. They still didn't like guests intruding on their space. They'd only recently gotten used to Mary. Yet one never knew when a book might start flapping its way through the air.

A black blur jumped onto her papers, sending the stack of letters scattering across the floor. The cat rammed into her pointed witch's hat, sending it tumbling next. "George!" She grabbed the cat before he could do any more damage to her papers or costume. The hat matched her black dress. She'd even tied a few strings to the broom to entice George to stay nearby as she greeted their guests. Celebrating All Hallows' Eve didn't feel right without a costume.

Lucas ambled in. "I heard George causing trouble. Did he lay across your writing again?"

"He knocked some letters off is all." Better than the time he sent half a manuscript she was editing across the floor. At least this time she wouldn't spend half the night putting the pages back in order. She let the cat go to gather up the letters on the floor, and without even an ounce of remorse for his actions, he wandered over to rub against Lucas's legs.

"You are a little devil," he said, voice full of affection, as he scratched George's head. George purred. George was only interested in Mary until Lucas came, the clear favorite.

Lucas's gaze strayed to the window and the overcast sky beyond. "I should go and put my costume on. Our guests will start arriving any minute."

"Another late night for you and Matthew, wasn't it?"

"Yes, but we got the departed soul to move on and gave the family some peace. Matthew has even given up on calling any of it devilry."

She smiled. "That sounds like good progress. You are kind to help those poor families. I'll go keep watch for our guests." When she got to the front entrance, movement drew her attention to the window. A small face pressed against the glass. She sighed. Any day they left the gates open, local children sneaked in to see the rumored haunted house.

Then Margaret jumped out of the bushes, sending the child screaming as he careened down the yard to the gate.

Lucas chuckled. "I'll go put my costume on."

"I'll see to my family."

She met Margaret outside, who was still cackling maniacally. She wore a bed sheet with eye holes cut out. The thin fabric let out a faint glow, subtle but still visible in the light of the setting sun, and the edges floated in the air as if suspended in water. Margaret always did like to show off her more creative glamour projects around this time of year. Upon closer inspection, Mary noticed that the white sheet sported little flowers embroidered across it. "Is that mother's sheet?"

"Yes. I didn't want to ruin any of my good ones."

Behind her a carriage pulled up. Papa waved out the window.

"Did you sneak onto the grounds again?"

"The gate was open. That doesn't count as sneaking in." Margaret skipped up the stairs toward the front door while Papa helped the footman with their luggage.

"You are only going to fuel the haunting rumors you know."

Margaret shrugged. "I could put on devil horns if you prefer." With a quick pinching motion at her temple, a pair of pointy reddish nubs began to protrude from behind her fingertips.

Mary winced. "Stick to the ghost." They headed inside, the strings trailing after her broom keeping George busy. If she wore him out, it might keep him away from the party food and decorations. It was either that or she'd have to stick him in the library, and that would upset the books. They didn't like getting stuck under a sleeping George.

"This place looks much nicer all cleaned up." Margaret spun in a circle as she took it all in. "But you should have let the overgrown bushes be until after the party. It would have been such great ambience."

"Leave the ambience to the storm coming. I hope everyone gets here before it hits." The dark clouds headed their way faster than she liked.

"The Steepes were on the same train as us. They should be here soon."

A hansom cab rolled up the driveway. "That must be Matthew." He'd been hinting at preparing a costume since he'd received the party invitation. All that did was leave her worried. She couldn't begin to guess what he had planned.

"I'll go take a peek at my room for the night and then meet you in the parlor," Margaret said. "Let me know if any more of those brats turn up. I'll give them a good scare!" Mary suddenly felt glad she grew up as the eldest.

"Father Holiday has arrived," the butler announced as the door swung open.

Matthew sashayed inside. His black outfit was complete with fangs and a flowing black cape she was certain had to have been borrowed from Lucas. Matthew tensed as he focused on something behind her.

"Lord Hallow," Lucas said from the stairs. Mary turned just as he pulled one of his stakes out to point it as his uncle. The hunter then. It felt a little backwards. She pressed a hand over her mouth to hold in the giggle that desperately wanted to escape.

Lucas stepped off the stairs and Matthew approached. Their serious expressions made them look ready to fight, just like the night of the confrontation between them.

"You'll never defeat me, human," Matthew said, dramatic enough for the theater stage.

"The story isn't over yet, vile creature."

Mary pressed her hand tighter over her mouth. The tension fell away as Lucas shifted to pat Matthew on the shoulder. "You didn't get caught in the storm, did you?"

"Not at all. I beat it here. Nice decorations, by the way." They headed for the parlor together. "I'm glad I got to carve jack o' lanterns with you this year."

"I am too." Lucas looked to Mary. "Let me know when the rest of the guests arrive."

"I'll let you know. And I like your costume. Very dashing. And very accurate too." She turned to Matthew. "I assume this is your handiwork, Father?"

"On the contrary. My dear cousin did all of this himself." Matthew slung an arm over Lucas's shoulder. "I edited my copy of *Twilight at Hollow Manor* to make it safe for him to read."

Mary's mouth opened in horror. "You've read it?" Embarrassment creeped up her spine. She wanted to go hide in the library. Her audience reading her story had never bothered her. Even Matthew having read it wasn't so bad. But Lucas? It felt too intimate. And what if he didn't like it? She couldn't bear the shame.

"Yes, and I prefer the hunter," Lucas said. "Anyone who drinks bl—" He cleared his throat. "Lord Hallow will have to work hard for redemption."

"Well I already finished the story and turned the rest in to the editor. Much too late to take your review into consideration. You'll just have to wait and see how it all unfolds." She'd been writing like mad whenever she visited the manor. She'd even started plotting out a new project that had been knocking in earnest at her imagination. Something involving ghosts.

Matthew tilted his head. "Oh come now. How does the story end?"

"I'm not saying." She turned to the window. "Oh look, there are the Steepes."

Martin helped Charlotte out of their carriage. As they walked arm in arm to the front door, Mary couldn't help but overhear their conversation "...I just don't think exiling Bertram to the countryside manor will be enough. If all the servants are quitting he clearly hasn't learned anything."

"It's only been a few months. Father is certain that by the time all the gossip surrounding the exhibition dies down, he'll return to his senses," Martin replied, scratching the back of his head. He didn't sound very confident.

"Well the last maid who was sent is my friend and I'm worried. The two of them will be all alone out there."

"My dear, despite what you may think of him I can assure you that Bertram is a perfect gentleman. He would never do anything untoward."

"She's not the one I'm worried about. If he pushes her over the edge, you'd better not fire her. He deserves whatever she does to him."

"Welcome," Mary called, knowing she'd need to get all the gossip later. "Thank you for coming to our party."

Charlotte beamed at her, all of her anxieties seeming to melt away. "Thank you for inviting us."

"This has been a good party," Lucas murmured against her ear. She sat in a chair by the fire while he stood behind her, leaning over the back of the chair.

Mary shivered, enjoying the way his breath tickled her neck. She agreed. The food had been a hit and everyone wore smiles. After the grief that dogged her footsteps these last few months, seeing everyone around her happy brought her peace.

She pointed to Martin and Roquefort, both men oblivious to the world around them as they talked. "What do you think those two are discussing?"

"Who knows? Probably some manner of obscure ancient magic. Once those two get going, it's nearly impossible for them to stop. I don't know which one I feel more sorry for." She giggled, leaning back into the chair and nuzzling against his cheek. She bared her neck, no longer afraid he might sink his teeth into them. At least not in a bad way. He ran a finger over the back of her neck, goosebumps following. "While we have a break in the storm, may I borrow you for a quick walk before the sun finishes setting? I have something I want to show you."

"Absolutely." They snuck out of the parlor, Margaret's off-key singing keeping everyone too distracted to notice them. With autumn setting in, she couldn't get enough of the moors and garden. The beauty inspired her to write, and the peace and quiet made it easy to focus. That is, once the new roof had been finished.

The week of the repairs had come with a lot of banging and shouting during her visit. Lucas had workers check every room for any pressing repairs needed. Most rooms just needed a good cleaning and updated furnishings, but the new railings, roof, and the bushes finally getting tamed from their overgrown states made the manor feel much more like a home than a setting for a horror story.

She held onto his arm as they headed into the garden. "I'm glad you agreed to the party. I like having everyone together and happy."

"It has been far too long since anyone hosted a gathering here. My mother used to love to throw dinner parties while Matthew and I ran off to go play as soon as we finished eating. I couldn't have planned any of this without you. Thank you."

Leaves drifted down from the trees along the garden path. George pounced on the nearest one. He rolled onto his back, chewing on the edge of the leaf as his back paws kicked at it.

She sighed in contentment. "Everything is beautiful here." They meandered through the garden, taking their time. When they reached the far end, Lucas paused at the archway like he always did, gazing up at the tower. He hadn't taken over the study. Not yet.

"I have something of yours I've been meaning to return for far too long," she admitted. "I feel guilty for holding on to it."

"What is it?"

She fished out his handkerchief. She'd been keeping it at her desk as a reminder of him when they were apart. "You dropped this at Roquefort's party. I found it by your carriage."

He smiled. "Keep it. My gift to you."

Instead of turning around as they usually did on their garden walks, he headed through the archway. A single jack-o-lantern stood beside the tower door, a perfect match for the carved pumpkins out front of the manor.

"Looks like the storm is almost here." She pointed at the sky behind the tower. "Perfect weather for our party." Some lightning would add great ambiance once night fell. And since all the guests were staying overnight, some longer, they didn't need to worry about traveling in the storm.

"My father always loved this time of year. As a child I found it terrifying. When I was three, apparently my father wore a costume that made me cry in terror."

She reached for his hand, enjoying the way he let her hold it when they were alone, especially days like today when they would be surrounded by others. He was a gentleman to his core, but that made him indulging her all the sweeter. "You are too gentle a soul for All Hallows' Eve is all."

They made their way up the spiral stairs. At the top she headed for the large window by the desk. The colorful moors beyond made for the best writing background anyone could ask for. It was no wonder Lucas's father had chosen this room to write his vampire story in. Off in the distance she could spot the bell tower of the village church. The modest chapel Matthew had transferred to wasn't far from it, though it wasn't quite as easy to spot.

"The view is amazing from up here."

"It is." He joined her at the window. For a minute they did nothing but stand and admire the view. She savored moments like this when she could just get lost in her thoughts and the countryside while having him at her side.

This must be love, she thought. Like what Charlotte had, and what her parent's marriage had been so sorely missing. Lately she'd poured her feelings into *Twilight at Hallow Manor*, having Alice fall deeper in love with Lord Hallow. She'd even spared the vampire from the Hunter's wrath, pinning all of the killings on the far more wicked vampire responsible for turning Lord Hallow. It eased Mary's conscience to make sure her main love interest wasn't a brutal murderer.

Mary was careful to not leave her writing or the published version lying about anywhere, too afraid Lucas would get his hands on it. Embarrassment burned in her cheeks as, despite her best efforts, Matthew had somehow managed to convince his cousin to read it anyway. She didn't like the idea of him peering into her story like that. It was like him taking a dive into her own experience of falling in love. A truly frightening notion, but somehow, just a little bit comforting.

"I want you to have this study as your own," Lucas said, his soft voice breaking the silence and startling her out of her worries.

"Me?"

"Yes." He turned to her, his hands folded behind his back. "A view like this deserves to be loved the way my father loved it. As much as I adore it, the light is too bright for me during the day. I think my father would be happy to have another writer make use of the room." He took her hand in his. The adoring way he looked at her stole her breath away.

She looked out at the beautiful sunset, giddy with excitement. "I don't know what to say, Lucas. Thank you so much."

"After all the misunderstandings our relationship started on, I wish to make my intentions clear." He lowered his tall form onto one knee, looking up into her eyes. "I want to marry you."

Her heart almost exploded. "Yes!" She threw her arms around him, nearly pushing him to the floor in her excitement. She kissed him, not caring whether it was proper or not. His arms entwined her waist as he kissed back, meeting her enthusiasm with his own. He spun her around and around as he stood, leaving Mary feeling positively weightless.

When they finally pulled away, faces flush, he gave her another smile. "I didn't mean for that to be my proposal, but if you are willing, I do have a ring back at the manor."

She squealed in delight. "Can we save the ring for tomorrow? Then we can share the news after you talk to Papa tonight. I think he would feel left out if you didn't ask for his blessing." She wanted him to feel involved. Like he wasn't forgotten. His opinion still mattered to her.

"I don't think that will be a problem." Lucas chuckled. "Do you remember how nervous I was when I came to get you before seeing *Romeo and Juliet?*"

"Is that when you asked? You certainly kept me waiting," she teased. The play had been an excuse to spend more time together a few weeks after they had walked out of *The String of Pearls*. Mary found it adorable just how shy Lucas seemed that evening, though she'd always assumed it was because of how close they were in public for the long train ride out of London.

"I confess it wasn't exactly my idea. While you were upstairs, he told me I was free to ask you for your hand as soon as I was ready. After a lot of stammering on my end, he told me he wouldn't rush me."

"He didn't." She covered her mouth with one hand. She'd never stopped to think her father would be expecting marriage already.

"He did."

"I'm sorry, I had no idea Papa would attempt to play matchmaker that aggressively."

"It's fine. I enjoy hearing his stories about my father. Besides, he wasn't wrong about my intentions in courting you." He held out his arms. "Any changes you want to make in the decor feel free. If you don't mind, I was considering moving some of the tapestries to the library where I can see them."

"The decorating can wait. We have a party to get back to." She pulled him in to steal a kiss.

"We won't make it back if you keep kissing me," he murmured against her lips.

"Let them wait a few more minutes."

Continue for a delicious quiche recipe. In the meantime, if you enjoyed this story please consider leaving a review. If you want to stay up to date on new releases, books news, and free short stories, you can join my newsletter(https://katevalentauthor.com/steeping-notes/)

Lucas' Crustless Quiche Recipe

Dear Charlotte,

Well I finally have it. It took a great deal of convincing, but Lucas shared his recipe for the quiche that you won't stop asking me about. It's his grandmother's recipe, so he's fairly protective of it. Except for the garlic. That he only added because he thought I loved the stuff. I swear he used an entire bulb when he made it the first time. Feel free to use less garlic if you aren't trying to keep any vampires away (ha!)

Ingredients:

- 1 cup mix of mushrooms (trumpets, oyster, crimini)

- 1 green onion

- 1 medium shallot

- 9 cloves garlic

- 3 strips bacon

- 8 large eggs

- 1 cup milk

- 1/4 cup white wine

- 1 teaspoon salt

- 1 cup shredded Gruyere cheese

- ½ teaspoon black pepper

- ½ teaspoon herbs de provence

- 1 slice of lemon and sprig of thyme for garnish (per slice)

Directions:
1. Chop the mushrooms roughly.

2. Slice the green onions, separating the whites from the greens.

3. Dice shallots and garlic.

4. Crack the eggs into a bowl, and discard the shells. Beat the eggs until the egg whites and yolks are fully combined.

5. Add the milk to the eggs. Add the salt and pepper. Beat until combined with the eggs.

6. Heat your pan over medium-low heat. Dry fry the mushrooms. Remove them from the pan when they are finished.

7. Cook the bacon. Remove it from the pan when it is done.

8. Keep the grease and add the sliced shallots and onion whites.

9. Cook the shallots and green onions until they are sizzling. They should start turning brown on the edges.

10. Add the cooked mushrooms and bacon back to the pan.

11. Add sliced garlic to the pan and cook until golden brown.

12. Deglaze pan with white wine, stirring up any brown bits with a wooden spoon.

13. Pour the egg and milk mixture into the pan and stir.

14. Cover the pan with a lid. Turn the heat down to low. Allow the eggs to cook until the quiche has solidified. It takes about 15 minutes.

15. Add the cheese on top and return to the oven until melted.

16. Sprinkle the sliced onions greens over the eggs and cheese.

17. Slice to serve. Garnish each slice with lemon and thyme.

You may notice the lack of crust. Apparently, the original recipe had called for one, but Lucas never quite figured out how to make it "The way *Grand-mère* used to," and so he never bothered. I think he just tossed the eggs into the skillet and threw the whole thing into the oven. Maybe you can give him some pointers next time you're over. Or better yet, you can bake one for me at your next submission of *Calamity in a Coffee Pot*. It's never a bad idea to butter up your editor, you know.

Your friend,
Mary

www.ingramcontent.com/pod-product-compliance
Lightning Source LLC
Chambersburg PA
CBHW050850190726
48286CB00007B/2307